COLD SHOT

Center Point
Large Print

Also by Dani Pettrey and available from
Center Point Large Print:

Sabotaged

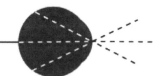

**This Large Print Book carries the
Seal of Approval of N.A.V.H.**

Chesapeake Valor
— Book One —

COLD SHOT

Dani Pettrey

CENTER POINT LARGE PRINT
THORNDIKE, MAINE

This Center Point Large Print edition is published
in the year 2016 by arrangement with Bethany House
Publishers, a division of Baker Publishing Group.

The text of this Large Print edition is unabridged.
In other aspects, this book may vary
from the original edition.
Printed in the United States of America
on permanent paper.
Set in 16-point Times New Roman type.

ISBN: 978-1-62899-900-6

Library of Congress Cataloging-in-Publication Data

Names: Pettrey, Dani, author.
Title: Cold shot / Dani Pettrey.
Description: Center Point Large Print edition. | Thorndike, Maine :
Center Point Large Print, 2016. | ©2016 | Series: Chesapeake valor ;
book 1
Identifiers: LCCN 2015047322 | ISBN 9781628999006
   (hardcover : alk. paper)
Subjects: LCSH: Large type books. | GSAFD: Suspense fiction.
Classification: LCC PS3616.E89 C65 2016 | DDC 813/.6—dc23
LC record available at http://lccn.loc.gov/2015047322

To Lisa:
For being a faithful friend,
sister at heart, and partner in crime.
Love you!

COLD SHOT

— 1 —

Fog wafted over the silent hilltop, dancing in eerie waves amidst the centuries-old trees, the weathered trunks the sole markers of the lost graves littering the grounds surrounding them.

Shoving his frost-nipped fingers into his stiff jeans pockets, Angus Reed shifted his weight, trying to pump some warmth into his limbs. His cousin Ralph moved slowly, methodically, over the grid they'd compiled.

Gazing up at the slip of a moon glimmering behind the clouds, he whispered, "Come on. Stay out just a while longer."

It was too risky to use any light other than the moon's, even if it was the observant ranger's night off. Angus shook his head. The man possessed a level of dedication and fastidious attention to detail the other rangers did not.

His leg twitched. The search was taking too long. "Anything?" They should have found it by now.

"Shh," Ralph hissed. "I gotta concentrate."

The twitching intensified. *Concentrate quicker.*

An owl screeched overhead, sending Angus's heart racing. He caught a glimpse of its shadow disappearing with the moonlight into the thickening cloud cover.

"Maybe we should come back another night."

Ralph's detector hummed to life.

Angus smiled. He *knew* it. Too many men had died on this hill. Many left to rot in mass graves, even more unaccounted for—just like his great-great-great-grandpappy.

Why should that woman and her team get all the treasure just because they had a sanctioned dig? His kin died defending this hill. Why should some anthro-archaeologist or whatever she was swoop in and steal what belonged to the families of those lost?

Nah. He was taking what was his—a chunk of the history his kin helped shape.

The detector whirred to a fevered pitch at the base of a gnarled oak tree, and Angus's shoulders slumped with hard-earned relief. *About time.*

"Told ya." Ralph snickered. "Get the shovel—and some light."

The thickening cloud cover left them no choice. They needed some light to work by. Resting the flashlight on the ground would hopefully limit the beam's reach.

Clutching the handle, he cut into the earth. A foot down, the tip of his metal shovel twanged off a hard shock of resistance.

Ralph gaped at him with a tooth-filled grin. Angus couldn't remember the last time he witnessed his burly cousin smile—the sight bringing the days of them as young 'uns running wild through the Pennsylvania countryside back with a *whoosh*.

Pulling a trowel from his bag, Angus aimed the light downward and set to work uncovering the source of resistance.

Griffin grabbed a flashlight from his desk drawer and slipped it into his belt loop. He preferred the stillness of night, nothing but the moonlight to guide his steps, but the moon had all but disappeared behind the burgeoning blackness of sky about to let loose with rain. Hopefully he'd get his rounds in before it started. Leave it to Hank to get married on a cold, soon-to-be very wet, November night.

Not that he minded swapping shifts. In fact, he far preferred patrolling the park after hours, without the usual throng of tourists—just him and the battle's casualties sharing the hallowed ground. He'd drive the necessary perimeter, then park behind Devil's Den and climb to his favorite lookout, which afforded him the best surveying spot outside of the tower.

His gun in his holster, he shrugged on his coat and zipped it up. Grabbing his hat off the hook by the station door, he stepped out into the brisk night. The air was thick and held the promise of rain, the fresh scent tantalizingly close.

Clearing the lower grounds, he made it to Devil's Den before the rain began. After parking his car, he took off on foot from the boulder-strewn area, heading for Little Round Top. Yes, there was a road winding around the back side of the hill famous for the 20th Maine's heroic standoff, but driving took the fun out of it. This time of year he was likely to see deer—even bats if he was silent enough—blending in with the darkness.

Cresting the rise, a faint glow caught his attention.

Halting, he listened.

Two muffled voices.

He crept closer, pulling his weapon. Vandals or relic hunters, most likely. Either way he wasn't approaching multiple unknowns unarmed.

"There it is!" a man hollered.

"Keep digging," a second man responded.

Griffin's jaw clenched as the men and the grave they were desecrating came into view.

"Looks like we found ourselves a soldier and some fine artifacts."

Griffin clicked on his flashlight, holding his weapon steady. "Oh, I'd say you found yourselves a whole lot more than that."

Finley's phone vibrated against her rib cage.

Please be an out.

Slipping it from her clutch nestled tightly between her body and the stiff chair arm in the darkened concert hall, she glanced at the number and recognition dawned.

Ranger McCray? *Seriously?* At nine o'clock on a Saturday night? The man really had no life outside of work. She looked over at the date her mother had set her up on and winced. Actually, she was only pretending at one. Had been ever since . . .

Blackness flashed before her eyes, and then the shining light. She blinked, her chest tightening, her palms moistening.

No. Not now. Not surrounded by all these people. Please.

Nauseated terror sloshed over her in a clawing rush, frustration and irritation following. How could it come on so fast?

Do the stupid breathing thing.

Sucking in what was supposed to be a deep inhale, her rib cage barely inched up, but she focused on the stage before her and forced herself to release the pitiful amount of air slowly, like a balloon squeaking out tiny spurts as it deflated. *One, two, three, four.*

She let the memory of panic drop, or at least pretended to. She was getting good at that—*pretending.* But she had no choice. She refused to let the world see what a mess she'd become. Least of all, a ranger who was too uptight for his own good—or anyone else's.

At least with Ranger McCray what you saw was what you got. He didn't tiptoe around her, which was refreshing, but then again, he didn't know. Though she doubted it would make a difference. The man possessed no filter, no sense of pretense, which she admired . . . at least half the time. The other half she wanted to throttle his ridiculously handsome neck.

God was using McCray and their time together as a test. She'd sensed it the first time they met, but it was a test she'd ignore. Despite what God thought, she was anything but ready for it.

Her phone vibrated again in her palm, and she looked back to it. Clicking on the voice message, she held it to her ear, attempting to ignore the offended looks of the other concert patrons.

"*Ms.* Scott," Ranger McCray began with *that* tone—his nerve-pricking emphasis on *Ms.,* which burrowed under her skin. How many times had she asked him to call her Finley?

"This is Chief Ranger McCray from Gettysburg National Military Park."

Like she didn't know who the infernal man was. If she'd had any idea the planned three-month dig would run so far past estimated completion, that she'd be forced to endure his brooding and incessant lectures about disturbing hallowed ground over and over, she never would have applied for the grant in the first place. It seemed a safe enough job. Controlled. Helpful. Just how she needed to spend her summer. But she hadn't foreseen Ranger McCray or the feelings he stirred—both the good and the bad.

"We've got a . . . situation. Could use your expertise. Come as soon as you get this."

What possible *situation* could he have with an archaeological dig at a Civil War battlefield at nine o'clock on a Saturday night?

He, of all people, would manage to find one.

Glancing over, she found Kirk's basset-hound-brown eyes staring at her. "Is everything copacetic?"

"Actually, no." Beginning with his use of the word *copacetic*. Was that the fourth or fifth time he'd used it tonight? She gripped her clutch. "Work emergency. I'm afraid I have to go."

Griffin tapped his booted foot. How long was this going to take? She lived an hour away, and it had already been an hour and a half.

He rested against the two-hundred-year-old oak, garnering a little shelter from the downpour.

Ralph and Angus Reed were now in the custody of Gettysburg police under charges of trespassing, vandalism, and grave desecration. Once Ms. Scott found time to arrive and determine the general age and possible identification of the remains, they'd know if further charges would apply. Feeling a storm in the air and in his knee, he'd quickly tarped the site as the first drops of rain fell, but the sooner she arrived, the sooner the proper processing could begin.

Twenty minutes later the storm subsided and

he bent to examine the condition of the remains, praying the tarp had done its duty.

Shining a flashlight on the exposed bone, he froze.

Was that . . . ?

He leaned closer, examining the ring still hanging around the metacarpal and what appeared to be soft tissue holding it there.

He swallowed.

If what he was looking at was in fact soft tissue, this was not a Civil War–era grave—it was a modern one.

— 2 —

Finley hastened up the steep incline, her three-inch heels sinking into the mud. A damp chill hovered thick in the air, a lingering effect of the crisp fall rain, which thankfully had ceased.

Vandals. That's what she'd assumed Ranger McCray's call had been about—some bored local teens deciding desecrating an archaeological dig would make a fun Saturday night outing—it'd happened before. But her dig was smack in the middle of the peach orchard, not up on Little Round Top, where the stalwart ranger was *"awaiting her presence"* according to Ranger Tim, who was now manning the office. Her curiosity was most certainly piqued.

Light emanated from the ridge as she neared, the beams mingling with the dancing fog in swirling fairylike motion. If she focused on it too long, it'd be dizzying.

"Does this sort of thing happen often in your line of work?" Kirk's leather loafers slipped on the slick earth and, in a move evocative of a Charlie Chaplin routine, he nearly did the splits before windmilling his arms and managing to rather quickly, albeit awkwardly, regain his stride.

It had been polite of him to offer to accompany her, but his overbearing insistence rubbed her wrong. Though without a vehicle of her own, since Kirk had picked her up for their date, she hadn't been left with much choice.

Heat radiated up her neck at the sight of Ranger McCray's physique—broad shoulders, taut muscles, and rugged features—illuminated by a combination of the shadowy moon breaking back through the wispy cloud cover and a series of flash and floodlights he'd set up in an oblong pattern over and around a large blue tarp.

The breathtakingly handsome man had been both the bane of her existence and source of tingly excitement for the past five months. It was an irksome and unwanted combination. The last thing she needed was a man in her life.

"Finley," Kirk said, his voice distant, despite his proximity.

"Glad you could finally make it, *Ms.* Scott." Griffin turned, his steel-blue eyes slowly taking in her attire. His lips quirked in a way that sent goose bumps rippling up her arm. "Nice dress."

Nice dress? She gaped down at her latest Anthropologie purchase—soft cream with strands of silver filigree. Had Ranger Grumpy really just complimented her? How did he always manage to throw her off her guard?

Before she could respond his gaze shifted over her right shoulder, his chiseled jaw lifting a notch. "Who's the stiff?"

"Stiff?" She followed his penetrating gaze to Kirk, standing uncomfortably still, the hem of his overcoat splattered with mud.

"Kirk Bellahue," he said, his flattened palm fastening his silk tie in place as he swooped forward to shake Griffin's hand.

His gaze shifted back to her. "You make a habit out of bringing dates to crime scenes?"

"You caught us in the middle of . . ." Her first date in over a year.

"A date. Yeah, I got that."

"Wait a second . . ." *Did he just say . . . ?* "I'm sorry—did you say *crime scene?*"

"I'm afraid so. Two knuckleheads thought they'd do a little relic hunting. Ended up uncovering a body—or what's left of one."

Yes, it was a crime to uncover a grave, to

exhume human remains without permission, but Griffin's demeanor seemed to indicate something more heinous.

"Come take a look." He strode toward the tarp. "I covered it as quickly as possible. The rain came on fast."

It'd been a gorgeous, clear night when they'd entered the concert hall.

"Didn't want the water compromising the remains."

Smart.

She moved in step with Griffin, and Kirk walked behind her. Pausing, she turned. "Kirk, I appreciate you driving me here. It was very thoughtful of you, but you should go."

His blond brows furrowed. "How will you get home?"

"I can take her," Griffin offered, nearly knocking her off her feet.

Had he just offered to . . . ? Her eyes narrowed. "Are you sure?"

"He doesn't belong here," Griffin said, lifting his chin at Kirk. "We need to secure the scene."

Of course. It was all business with Ranger McCray, though for some odd reason she felt more comfortable with Ranger Grumpy taking her home than Kirk, whose appraising gaze flickered between the two of them.

"I'll call you," she finally said, hoping that would help move him along. Loath as she was to admit Ranger McCray was ever right, in this case he was. Kirk didn't belong there, and the quicker he left the more at ease she'd feel. "Thank you for tonight and for your understanding." She said it as matter-of-factly as she could manage without sounding rude, hoping to cut off any further pro-test on his part.

She had a job to do, and she wanted him gone.

It worked, and after an extremely awkward hug, Kirk left her and Ranger McCray alone on the hilltop. She took in Griffin's pensive expression, his tight brow, and wondered at the source of *his* discomfort. Apparently she wasn't the only one on edge.

Griffin pulled back the tarp, droplets of rain-water drizzling to the ground at their feet, the loamy scent of soil filling the air. The skeleton was only very partially uncovered—just a fraction of the deceased's lower right arm—hand to ulna.

"Here." Griffin angled the flashlight beam on the finger bones.

She squatted beside him, her heels slipping into the earth. "Is that . . . ?" Was she looking at soft tissue draped between the metacarpals and phalanges?

No way would a Civil War soldier's remains still possess any degree of soft tissue. Now Griffin's grim use of the term *crime scene* made sense. If this was in fact soft tissue—she'd have to examine it back at the lab before pronouncing it as a certainty—what they were looking at was a modern victim.

Her gaze swung to Griffin beside her, his breath coming out in white puffs in the cool, damp air. It was an extremely keen observation from a park ranger, even if he was official law enforcement.

He cocked his head at her staring. "Yes?"

"Sorry." She blinked. "I was just thinking what a great observation you had."

He shrugged off the compliment. Of course he would.

She pulled her work gloves from her clutch and set the silver sequined purse aside.

Griffin's brows arched. "You always carry work gloves in your purse on date night?"

She slipped them on. "Unfortunately . . ." The rubber snapped against her skin as she released the edge. "You never know when remains might be discovered, and I like to be prepared."

"Minus the killer dress and heels."

Killer dress? What was up with Ranger Grumpy tonight? Two compliments in a row. She smirked, her playfulness returning in the most surprising of circumstances with the most unanticipated person. "You'd be surprised what I can do in a dress."

He nearly choked on a cough. "Is that right?" A

21

smidge of actual amusement lilted in his baritone voice.

She allowed the pleasure that filled her to simmer for a moment—it'd been far too long—but then she got on with business. "I need to call in a crime scene investigator to help me process the scene." She knew exactly whom to call. The one CSI she could truly rely on.

Griffin nodded. "If there's any chance we're dealing with a more recent body we'll need to alert the Bureau, as we're on federal land. I have a friend I can request. He's one of the best."

"Fine with me. Though I can't confirm the date of the remains until after a thorough exam at my lab."

"I understand."

"It'll be best if we wait until daylight for excavation. It's too easy to miss something in the dark, even with the lighting you've brought in. In the meantime, I'll call my guy and you call yours. And then I can get started setting up a primary grid and mapping it."

"Just let me know how I can help."

"Any chance you have a change of clothes in the ranger station?" Not that she couldn't perform her duties in the dress, but it was such a pretty one, she hated to ruin it.

"I'm sure we can find you something more . . . *functional*. In the meantime . . ." He shrugged off his jacket and draped it across her shoulders. "This should help."

Warmth enveloped her. It smelled of evergreen and him, and for the first time in a long time she felt safe. What was up with that?

— 3 —

Griffin put a call in to Declan Grey. If he was going to have to put up with federal agents traipsing through his park, he wanted Declan and, fortunately, the jurisdiction fit. Griffin preferred to avoid reminders of the past, but he couldn't manage to cut ties completely—cutting his "brothers" from his life would almost be like cutting off his own arm—so he and Declan had remained in pretty regular contact since college.

He shrugged into his secondary fleece, a surprising amount of pleasure filling him at seeing Finley's petite frame drowning in his ranger jacket. He'd been drawn to the woman ever since she'd arrived at his park, but as history had painfully proven, his instincts sucked, hence his boorish behavior. Anything to keep a wall of indifference between them. But tonight . . . in *that* dress . . . it was going to require massive amounts of restraint on his part to behave. The woman was mesmerizing.

Grabbing the thermos he'd filled with coffee

and tucking two plastic mugs in his oversized hand-warming pocket, he headed out of the station and up the well-worn path to Little Round Top.

He crested the ridge and found her sketching the initial scene. Her precision was impeccable.

She jumped at his approach.

"Sorry. Didn't mean to startle you."

She brushed her auburn hair back. "It's fine. I was just . . . concentrating."

He lifted the caffeine-filled thermos. "I brought fuel." It was going to be a loooonnnng night—at least she was going to change out of the killer dress. "And"—he lifted the pile of clothes—"a change of attire." He'd tried to talk her into waiting inside the warm ranger station until the CSI and Declan arrived, but she refused to leave the scene.

"Thanks." She took the sweatpants and sweatshirt and moved behind the giant oak that had been holding him up earlier.

Was she . . . ? Heat rushed his cheeks, and he quickly turned his back, though the twenty-hand span of the trunk fully shielded her. "Don't you want to use the restroom or ranger station?" The woman never ceased to surprise him. Talk about unnerving and captivating. Good thing she'd be gone in a day.

"I can put the new outfit on before taking my dress off."

How on earth . . . ?

"I swam growing up. You had to learn to change at all sorts of meets with all sorts of accommodations—or lack thereof." She stepped from behind the tree and draped her dress over a low-lying tree limb—now clad fully in his clothes. They dwarfed her petite frame, but she looked no less striking. Something about her in his clothes . . . Attraction pulsed through him. *Great.*

She kicked off her heels, took the coffee mug he offered, and sank to the ground, pulling her knees to her chest and perching the sketchbook against her thighs. "Thanks." She glanced around, her big blue eyes a bit wider than usual. "Lots of strange sounds out here at night."

"A lot of critters call the park home." He yanked a couple packets of his homemade trail mix from his pocket and offered her one as he sank to the ground beside her—having laid out a second tarp to keep them dry. "Wasn't sure how much of your date I interrupted."

"We had dinner, but I'm still famished." She opened the trail mix with one hand while cupping the mug in her other. "I hate places that serve miniscule food and call it gourmet. I mean, who actually eats like that?" She tilted her head back and tapped some trail mix into her mouth. "Wow," she said after swallowing. "This is good. Where'd you get it?" She jiggled some more out of the bag.

"I made it." He popped a handful into his own mouth.

"Really. Hmm."

"Hmm?"

"Oh. Just didn't picture you as the cooking sort, but I suppose trail mix isn't cooking exactly, and it does fit well with the whole outdoorsy thing you've got going on."

He arched a brow. "Outdoorsy thing?"

"You know . . . I can tell you enjoy spending time outside, and you're built like someone who . . ." She swallowed hard.

"Someone who?" he pressed.

"Is . . . athletic . . ." She cleared her throat. "Fit." She tried to shrug off the embarrassment flushing her face in the harsh glow of the floodlights.

He popped a handful of trail mix in his mouth, smothering a grin. So Finley Scott thought *him* attractive. The feeling was absolutely mutual, but it didn't make any sense, which yet again proved his instincts were bunk. Such a shame. The woman was . . . *enchanting.*

She spent the next two hours making chitchat, clearly not a fan of the dark or the silence. Two things he loved.

"I'm guessing you're not a fan of camping?" he said.

Her brows arched. "Why do you say that?"

"You don't seem to be enjoying the atmosphere—crime scene aside, of course."

She picked at what remained of her trail mix. "Never camped growing up, but we did spent a lot of nights on our sailboat. I loved sleeping up on deck under the stars." A soft smile curled on her lips at the remembrance.

Interesting. So why the palpable unease? With her profession she had to be used to crime scenes. Was it him that was making her so uncomfortable?

The distinct throaty wail of a Triumph's exhaust rasped in the distance, coiling Griffin's muscles. It couldn't be. "The CSI guy you called . . ."

"Yeah?"

The motorcycle pulled into the lot on the back side of Little Round Top.

"His name wasn't, by any chance, Parker Mitchell, was it?"

Her brows furrowed. "Yeah. . . . How'd you know?"

He pinched the bridge of his nose. Of all the possible crime scene investigators . . .

— 4 —

Finley shifted to stand, and Griffin offered his hand. She took it, her fingers dainty in his hold.

She looked up at him, something shifting in her gaze, but he couldn't read what.

How was that possible? He could read *every-one*. Well, everyone but . . .

Parker stepped over the rise.

Finley slipped her hand from Griffin's and moved to greet him. "Ranger McCray, this is—"

"Hey, Griff." Parker's lilting Irish brogue tugged a million memories to the surface.

He greeted Parker with a nod, ignoring the surge of adrenaline burning his limbs at the sight of his other "brother."

Finley glanced between them, and he prayed somehow the tension remained hidden. He didn't want to go there.

"You two know each other?" she asked.

That cocky smile he hated curled on Parker's lips, above the ridiculous goatee the man had grown since they'd last seen each other. "Now that's a loaded question."

Griffin swallowed. *Misdirect. Quick.* "Declan's on his way," he said.

"Declan." Parker's smile widened. "A Pirates reunion, then. Minus one, of course."

Minus the one who'd held them all together after . . . He choked that thought.

Finley's blue eyes blinked up at him. "Pirates?"

He exhaled. So much for keeping memories in the past. "It was the name of our Little League baseball team."

"Little League?" Her brows furrowed. "You two grew up together?"

Griffin sloughed his balled fist into his jacket pocket. "Afraid so."

Parker stepped to Finley. "How you doing, whiz kid?" He pressed a kiss to the top of her head, and Griffin's gut knotted.

"Whiz kid?" he asked, trying to ignore the irrational jealousy flaming inside.

Parker draped his arm around Finley's shoulders, only stoking the fire. "Finley is amazingly brilliant."

Coming from Parker, that was saying a lot. Not that he'd ever need to utter those words. Parker was cocky enough without any comments on his intelligence. If only he possessed common sense, responsibility, trustworthiness . . .

"She was the youngest doctoral graduate in her field at Penn State," Parker said, finally releasing hold of Finley.

The grip on Griffin's chest eased as Parker stepped away from her. "Really?"

Finley shrugged. "I went into my undergrad with a lot of AP credits. I'm what you'd call a knowledge nerd."

She was the sexiest nerd he'd ever seen.

He'd known she was intelligent but hadn't bothered looking into her past. He didn't like people judging him by his, so he figured it only fair to extend others the same grace. He judged on what he saw—or tried his best to stick to that. Unfortunately *his* best had cost someone her life.

• • •

Finley sat cross-legged, her back against the rough tree trunk, observing the palpable strain between Griffin and Parker as the night passed uncomfortably. She hated the dark surrounding her, but Griffin and Parker's presence brought her a measure of comfort, made the fear itching to burst open remain beneath the surface.

Please, Father, don't let Griffin, of all people, see me freak out. Settle the fear. He's not here, and I'm not alone. I'm safe.

She mentally repeated the phrase over and over until the burgeoning panic simmered. She was safe. She didn't really believe the words, but they worked enough to keep the façade in place.

Taking a deep breath, she shifted her attention to the two men with her.

What was the deal with them?

She'd known Parker for a year, ever since he'd been called in on the case that nearly destroyed her. He'd been the freelance investigator hired by the deceased's family to help solve their daughter's cold case when the county-appointed one had completely dropped the ball.

She'd only met Griffin a few months ago, but she felt she knew the straight-laced ranger better. And yet . . .

She gazed between the two men, startled at the depth of emotion welling on Ranger McCray's pinched face. She wondered if she really knew him at all.

He stood. "Since we can't do anything until dawn and you two are here to keep the site secure, I'm going to finish my rounds."

She got to her feet, thankful Parker had swung by her office just down the hall from his at the medical examiner's and grabbed her extra pair of tennis shoes. "I'll go with you."

Griffin quirked a brow.

"I'm getting restless just sitting. Parker can keep an eye on things. You don't mind, do you?" she asked.

Parker lifted the hand casually draped across his knee in assent. "Of course not, love."

Dark brown hair, deep green eyes, and a dynamic smile. Most women went nuts over the handsome man, and his gorgeous Irish accent only made him more attractive to most. But she'd never been attracted to him in that way. She appreciated his good looks and intellect but wasn't drawn to them like a moth to a flame.

Griffin stiffened beside her. *Curious.* Was his discomfort because she was interrupting his solitude by joining him or because of Parker's term of affection? Either way it didn't matter. Walking would help ease the tightness in her belly. It always did.

She moved to Griffin's side. "I'll follow your lead."

He hesitated a moment but then nodded and glanced over his shoulder at Parker. "Back in an hour."

Parker lifted his chin.

Seriously. What was going on between these guys?

Griffin kept his stride firm, steadfast, the release of adrenaline a welcome relief. He hadn't expected Finley showing up with a date to bug him so much. Regardless of his attraction, he'd never pursue her. The fact that his gut told him to go for it was proof enough not to.

But then hearing Parker call her "love"? *Ugh.* It had burrowed like a chigger under his skin— constant inflamed irritation gnawing at the surface.

"So . . ." she said, " . . . you and Parker grew up together?"

The lady didn't waste any time. He kept his stride brisk. "Yep."

"Small world."

He moved through the trees, darkness wrapping around them as the floodlights faded in the distance. "Yep." Warmth filled his limbs as they wove through the narrow trunks lining the shallow gulley.

Reaching the top of the small ravine, the hairs along the nape of his neck pricked. Instinct kicked in and he snaked an arm around Finley's waist, pulling her to him.

Panic surged in her eyes, and she struggled against his hold.

He quickly released her. "Sorry," he whispered. "Didn't mean to startle you. I heard something." He gestured to the tree line.

"Oh." Pink flushed her cheeks in the flashlight's beam.

He held his finger to his lip, indicating silence, and cut the light.

She hovered beside him as he scoured the tree line, the distinct sensation of being watched raking over him.

He didn't see anyone or hear anything further, but something held fast to his gut. Lowering his mouth, he whispered in her ear. "Take my hand." He reached out for her.

She placed her palm against his, and he wrapped his fingers around hers, biting back a groan. Why did she have to feel so perfect?

Fixing his focus where it needed to be, he stalked toward the copse of trees, Finley fastened to his side.

Leaves crunched to the south of them—just the briefest whisper of sound, but distinct. Pulling his weapon, he ignored the concern on Finley's face and continued forward. Twenty more strides and he stopped to listen again.

Finley's hand tensed in his.

An owl hooted, and a small critter scampered through the underbrush behind them. Perhaps what he'd heard had just been an animal after all, but the sense of a threat wouldn't release its hold.

Clicking his flashlight on, he reswept the area. *Nothing.*

Hmm. Maybe it was time to move on. He was just about to turn around when something scraped on their right, the sound of a jacket sleeve raking along a tree limb.

His vision narrowing, heart thudding, he tugged Finley into a full-out run. The beam of his flashlight bounced off the trunks surrounding them as they jumped over tangled roots and through sloshy ground cover.

Trees whizzed by, inches from his face. He ducked and swayed, praying Finley followed his lead.

A small yelp escaped her lips as she flailed forward. He tugged her hand upward, righting her.

He paused, his breath deep but even. "Are you okay?"

"Just caught my ankle on a root. I'll be fine."

"Are you okay to keep going?" He wouldn't leave her behind. Not with the current unknowns. Who was out there? They clearly weren't alone.

"Yes." She rested her full weight on her ankle and winced. "I'll be fine."

No she wouldn't. Not at the clip he needed. "Let's get you back to the site."

"Please, it's a minor twist, if anything. I'm good. Let's go."

"You sure?"

"Positive." She started moving at a decent clip. *Impressive.*

They tracked back through the woods, reaching the nearest road in time to see taillights disappearing in the distance.

Someone *had* been there. He knew it. But who, and why?

— 5 —

Griffin watched the strobe of Parker's flash reflecting off the red-hued sky. *Bad day to be on the water.*

He shook his head, the nautical knowledge as much a part of him as the blood flowing through his veins. He glanced at Parker, and then to the parking lot at the black Expedition pulling into a slot. Declan climbed out, slipping his aviator sunglasses in place. Maritime culture flowed through them all, binding them in yet one more unbreakable way.

He glanced at Finley still moving gingerly on her ankle. He should have made her stop. Their nighttime observer might simply have been somebody curious to check out the rumors no doubt swirling around town about a body being found, but the restlessness in his gut wouldn't cease.

Finley had grown quieter after the incident, uneasy. Perhaps it had shaken her more than he realized. He felt bad about that. He hadn't meant to startle her. He'd just followed his gut, which usually ended badly. Would he never learn?

"Griffin," Declan said, approaching. Dressed in a white dress shirt and grey dress pants, his light brown hair short and closely trimmed around the ears, he looked every bit a Fed—even on a Sunday.

"Thanks for coming." He shook his friend's hand.

Parker paused his work. "Hey, man." He gave Declan a man hug—straight arm—pat on the back—more chest bump than actual hug, but still far too touchy-feely for Griffin's taste. "Glad you could make it."

"Griff said dawn, but I'm sure you were here hours ago." He lowered his glasses, shifting his attention to Finley. "I don't believe we've had the pleasure."

Griffin made the introduction. "Declan Grey, Dr. Finley Scott."

"Glad to meet you." She shook Declan's hand, and Griffin tried to ignore the irritation Declan's overly pleasant smile at Finley had on him. It was no wonder both he and Parker were flirtatious—Finley was gorgeous—but he didn't have to like it.

"I hear you three go back quite a ways," she said.

Declan glanced at Parker, his brown eyes filling with pleasure, or at least nostalgia. "You telling stories out of school again?"

"Just the good ones." He winked.

"Actually," Finley said, "all I've heard is that you used to play Little League together."

"Which is more than enough background on us," Griff said, needing to nip any further conversation on that topic in the bud. "We need to focus on the job at hand."

Parker chuckled. "There's the Griff we all know. Work. Work. Work."

"Work is how stuff gets done." Adherence to rules. Integrity. Focus. Not allowing feelings to intervene or emotions to distract. That's how people got hurt.

"Speaking of work . . ." Declan said, stepping to the grave's edge. At least one of his friends knew how to take work seriously, life seriously. "What do we have here, Dr. Scott?"

"A lot of work ahead of us. I've set up and mapped the grid. Parker will assist with collecting samples as well as photographing the scene."

Declan arched his brow at Parker. "Don't you usually have an assistant?"

"She's out of town right now. Could have mustered someone up, but not the best on such late notice. Don't worry, I know how to photograph a scene, and I'll have my photographer run through all the shots when she returns tomorrow morning."

"No problem," Finley said. "Griffin, would you mind taking notes as we go? Don't worry, I'll walk you through it."

Parker knelt by the grave. "He won't have a problem."

Griffin gave him a death glare. If he brought up his job with the Baltimore PD or his sniper expertise . . . it would only fuel questions on Finley's part—ones he most definitely did *not* want to answer.

Reaching for the sketchpad and pencil she held out, he flipped to a fresh page.

"Let's get started." She shifted naturally into her concentrated work mode that was such a pleasure to watch. "Let's begin with surface surveying and recovery, then we'll remove the top layer of soil and vegetation and progress to a bisection from there."

"What kind of bullet caused that?" Parker asked, snapping a close-up of the victim's head. He turned to Griffin at the same time Declan did.

Finley's brows pinched. "Why are you both looking at Griffin?" What was the deal with him? His mastery over the situation in the woods— hearing something she never would have if he hadn't stilled her, zeroing in on whomever was watching, which still had her shaken—and now everyone's deference to his apparent ballistics knowledge. Clearly there was more to Ranger McCray than met the eye. She just wished he didn't intrigue her so. He was not where her thoughts ought to be focused.

"Because Griffin is—" Declan said.

"I know something about bullets," Griffin cut him off, kneeling to examine the wound. "My initial guess would be a 7.62 millimeter."

Finley pursed her lips to speak, but Declan jumped in, interrupting her. "Any way to tell the distance?"

Griffin shook his head. "Not enough information. I mean, I can tell you it wasn't at close range—that would have caused significantly more damage—but I'm sure Dr. Scott will be able to confirm specifics with her exam."

What was it about Griffin that he or they didn't want her to know? Uneasiness sloshed in her gut. She needed to be able to trust the people around her. It was essential.

"I'm done with this round," Parker said, lowering the camera to his side, clearing them to move forward with the next level of samples and evidence collection.

Thankful for the need to focus, she shifted her attention to what they'd found so far—remnants of a battered Las Vegas 51s baseball hat and hair fibers.

She moved on to measuring the bullet wound, and Griffin was correct. The victim had been shot dead center of the forehead with a 7.62 mm bullet, but she still wouldn't make any official declarations or rulings until her full exam had been performed at the lab. She had worked enough cases to know when to remain silent. Reporters were already lining the parking lots below; news spread like lightning these days.

Taking into account the graduation ring—with no obvious identifying details—baseball hat, and the minor root etching on the bones, there was no doubt they were dealing with a modern body dump. Based on the initial analysis, she'd guess sometime in the last year.

"How long has he or she been in the ground?" Declan asked.

"I can't comment until I perform my exam," she said.

"Are we dealing with male or female?"

"Again, I can't comment until I perform my exam."

"Can you estimate?" Griffin asked.

Of course Griffin felt a stake in this. The victim had been found on his grounds, his watch.

"I'd prefer not to. An incorrect estimation can start the investigation out on the wrong foot. Once astray it's much harder to redirect to the right path."

Griffin nodded. "I can respect that."

"How soon can you start getting me results?" Declan asked.

"One step at a time. The first is to get the remains transported to the lab."

A flurry of reporters had set up camp at the edge of the crime scene tape—they'd been able to secure a wide perimeter, but the reporters had flocked all the same. They always did.

And he'd blended in perfectly. Even asked a question or two. Just enough to get the necessary information.

They'd found her. He was sure of it.

Time to make the call.

— 6 —

Finley settled back for the ride to the lab, still surprised Griffin had offered to drive her. She shifted her focus to her surroundings, trying to both distract herself from the fact that she was alone with a man in his vehicle and to also learn as much as she could about said man, since a talker he was not.

She took mental inventory of the contents of his truck. A pack of sunflower seeds sat in the center console, a coffee tumbler in the cup holder, and a pair of Oakley sunglasses in the pocket of the overhead visor. An O's decal decorated the glove box. So he was an Orioles fan.

She let the contents sink in, imagining what sort of person the owner would be if he weren't present. It matched the picture she had in her mind of the man beside her, but after his interaction with Parker and Declan, it was clear he was hiding something. Question was, what?

Start subtle.

"Have you always been a park ranger?"

He glanced over without fully turning his head, his gaze on the road. "No."

"What'd you do before?"

"Something different."

"I figured as much." She stared at his silence. Was he seriously going to ignore her question? "Such as?" she prodded. Clearly it involved ballistics knowledge.

He tapped his thumb against the steering wheel. "How well do you know Parker?"

Was this his way of answering or avoiding her question? "We've worked together off and on for a year."

"Just worked together?" His posture was relaxed, his left arm casually extended, his hand draped over the wheel, but something told her this was no casual question. She studied the tightness of his jaw. Was he jealous? No way, this was Ranger McCray. Strong, stalwart, confident. Certainly not interested in her.

"Is it a complicated question?" he ventured.

He still hadn't answered hers. "Was mine?"

His lips cracked into a smile, but infuriatingly, he still said nothing, so she returned the favor.

"Well?" Tightness edged the man's voice.

He lowered his, still in the building. "They have her at the ME's office."

"And?"

"Waiting on a positive ID."

"And Tanner?"

"I'm closing in."

"I don't like it."

"You want me to strike preemptively?"

"If they ID our girl, it'll lead them straight to our door. Make sure that doesn't happen."

Finley glanced at the clock. Where was John, the lab tech, with Jane Doe's body? After arriving at the lab, she'd left the annoyingly silent Griffin in the lounge with Declan. What was he hiding about his past work? And why from her?

Parker had disappeared to his lab as usual when they had a new case, and she'd called to ask John to transport Jane Doe to the exam room nearly twenty minutes ago.

Five frustrating minutes later, she decided to take matters into her own hands.

Griffin and Declan remained in the lounge conversing, neither appearing to notice her pass by the open door. Her curiosity about their relationship along with Griffin's knowledge of ballistics rose, but she remained on task, stalking down the dimly lit corridor toward the arrival bay.

Don't focus on the darkness. You aren't alone. It's not the same. He's gone. He can't hurt you anymore.

Frustrated she'd allowed herself to get worked up again, she chugged down a soothing breath as she turned the corner. *I am safe.* How many times did she have to work to convince herself of that?

"Give it time," everyone said.

She was tired of giving it time. It'd been long enough.

She just wanted to feel normal again.

Wrapping her fingers around the cold steel handle, she pushed the door in.

John lay facedown on the floor, blood pooling around his head. "John!" She shrieked, rushing toward him, but movement shifted her attention. A man in black hefted Jane Doe's bagged body onto a stretcher.

"Hey!"

He looked up, but the room was too dark to make out the details of his face—and he was wearing a dark hoodie pulled low to his eyes.

His right arm swung up and instinct urged her to hit the ground. She collided with the cold tiles as a shot whizzed overhead with a soft whir, lodging in the wall behind her.

As another shot collided with the steel she dove for the door and scrambled for the janitorial closet across the hall.

Her pulse throbbing in her throat, she reached the closet and shut the door, her chest rising and falling in rapid pace with her breath.

Please, Father . . . was all she could manage through the terror gripping her. Her heart ticking in her throat, she waited.

Listening for footsteps was nearly impossible over the hammering in her ears.

She waited, each breath labored, shallow, her chest tightening.

He wasn't coming.

Relief filled her . . . but then the realization hit.

He is taking Jane Doe.

As petrified as she was, she couldn't let him do that. Couldn't let him deny Jane Doe her real name or her family closure. It's *why* she did what she did—to bring justice to those who could no longer fight for themselves. Though she was weak, her Savior was strong.

Swallowing her fear, she cracked the door and with clammy hands gripped the edge, staring into the corridor.

Please, Father, help me to be brave.

Something squeaked to her right. Her heart

racing, she leaned farther into the hall. The man was wheeling Jane Doe's body away.

Griffin glanced at the hall. He'd heard something. It was muffled, but . . .

Declan cocked his head. "What's wrong?"

"I thought I heard . . ."

"What?"

"A gunshot."

"Trust me, if there was a gunshot in the ME's office, we'd all be on full alert."

Griffin strode to the door. "It sounded like a silencer."

"Silencer?" Declan followed him into the hall. "Then how did you . . . Never mind." He shook his head.

Griffin moved toward the arrival bay, toward the origin of the sound. "It came from this direction."

Finley's silhouette darted down the side hall with a mop poised upright in her hands. *What on earth?* He looked back at Declan.

"This way," he said. "We can cut her off."

Following Declan around the bend, they froze as they reached the guard station. The guard was slumped sideways in his chair, blood trickling from his nose.

Heat flared in Griffin's chest, spreading through his limbs. *Finley.*

The outside bay door opened, and he raced for

it, pulling the fire alarm as he went, Declan fast on his heels.

Don't be stupid, Finley.

Red lights whirled along the beige walls, intensifying his adrenaline rush.

Sirens shrilled nearby—the fire station only two blocks over.

Hammering through the bay doors he found Finley on the ground, her arms wrapped around the metal stretcher leg.

Was that Jane Doe?

A police cruiser and fire truck approached, their lights radiating out over the darkness, illuminating a black van as it sped away.

He dropped to the ground and lifted her onto his lap. "Finley?"

She groggily came to, blinking. "Hey." She smiled. "You called me Finley."

He smiled despite the dire circumstances.

Declan rushed past them, firing at the van tearing out of the parking lot.

Griffin smoothed the hair from Finley's brow, checking her for signs of injury. "What happened?"

"That man killed John and tried to steal Jane Doe."

"So you decided to stop him with a mop?"

"It's all I could find. I jammed it through the stretcher wheel spokes, and he went flailing forward with his momentum. Unfortunately, I did too. Last thing I remember seeing was the metal stretcher edge in front of my face and emergency lights swirling in the distance. Good call on the alarm."

"The benefits of having a police and fire station within walking distance."

An EMT knelt at Finley's side. "Let me take a look at you."

She waved him off as another moved to John. "I'm fine." But it was clearly too late for John.

"Looks like you took a knock to the head." The EMT insisted on examining her. "This'll just take a minute."

She started to protest, but Griffin cut her off. "Let the man do his job."

She nodded and then winced, clearly regretting the motion.

Declan returned.

Griffin didn't have to ask—his friend's angry face said it all. The man got away.

"I appreciate you offering to stay," Finley said as Griffin accompanied her back toward her exam room and away from the chaos. "But it's not necessary."

"Yes it is." Someone had broken into the medical examiner's office, for goodness' sake— had killed the lab tech, knocked out the security guard, and taken a shot at Finley. It was the definition of an unsafe environment, and his years in SWAT had trained him perfectly for such things.

"I won't be alone. As you can see. . . ." She gestured to the spinning red-and-blue lights outside the corridor windows. "The cops are here in abundance."

"They aren't going to be in the lab with you." Only on the perimeter after the building was deemed secure, if they followed standard protocol. That wasn't good enough.

"Parker will be here. He won't leave until he's worked every piece of evidence. Trust me—I know him."

That's exactly what he'd thought too until . . .

Parker rushed into the exam room. "What happened?" His worried gaze shifted to Finley, and he stepped toward her. "Are you okay?"

She rubbed her arms. "I'm fine, but John's dead."

"What?" Parker's eyes widened.

"And he tried to kill Finley too." Outrage spewed from Griffin's lips.

"I'm so sorry." Parker grasped her shoulders. "I had my headphones on, and my lab doesn't have a window. . . . It took me a moment to figure out what was happening. Any idea who he was?"

Finley shook her head. "I only saw him briefly and not well, but I didn't recognize him."

"What about security footage?" Griffin asked. The ME's building had to be decked out with it.

"Police say the man kept his head down, hoodie on. They got no clear image," Declan said, entering and leaning against the counter.

"Any idea why someone would try to steal the body?" Griffin asked, attempting to ignore the fact Parker's hands were still on Finley's shoulders.

Finley inhaled. "To prevent ID would be my best guess."

"Which means the killer is aware we found her." And was likely the same person they'd chased through the woods last night.

"Which means he's close," Declan said, echoing Griffin's thoughts.

He looked at the bruise on Finley's forehead. "Too close."

He watched them through his scope. The same group from the crime scene, now all at the ME's lab. They were going to work this one hard.

His jaw tightened.

Tonight's events had taken an unexpected and decidedly unsatisfactory turn.

His finger itched to pull the trigger, but a dead forensic anthropologist would only stir the hornet's nest.

He held his breath, wanting—no, *aching*—to squeeze the trigger, but he released his hold and rolled off his stomach.

Standing, he took one last glance over his

shoulder, the distance too far to see them with-out the aid of a scope. This wouldn't be the last time he had them in his sights, and next time—when the timing was right—he'd happily pull the trigger.

— 7 —

Finley pulled on her gloves. The attempt at body snatching had seriously flared her curiosity. Who, exactly, was Jane Doe?

She turned on her microphone and began her analysis of the remains, recording the pertinent information—date, location, starting time of analysis, and names of everyone present. Next she moved on to radiographing—obtaining dental images, and x-raying the entire skeleton, paying particular attention to the skull wound, which was almost certainly the cause of death.

She retained two lumbar vertebrae in their original state before cleaning the rest of the bones and laying them out in a systematic manner—distinguishing left from right, inventorying each bone and tooth, and photographing the entire skeleton in one frame.

Recording the condition of the remains, she moved on to the preliminary identification.

Race—Caucasian, based on the victim's phenotypic traits: shape of the head, nose and face, stature, and proportions of the upper and lower limbs.

Sex—female, based on her assessment of the pelvis, femoral head, and skull.

Age—thirty years plus or minus, based on dental development, tooth eruption, bone length, and the appearance and fusion of growth centers in the bone.

Next she moved on to individual identification, searching for evidence of trauma and developmental anomalies, wrapping each stage up with supporting photographic evidence.

Parker lounged on the open counter opposite her, watching as he always did. Griffin stood steadfastly still on the perimeter, and Declan paced *and paced and paced.*

It took time to distinguish injuries from medical treatments and therapies from those resulting from trauma. Each bone examined for cracks or breaks. Each one examined for contact with metal or other foreign objects.

She wrapped up her exam by noting the finishing time and turning off the microphone. She'd go to her office, replay the recording, and write up her official report.

"Well?" Declan said.

"Caucasian female. Age thirty, plus or minus. Major trauma to the front of the skull. Based on the measurements I took and the bullet collected, Griffin was correct in his assessment of the caliber size. The wound occurring perimortem with low velocity."

"Which would make that her cause of death?" Declan pressed.

"It appears so, but the ME will make an official ruling based on my findings."

"How low a velocity? I mean, what kind of distance are we looking at?"

"The entrance hole is circular, beveled internally, and sharply edged. The fracturing wasn't rapid like we'd see in a higher velocity shot, though there clearly is no exit wound."

"Which suggests . . ."

"With that caliber bullet, low velocity indicates distance, and the trace evidence found on both the projectile and her skull, I'd say the bullet passed through something or more than one something based on the two distinct trace fragments Parker will finish analyzing."

"Any other signs of trauma?"

"Injuries, but ones that occurred years ago. I believe our victim suffered from osteogenesis imperfecta."

"And that would be?"

"It's a congenital bone disorder characterized by brittle bones that fracture easily. I count a half-dozen fractures from what appears to be her formative—childhood and teen—years."

"But that has nothing to do with her murder?"

"It's just another piece of the puzzle that helps

us hopefully get one step closer to identifying Jane Doe." She glanced to Parker. "Any results from the samples we took on site?"

"Hair—blond. Blood matted and high in chlorine."

"A swimmer? Makes sense. Any contact sports would have been too dangerous with osteo-genesis imperfecta. Hair follicle?"

"Afraid not."

"I assume you're running the blood sample?"

"AB positive."

"Anything else?"

"There were a couple types of particles around what appears to be the bullet hole through her cap."

"Any idea?"

"It's still running through the database analyzer, but the first appears to be glass."

"Glass?"

"Yes."

"I didn't see any evidence of trauma to the head other than the gunshot wound. Hmm." She frowned. "And the second?"

"Tougher to say. We have only fine shards. Under the microscope it appears to be some sort of plastic, but again, it's running through the database analyzer, and that takes time."

"Okay, so if the bullet passed through glass and plastic, let's surmise for now, we're talking a shot through two other objects with a direct hit to her apricot based on the skull trauma, which would have killed her instantly," Declan said, glancing at Griffin.

Finley's brows arched. "Apricot?"

"Medulla oblongata," Griffin said.

"We also know the velocity at impact was fairly low, which could indicate a shot from some distance." Declan continued to keep his gaze fixed on Griffin.

"Yes," she said slowly, wondering where this was going.

Declan exhaled. "I think we're dealing with a sniper."

— 8 —

Griffin swallowed. It had been one year, five months, and fourteen days since his sniper expertise had last been called on. At least tonight they were just asking for his knowledge, not his skill. But it was only a matter of time before Finley would learn the truth about him. About what kind of man he really was. One who couldn't pull the trigger when it mattered.

"Sniper?" Declan asked again.

Griffin shook off his thoughts of Finley and focused on the task at hand. "It's possible. It'll help if I examine the bullet."

Finley nodded, confusion marring her brow. "Okay."

It wouldn't be long before her questions came more rapidly. It was clear what he'd done for a living.

Following Parker to his lab, Griffin pulled on a pair of gloves and studied the bullet under the light, tension searing through him. He exhaled and studied what had no doubt killed Jane Doe. "See the scarring around the base of the projectile?" he said.

They all studied the area his finger pointed out.

"That happens as a result of crimping during the loading process. I've seen this occur on 7.62 x 54 millimeter rounds, and that narrows down our weapon significantly. It could be an older Mosin, which is a WWII sniper rifle, but more likely you're looking at a modern Dragunov."

"Which is . . ."

"A sniper rifle still in use by Russian special ops."

"So *if* we're dealing with a sniper," Finley asked, "does that mean our sniper is Russian?"

"No. It just means that's his weapon of choice, which could indicate he was in service overseas in that region. Black ops, for example," he explained, "often use the weapon of the country they are entering to distance themselves even further from U.S. affiliation. To blend in."

"And you know this how?"

Griffin's jaw tensed, but before he could answer Declan cut in.

"So if we're dealing with a Dragunov . . . you can determine distance based on velocity at impact?"

Thanks for the redirect, bro. "Yes."

"Good." Declan slapped him on the back. "Get on that."

"You got it."

Finley's curiosity was nearly boiling over. He saw it in her eyes, the firestorm of questions poised on her lips.

"Let me do some calculations," he said, hoping to stall her inquiry. "Do you have a calculator I can use?"

Parker retrieved one and handed it to him. "Be my guest."

Minutes later, Griffin looked up.

"Well?" Declan asked.

"I'd say you're looking at a shot around fifteen hundred meters."

Declan's eyes widened. "Fifteen hundred meters? Only a—"

Griffin exhaled. "I'd say a hundred guys worldwide could take a shot like that, but you also should take into consideration the fact that he used a standard round."

"Which means?"

"A lot of snipers will load their own ammunition to exact specifications, each round minimizing ballistic variances. These guys can shoot a three-round group no larger than the size of a quarter at a thousand yards. The fact this guy made that shot with factory-load ammunition indicates rare skills."

"So we're definitely dealing with a sniper?"

Griffin rested his palms on his thighs. "I'm afraid so."

"What else can you tell us about him?" Declan asked. "Anything off of what we have so far?"

"The bullet is steel-jacketed. He used a Russian rifle. Based on the forensics you presented, I'd say it was a calculated but quickly chosen shot to take. Going through glass, if that's what we're dealing with, makes the shot harder and containment sloppier. Shattered glass equals noise and debris. Certainly not ideal conditions, which leads me to believe he needed to take that shot then."

"Why?"

"That's your area of expertise."

"So what happened after the shot?"

"Someone buried the body."

"The sniper?"

Griffin shook his head. "Not usually part of a sniper's arsenal."

"So it was important to take the shot right then and afterward hide the body?"

"Yeah, so it appears, based on the evidence."

"Any chance we're looking at a professional hit?"

"Possibly, but *if* we were talking about a paid assassination—there are easier planned shots to take. Unless . . ."

"Unless?"

"Unless she spotted him, but at fifteen hundred meters away that's impossible."

"You're telling me if a sniper had you in his crosshairs, you wouldn't know it?"

A trained sniper might sense it—have a gut instinct—but the chances of the victim being a sniper were practically zero. There were female snipers, but they were by far the minority.

"Results on the fragments are in," Parker said, turning from the computer.

"And?" Griffin waited. This was Parker's area of expertise, and he was good at his job. If only he'd acquired his talent sooner.

"It's glass. Most commonly used in the automotive industry for car windows."

"Can you narrow it down to makes and models?"

Parker nodded. "Already working on it."

"And the second fragment type?"

"Plastic."

"Used in?"

"It's a translucent plastic that has a number of applications, but I should be able to narrow it down further too."

"Good," Declan said. "You work on that, and . . . Griff?"

He inhaled, knowing what was coming. "Yeah?"

"You still have your connections?"

"Yes." They didn't go away. Once a sniper, always a sniper.

"Could you ask around? See if anyone heard anything about a hit in . . ." Declan turned to Finley. "Have you estimated time of death?"

"Based on the soft tissue remaining, the state of the victim's clothes, and the minimal root etching on her bones . . . I'd say we're looking at under a year."

"Based on the larva remnants," Parker added. "I'd say late winter, early spring,"

"Which would explain why the grave was so shallow," Finley said. "And why he covered it with rocks. He needed the extra coverage."

Griffin raked a hand through his hair. "I still can't believe none of us noticed the smell." A recent dead body had been decomposing in their park. On a hill he'd walked a thousand times.

"The cold would have delayed decomp, hence the soft tissue," Parker said.

"But the summer months?"

"Which is what the bug life shows. There was still plenty to feed off of in the warmer months, but the grave was located quite brilliantly. Up on a hill, shaded, not a lot of standing water, which keeps things dry and slows decomp. Even the rocks prevent rodents from digging in, and last March we had that horrific snow and ice storm.

If she were buried not long before it, the snow would seal her in quite nicely."

Griffin's eyes narrowed. "That almost sounds like admiration in your voice."

Parker shook his head. "No. Just find the man's knowledge of body disposal and of the area quite intriguing."

"Which means we're not dealing with a first timer," Declan remarked.

Familiar with the area. Something kicked around in Griffin's mind. "We found a dead deer carcass up on Little Round Top last spring. April, maybe." He wrinkled his nose. "The smell lingered awhile, even though we moved the carcass farther back into the woods."

Parker rubbed his chin, fingers moving across his ridiculous goatee. "Was the deer's cause of death apparent?"

"Our guess was hunter or poacher. Looked like it might have been an arrow wound to the heart, but scavengers had already gone to work so it's hard to say."

"Let's surmise it was a poacher," Parker continued. "Why leave his kill?"

"No idea. Maybe got startled off. Maybe was just in it for the sport—sadly we see that happen a fair amount."

"Could be Jane Doe's killer knew the corpse would start decomp once the temperatures warmed so he provided an explanation."

"But that either means he hung around the month or two we're talking about or returned to throw us off."

"That would be a truly frightening possibility," Declan said.

"Why?" Finley asked.

"Because it indicates we're dealing with a clever killer, one who thinks through every detail," Parker began.

"And one a lot closer to home than I'd care to consider," Griffin said.

"So"—Declan turned to Griffin—"your asking questions of your sniper contacts may prove our best lead. Ask about hits this past winter, early spring, and a sniper who prefers to use a Dragunov."

"I'll ask around, but snipers aren't exactly the chatty sort."

"What? A charming guy like you? Surely you'll have no trouble," Declan said with a cheesy grin.

Griffin lifted his chin a notch. "Funny." He *could* be charming if he chose to be, but snipers certainly weren't the group to do so with. "I know a guy I can check with. He's a retired Marine sniper. Served in Vietnam. Runs a shooting range about an hour outside of Gettysburg. Nice range. He knows the area fairly well, but just because Jane Doe was shot local or at least buried local, doesn't mean the shooter is. Parker's theory about him returning to the crime scene is just a theory." Parker was great at those. Results were a different matter.

Parker cocked his head. "Never said otherwise."

"How soon can you head to the range?" Declan quickly asked. Always the peacekeeper, or at least he attempted to be.

"I can go tomorrow after my shift."

"Great."

"In the meantime, I'll keep working the trace evidence," Parker said, turning back to his equipment.

"Let's plan on meeting here tomorrow night," Declan said. "Say . . . six? We can go over the progress we've made, share a bite to eat."

Parker and Griffin looked at each other, and after a moment's hesitation Griffin nodded. If he could help bring a killer to justice just by asking some questions and relaying those answers, he was in. It didn't mean he had to like the close proximity to Parker.

"Sounds great," Finley said, clearly wanting to remain in the loop.

Declan stepped from the counter he'd been leaning against. "I'll get started searching missing persons reports now that we have a descrip-tion and key parameters." He smiled, clearly enjoying all of them being together again. Of course he would.

Declan waved and disappeared down the hall.

"I should head back to my office," Finley said. "Got a lot of work ahead of me."

Griffin followed her out. "Can I wait and give you a lift?" He wanted to see her safely home.

"Thanks, but I'll be a while. I'll have Parker give me a ride. He'll be here just as late and lives not far from me."

Griffin swallowed, not wanting to think about Parker seeing Finley home for a multitude of reasons. "Okay. See you later," he said, ducking out before she could respond. He'd feel better personally seeing her home, but maybe this way was better after all—it wouldn't give her a chance to prod into his past.

He maintained a quick pace down the corridor, the soles of his Merrill boots squeaking on the freshly mopped floor, the abrasive scent of Lysol wafting like a thick cloud in the air between the dropped ceiling and cinderblock walls.

Within seconds, Finley's springy steps echoed down the hall after him.

He hung his head. He should have known better. She was far too inquisitive.

"Hey," she said, hurrying to catch up. "You left quickly."

"Wanted to let you get to work."

"Thanks, but the least I can do is walk you out. You probably just saved my life."

He hated to think of her being in danger, but

his gut told him she still was—at least until Jane Doe was ID'd.

"So you were a sniper?" Finley said.

"Yes." He kept moving toward the outer door, not planning on going into detail. Especially not the gritty ones that haunted him at night. Not the ones that would destroy any respect she might hold for him.

"That must have been an unusual job."

Most people used *interesting* or *hard*. "That it was." When he pushed through the metal door out into the parking lot, small flakes of snow—unusual for November—fluttered around them.

She leaned against the stair rail, staring up at him with wide blue eyes. "Why the career change?" She asked so innocently, so sweetly, he didn't have the heart to shut her out—at least not fully.

He wrapped his scarf around his neck and tucked the ends into his pea coat. "Couldn't do it anymore."

She nodded, understanding filling her eyes. He couldn't linger there, couldn't handle the pity that usually followed. He allowed his gaze to follow the curve of her cheek down along her delicate chin and then up to her lips—pink and full and cracked ever so slightly, her breath evaporating in the cold night air. She tilted her head back, and he made the mistake of looking her in the eyes, surprised to find longing, not pity, residing there.

He swallowed hard and took a deliberate step back. "Good night, Ms. Scott."

Disappointment filled her eyes. "I thought we were past that."

He scanned the parking lot, the unsettling sensation of being watched raking over him again. "You should get back inside."

"Why?" She stiffened as his gaze swept the parking lot. "What's wrong?"

"Just humor me." Placing a hand on her slender waist, he directed her back inside and, ignoring the perplexed expression on her face, shut the door behind her, making sure it was locked before taking a solid walk around the perimeter. Cops still maintained a presence for now, but he'd feel a whole lot better after Jane Doe was ID'd and Finley Scott was no longer involved.

"Tonight *clearly* did not go as planned," he said over the burner cell.

He swallowed hard. "I'm afraid not."

"You know what needs to be done?"

"Yes."

"Good. Don't screw it up."

— 9 —

The following afternoon Griffin stood at the edge of the crime-scene tape surrounding the grave on Little Round Top. Soon it would be removed and things would go back to routine.

Routine—something he typically valued. However, going back to routine also meant Finley's archaeological dig officially wrapped up today. No more daily interactions with the vivacious Dr. Scott. The thought of not seeing her on a regular basis left him . . . *empty,* and that was unacceptable. A clear warning sign he needed to stay away.

He rubbed the back of his neck. It was a good thing she was leaving, even if it felt anything but.

"Hey there." Her voice echoed behind him.

He turned to find her cresting the hill from the lower parking lot.

"Figured this is where you'd be." She was decked out in her dig coveralls and a pair of polka-dot rubber boots, and was still breathtaking.

He tried to suppress the pleasure her presence triggered. "Didn't expect to see you here today."

"What can I say?" She shrugged. "Couldn't stay away."

His shoulders broadened with his smile. "Really?"

She gestured to the grave. "I see you couldn't either."

The grave. *Right.* Of course that's what she was talking about, and she was correct in that sense. A woman being found in his park, on his watch—he most definitely wanted to see her killer brought to justice. But that wasn't where his thoughts had been since Finley appeared.

She linked her arms across her chest, her auburn hair vibrant as it slipped from her dark green knit hat along her shoulders and partway down her back. "Anything new pop out at you?"

"Nah. I was more trying to take in the surrounding area now that the circus has died down. I figure it stands to reason if she was buried here, she may have been killed close by. I'm scoping out the possible shooting terrain, though it's crazy to think someone could have been murdered in the park and none of us knew."

"It's over nine square miles to patrol, and I imagine you only have one officer on duty during off hours. No way to patrol it all at once. Besides, he hid her grave well."

"Yeah, he's not only a skilled shot, but his willingness to get his hands dirty, *if* he's the one who buried her, indicates a paid hit and disposal to me." He glanced at his watch, hating to leave

Finley now that she'd just arrived, but he needed to head for the range. "I'm sorry, but I'm going to have to duck out."

"Heading for the shooting range?"

"Yeah. I told Declan I'd head up after my shift, so I better get going before it closes." It was an outdoor range, and the sun was setting earlier and earlier.

She rocked back on her boots, the ground still a wee bit damp from all the rain. "How about I come with?"

"What?" She wanted to accompany him to a shooting range?

"Sebastian's got the dig wrap-up under control. It's his day and he's an eager grad student. Don't want to crush his joy. Besides, I've got nothing better to do."

"Shooting ranges aren't exactly glamorous."

She glanced at him sideways. "Not sure what that statement implies about me, but I'm guessing that's your way of saying I won't fit in?"

He could only imagine the men's reaction when she waltzed in.

She tucked her hands in her pockets. "Look at it this way. It'll appear more natural if you're teaching a friend to shoot and we happen to ask some questions, rather then you going in just to get some answers, right?"

"Y . . . e . . . ah."

"Good. Now that that's settled, let me change

69

out of my dig clothes. I've got a duffel in my car. I won't be but ten minutes."

Nine minutes later, Griffin leaned against his truck, a cup of coffee in hand, a second one waiting in the passenger's side cup holder for Finley. True to her word, she was striding toward him in under ten, her work attire replaced by a pair of dark jeans, black boots cresting her knees, a bright blue silky top, and a snug-fitting black fleece lined with blue.

Heads would turn when she entered the shooting range, though they'd turn no matter what she was wearing. The lady was gorgeous. Yet another reason spending time together was a very, *very* bad idea. He just wished he wasn't so happy about it.

Finley looked over at Griffin, the afternoon sun silhouetting his chiseled features. Why was he no longer a sniper?

"So"—she shifted to face him—"tell me about being a sniper."

"It's a job of precision, discipline, and mastery."

"How'd you prepare for the profession?"

He explained his love of target shooting from a young age, his training with the police force, and an auxiliary class he'd been handpicked to participate in at Quantico for extra training in handling any form of domestic terrorist attack or hostage situation.

"Sounds like you really felt called to do the job and excelled at it."

"I . . . *did*." The word lodged thick in his throat, the syllable creaking out.

She was pushing her luck. Pressing a private man to share. But she was intrigued.

"May I ask what happened?"

He exhaled. "I was a tactical officer with the Baltimore Police Department's SWAT unit," he began. "I specialized in hostage situations." His body tensed. "There was a call. A hostage situation the summer before last. I arrived on the scene. A man was holding a woman at gunpoint—an attempted rape interrupted. Someone heard her scream and grabbed two patrol officers he'd seen at the corner diner.

"They quickly boxed the perp in. He was stuck and knew it, so he put a gun to the woman's head and threatened to shoot if they didn't let him go. Hostage negotiators and SWAT were called in. We had him cornered in the woman's building.

"The negotiator was talking him down, or so we thought, when he burst out the door, the gun to the woman's head, trying to make a run for it. I had the shot but hesitated." His jaw tightened. "I knew the guy. Tim Bowers. We went to the same gym. Played racquetball weekly. Shared lunch afterward."

"It's only natural it gave you pause."

"It may be a natural civilian reaction, but not a sniper's. I had target acquisition and a clear shot. When I hesitated, Tim moved and the sniper on the adjacent roof took the shot. He wasn't as good. He didn't kill Tim, at least not outright. Tim pulled the trigger, instantly killing Judith Connelly, before collapsing to the ground. An innocent woman is dead because of me."

"You weren't the one holding her hostage, and you certainly weren't the one who pulled the trigger."

Pain etched across his face. "Exactly."

Stupid choice of words. "I mean Tim Bowers is responsible for Judith's death. Not you."

"It was my job to protect her. I was trained to pull the trigger once I had the shot. Not to allow emotion to infringe."

Griffin pulled into the Red Barn parking lot and cut the engine. He didn't blame Finley for being curious, and for some reason he felt compelled to share the truth with her. It was time. Better she knew up front.

Stepping from the truck, he inhaled a deep breath of the crisp air.

The gun store and shooting range office occupied a revamped big red barn. The range was located on the far side of an old wheat field—several fields, actually.

It didn't take more than Finley stepping from

his truck for heads to turn, the few men in the parking lot already enraptured.

He rested his hand on the small of her back, ignoring how much he loved the sensation. It was a presumptuous move on his part, but he felt protective of the lady, and her soft smile up at him said she didn't mind the gesture. "Let's head inside."

"Griff," the older man working the counter said as they stepped inside. "I see you've brought a friend." The old man's grey eyes perked.

Griffin's hand remained steadfast on the gentle curve of Finley's back. "Hey. May I introduce Finley Scott."

"Finley," the man said with a nod. "Unusual name."

"Unique lady," Griffin said. He kept his eyes on Gunny but could feel the smile on Finley's lips without seeing it.

"You ever shot before?" Gunny asked Finley.

"No, sir, but I've been wanting to learn."

"Sir?" He shook his head with a wheezy chuckle. "Don't think I've ever been a 'sir.' "

"Oh, I'm sorry . . ." Her brow creased.

"You," he said with a smile, "can call me Gunny."

"Gunny?"

"It's what everyone calls me."

"Gunny was a Marine gunnery sergeant and the name stuck," Griffin explained.

"Oh," she said. "Thank you so much for your service to our country."

His eyes sparkled with pride. "Don't get much thanks these days. Though back during 'Nam when I served it was a lot worse."

"I'm sorry about that."

"You weren't even alive then."

"The tail end."

"But far too young to remember."

"I've worked—" Thankfully she cut herself off. "I studied the effects of war on casualties."

"Ah." Gunny went back to cleaning his gun. "Reading's one thing. Living it, another." He lifted his chin. "Griff can attest to that."

Griffin nodded solemnly.

"Don't tell me you're still hiding?"

"It was a career change, Gun."

"Same diff." The old man shrugged.

Could he come shoot at the range one time without Gunny bringing that up?

"The lady and I would like a lane."

"You got your equipment?"

"Yep."

"Take lane four, and good luck, missy. I'll be curious to see if you do as well as I'm anticipating."

"Oh, like I said, I've never shot a gun before."

"Doesn't mean you don't possess the innate skill. For some people it's like breathing—comes naturally. Like, Griff, here. He tell you—"

Griffin held up his hand. "Let's not bore poor Finley with old stories."

"Not that old."

Griffin lifted the target paper. "Thanks, Gunny."

Gunny waved with a smile, his gaze full of mirth.

"He seemed nice," Finley said as they exited through the rear of the building.

"Ornery is more like it."

"Why didn't you ask him any questions?"

"After we shoot."

— 10 —

The range was pretty quiet this time of day. Only a handful of men occupied the various lanes, a wooden-roofed structure protecting them from glare and weather.

Gunny had put them on lane four, which allowed for targets out to three hundred yards, but they'd start at twenty-five for Finley.

He fastened his target down range and strode back to her, noticing that her auburn hair was striking in the late-afternoon sunlight.

She nibbled at her bottom lip.

"You nervous?" he asked, picking up his .22 pistol.

"A little." She shifted from foot to foot, the crisp fall air biting. "But also excited." Her blue eyes shone with enthusiasm. "I've been wanting to learn to shoot."

"Any particular reason?"

She pushed her hands into her jean pockets, toeing the concrete slab with her shoe. "Just think it's a good skill for a woman to have."

There clearly was more reason behind her desire to learn to shoot, but he wouldn't prod. He, of all people, appreciated privacy. "Before we start we need to go over the safety instruction portion of our afternoon."

"Of course."

"First, you always want to make sure you start with the safety on." He stood behind her, wrapped his arms around her waist and placed his hands over hers. Fireworks shot through him, ricocheting along his nerve endings.

She smiled softly back at him . . . *surprise* in her eyes.

Why surprise?

Was her heart racing too?

He should have never let her come along. Time spent with Finley Scott was *dangerous*.

He swallowed, his throat dry, but managed to continue, "Always point it down range."

"How's this?" she asked.

Perfection. "Great," he managed to grit out. "You're lined up perfectly. Now, you want to release the safety and move your finger from the trigger guard onto the trigger."

She listened intently, doing as instructed.

"Next, get a good sight picture."

Nodding, her silky hair brushed his cheek, tickling his jaw.

She was ready, but he was so hesitant to let go, knowing he'd probably never get to hold her in his arms like this again.

"Once you have the sight picture, you begin to squeeze the trigger. Nice and smooth."

"Got it."

Ever so reluctantly, he moved his arms away and took a step back, his heart still racing. This was very, *very* bad.

Her shot, however, was anything but. The gun reported, and a quick glance through the binoculars confirmed she'd hit the bull's-eye. "Great job."

"Really?" She glanced up, beaming—her eyes glistening, her cheeks rosy, her smile forming an adorable dimple in the hollow of her right cheek.

Her happiness was contagious and her presence addictive. There was just something about the woman that held him fast.

"Take a look," he said, handing her the binoculars.

She glanced back with pleasure lingering on her lips at the sight of her bull's-eye. "I credit having a great teacher."

He smiled. Of course she'd say that. "Wanna go again?"

"Absolutely!"

An hour later, they decided it was best to return to the purpose of their visit—asking questions. Finley had garnered quite the fan base, with the men swinging by to congratulate her on her natural shooting skills.

Griffin knew a few of the men, so he started yammering, first asking about the Dragunov, feigning interest in possibly purchasing one—not that he'd actually mind adding one to his collection. It was an impressive weapon.

Nearly all the guys suggested he talk with a man named Vern Michaels. Michaels was a former decorated sniper who'd lost his right leg during the first Gulf War and who shot at the range daily.

"If anyone knows anything useful, what shooters have that rifle, where to seek further answers, Vern's your guy," Tag said.

"Thanks, man." Griffin shook Tag's hand and that of his friend, Bill. Tag and Griff had competed against each other during numerous competitions, taking first and second place three years running in the Junior Olympics.

"Missed you at Mammoth last year," Tag said.

"Yeah." Griffin rubbed the back of his neck, conscious of Finley's curious attention. "Needed a break." How could he compete in shooting competitions after what happened?

"Well, it's good to see you, man. Hope to see you on the competition range next year."

Griffin nodded, letting his answer appear open-ended, but he'd already made up his mind. No more awards for a skill he'd failed at when a woman's life had hung in the balance.

"I heard the lady is quite a shot," Gunny said with a denture-filled grin as they reentered the store.

Of course news traveled fast. Hopefully the answer they sought did the same.

"What time is Vern Michaels usually in?" Daily snipers like Vern were nothing if not routine and in-the-know. Sounded like he was the perfect connection. If anyone knew snipers in the area, it'd be a daily guy like Michaels.

Gunny's eyes narrowed. "What's your interest in Vern?"

Of course Gunny would be protective of his regulars.

"I've got some questions about a rifle. Heard he's the guy to ask."

Gunny lifted his arms, indicting the vast weapon stock enclosing him in glass cases along the U-shaped counter he stood behind. "Did it ever occur to you I might know a thing or two?"

"Of course. I was planning on asking you. Figured I'd check with Vern too. The more insight, the better."

"Which rifle you interested in?"

"Dragunov."

Gunny's jaw tightened. "Why that weapon?"

Griffin glanced around to be certain there weren't any listening ears, then leaned in and lowered his voice. "We're investigating a sniper hit that took place last winter."

"Or early spring," Finley added.

Gunny's lips thinned. "Is that right? And you figured my clientele were the ones to question?"

"No. It's not like I think someone here . . . I just figured it was best to start at a place I know." Though asking questions like this in your own backyard was frowned upon.

Gunny's eyes narrowed, his jaw shifting. "Is this about that Gettysburg grave?"

Griffin nodded.

"You heard?" Finley asked.

"Been all over the news. I know Griffin works there. Now he's in here asking about a hit." His pale lips thinned again. "Not hard to put two and two together. Even for an old bird like me."

"Any thoughts?"

"Haven't seen a Dragunov around here, but Vern's pretty established in the area. He probably knows which shooters prefer that particular rifle, but that's assuming your sniper is local."

"Or regional," Griffin added.

"Hate to think we have a sniper for hire any-where around these parts."

"So there are none that you've heard of?"

Color imbued Gunny's pallid cheeks. "What did I just say?"

Got it. Gunny was done answering. "Thanks for your time."

He arched his greying brows. "I assume you'll be back?"

"Unless you want to give me Vern's home address?"

Gunny looked at him as if about to say *"Have you lost your mind, boy?"*

"Right. See you tomorrow, then."

"Wonderful." He didn't bother hiding his annoyance.

"Why's he so irritated?" Finley asked as they made their way to the door.

"Because we're using his business to seek out a killer."

She glanced back at the older man. "You think Gunny suspects who the killer might be?"

Griffin exhaled. "I think Gunny is bright enough to know there are a lot of really skilled shooters in the area—probably a handful of snipers, between the SWAT teams in the region and former military that have come back home following their service. Stands to reason our killer could be from around here or a transplant to the area. If he's not local, he's highly vested in keeping his and our vic's identity concealed."

• • •

The sun was beginning to set, and only a few vehicles remained in the dirt parking lot as they stepped outside, the air temperature a good ten degrees cooler than when they'd entered.

Finley turned to question Griffin about what Gunny might suspect, but his eyes widened and he suddenly grew still. Cocking his head slightly to the right, he squinted, studying the wooded slope to their right for the briefest of seconds before hollering, "Get down!"

Instinct kicked in and Finley dropped to the dirt, her elbows absorbing the brunt of the hit. What was happening? Panic seared through her like a knife fileting a fish—rapid and gut-wrenching.

Griffin rolled underneath the truck to her side and pulled her behind the wheel well, his arms holding her fast.

"What's happening?" Her pulse whooshed in a frantic frenzy.

"Sniper, I think. Twelve o'clock. About eight hundred meters out."

"A sniper? You don't . . . ?" Of course it was *him*. What were the chances another sniper would have them in his sights? "What do we do?"

"Get in the truck, lay low on the floorboard. I'm going after him." He opened the door for her, helping her inside.

"You're going to do *what?*"

"Find out who's tracking us." He shut the door.

The truck's floorboard was cold. The thickly grooved plastic mats pressed hard into her neck, arms, and legs as she lay curled up, wedged between the pedals and driver's seat. Memories of being stuffed in a car's trunk choked her, making it difficult to breathe. She fought to draw in a decent breath as cold sweat beaded on her skin. A chill washed over her, and her thoughts shifted to Griffin.

How could he head out after a killer? Did he possess no fear?

Squeezing her eyes shut, she prayed.

Please, Jesus, let him be okay. Let us be okay. Help me to breathe. Help me to calm down. Help keep us safe.

She continued to pour her heart out in a rush, begging her Savior to protect them. Every minute Griffin didn't return, the panic threatening to engulf her increased.

Please, Lord.

Griffin opened his truck door, and Finley bolted upright, knocking her head on the bottom of the steering wheel.

"It's me." He rested a reassuring hand on her arm. "Sorry I startled you."

She rubbed her head, her limbs trembling. "Is he gone?"

He nodded. "It's safe now." He helped her up

into his seat. "Let me take a look at your head. That was a pretty good conk you took."

He brushed back her hair, cupping her face as gently as he could, her skin cold and damp beneath his touch. She was terrified.

"Let me get the truck warming." He pulled his key from his pocket and, reaching around her, started the engine. Then he moved back to examine her forehead.

"What happened out there?"

"He was gone by the time I reached the place he'd set up." A welt was already forming at the base of her hairline. "Let me see if I've got an ice pack in my first-aid kit." He moved to grab it, but she clasped hold of his arm.

"How'd you know he was out there, watching us? Did you see him?"

"I caught a hint of light where a reflection shouldn't have been. Besides that, I sensed him."

"Sensed him?"

"It's part of sniper training. You have to learn counter-sniping—learn to spot or sense your enemy."

"Not to question you . . ."

He laughed. "But . . . ?" Curiosity and pursuing facts was part of her makeup, and what made her so impressively good at her job.

"If he was gone when you got there, how can you be certain he was there in the first place?"

"Indentation in the dried grass."

"Was he going to shoot us?"

"I don't believe so."

She frowned. "Why not? I don't understand."

"He would have had a better shot before we reached the truck." It may not have been the ideal shot, especially if she was the intended target, but it would have been the best opportunity. Once they reached the truck he'd lost his line of sight.

If she'd been the intended target . . .

He inhaled, then slowly released his breath, attempting to quell his rage. If anything happened to her . . .

He would *not* allow that to happen. Not on his watch. "From now on you're glued to me," he said.

Her nose crinkled in that adorable way that made him smile despite the circumstances. "What?"

"I can't be positive he was simply watching us. He could have been waiting for the opportune moment to strike. Either way, until we catch this guy, you're stuck with me." He'd brook no argument on the matter.

Much to his astonishment, she simply nodded in assent, and gratitude filled him at her lack of protest. Being in a sniper's crosshairs could have that effect.

Thank you, Father, for protecting us today. Please equip me to protect Finley. Shield us in the shelter of your wings. Put a hedge of protection around us, and lead us to Jane Doe's killer before he reaches us.

He was coming for them. Griffin felt it in his bones. The man was fixed on them.

Glancing at the sky, he was thankful the encroaching darkness would provide them with an added layer of cover.

He truly believed their watcher was simply that—a watcher, at least for now, but he wasn't taking any chances—not when it came to Finley. He was shifting into full protection mode, deciding just then to take a leave of absence until he was certain she was out of any danger. He had plenty of vacation time to use up.

"How did he know we'd be at the range?" she asked, still shivering.

He cranked up the heat as they pulled out of the lot.

"Did he follow us there? Was he one of the men we spoke to? Did he go out to wait for us?"

That was an awful thought—that they'd been face-to-face with Jane Doe's killer—but he was more concerned the man had followed them there. That he'd been on them all along.

— 11 —

Finley and Griffin entered the lab shortly after six that night, her heart still jerking with flutters every few beats, flipping and tossing in a disconcerting manner. Whether from the close call and the knowledge of being in a sniper's crosshairs or from the knowledge that Griffin would be glued to her, she couldn't be certain. Either way, her heart was hammering.

Patricia, the saint who kept the lab running and properly stocked, approached dressed in her overcoat and scarf.

"How are you doing?" Finley greeted her, praying she didn't ask in return.

"I still can't believe John is gone."

"Me either."

With a sigh, Patricia shook her head. "I hate to rush off, but I've got a half hour to pick Matt up from indoor soccer practice, and with 95 traffic this time of day . . . I'm really pushing it. "

"Drive safe."

"Thanks. Oh, UPS delivered a package a few hours ago. I told him to leave it on your desk as usual."

"Thanks."

Patricia smiled. "You *two* have a nice night." Swiping her card through the reader, she gave

Finley a quick wink before the automated doors swung open and she stepped out of the lab.

Attempting to ignore Patricia's prodding, she focused on the large digital clock on the wall— the neon-blue numbers bright against the black rectangular background. "Everyone else should be here soon. Want a cup of coffee or espresso while we wait?"

"Sure. I'd love a double espresso."

"No idea how you'll sleep tonight after that, but you got it." Or how his body could take any more adrenaline. She was still wired—her nerve endings tingling through her fingertips and toes.

Leading the way to her office, she dropped her bag on the navy sofa piled high with navy-and-white coastal-themed pillows—images of sea turtles, crabs, and starfish lining the fluffy back. She didn't get to spend much time on the sofa, but it was a nice place to sit and read when she had research to do.

She moved to the espresso machine she'd picked up on her last trip to Rome and turned it on. The machine purred to life while she ground the illy beans—the deep scent of roasted coffee filled the air. She tamped the espresso grounds into the container, slid it in place, and hit the On button. The machine set to work, steaming with a high-pitched whistle before the ebony liquid streamed out. She waited for the froth to drop, and then hit the Off button and handed him his cup.

"Thanks. Smells delicious. And you too?" His eyes widened. "I mean . . . Aren't *you* having espresso *too?*" He leaned against the counter and took a sip, his cheeks slightly red-tinged beneath his evening scruff. Never thought she'd see the day when Ranger McCray was embarrassed.

She pulled another silver illy coffee container out of the cabinet. "Decaf."

He smirked. "Where's the fun in that?"

"Trust me, you don't want to see me without sleep." She began the process all over, again reveling in the soothing scent of the beans.

Griffin lifted the small blue cup to his lips. "I already have." He took another sip.

She lifted a brow. When had he seen her without sleep? "Oh . . . right." The night they'd found Jane Doe. They had stayed up all night. "Your coffee helped."

"I'm glad, but this . . ." He lifted the cup. "Is divinely better."

"It's hard to beat illy." It was the best.

They took a seat on her sofa, and she kicked her feet up onto the ottoman. The hammering of her heart finally slowed to a peaceful, contented beat. She had been utterly grateful for Griffin's steadfast presence that night and again today. He'd helped calm her, despite the threat of danger. She'd seriously thought their midnight visitor at

Gettysburg had just been a local curious about their find, but after their close call with the sniper today, she was rethinking it all. She glanced to her desk, remembering the package Patricia had mentioned, and frowned. "That's weird."

"What is?"

"Patricia said UPS left a package on my desk, but there's nothing there." She stood and moved to it, searching the desktop and all around it in case the package had dropped, but there was no package to be found.

Griffin helped her search the rest of her office.

"Any chance someone else picked it up?" he asked when they'd finished a full sweep of the room.

She shook her head. "Not without me signing off on it first." They had a set protocol everyone followed.

"Maybe it got delivered to the wrong office."

"Ed knows my office. I always make him a cappuccino to go when he drops by."

"Maybe it wasn't Ed."

"Hmm. I suppose someone could be filling in." It'd happened a time or two. "Patricia never said Ed. Just said the UPS man."

"I'll bet that's it."

"What's it?" Declan asked from the doorway, lifting his brows with a cheeky grin. "Hope I'm not interrupting anything."

Finley restrained a frown. She wasn't ready to

lose her alone time with Griffin yet. She felt like she was finally getting to really know him, to see beyond the gruff exterior he liked to keep in place.

Watching him in action today . . . feeling his protective hand on her back . . . His strong arms wrapped around her—for as short a time as it may have been—had stirred feelings she hadn't felt since before . . .

Her stomach knotted.

On the other hand, the sniper situation had also stirred feelings she battled daily—fear and vulnerability. Nothing new. Not since last year. Not since Brent Howard.

Declan hopped up on the edge of Finley's conference table. "Whatcha two up to?"

"Trying to hunt down a missing package," Griffin said.

"Great." Declan clapped his hands together. "I'll help."

"Help with what?" Parker asked as he strode in.

"We're apparently searching for a missing package," Declan said.

"Don't worry about it," she said, trying to settle the unease churning inside from the mere thought of Brent Howard. "I'll check with the rest of the staff tomorrow. I'm sure it's here somewhere." Hopefully it didn't hold anything too time sensitive.

"Chinese is ready in the lounge," Declan said.

"Great." Finley placed a hand over her rumbling stomach. "I'm starved."

And she hoped the food would settle the queasiness. She'd had another night terror last night, no doubt triggered by the finding of Jane Doe's body. She had to get over this. It was her profession, and she refused to let Brent Howard affect her love of her job. He'd already stolen her peace. She wouldn't let him have any more.

Please, Lord, let this case be straightforward from here on out. Don't let it turn into another Howard case.

But she knew in her heart this case was going to be anything but straightforward. God seemed to think her way stronger than she was.

Griffin entered the lounge to find a tall, slender blonde waiting.

"Everyone, I'd like you to meet my photographer, Avery Tate," Parker said, swooping in behind him. "Avery, this is Chief Ranger Griffin McCray."

She nodded at him with a smile, and Griffin returned the gesture.

"And this"—Parker clamped Declan on the shoulder as he entered—"is Federal Agent Declan Grey."

Avery looked between the men, and her eyes narrowed with a twinkle. "*The* Griffin and Declan?"

Declan smiled. "So you *are* telling stories out of school again?"

"Like I said, only the good ones." Parker winked.

Great. Griffin sighed. He had no desire for a walk down memory lane.

"And this . . ." Parker said, "is the renowned Dr. Scott."

Avery extended a hand. "It's a pleasure, Dr. Scott."

"Finley, please."

Avery nodded.

"Now that we're all acquainted, how about we eat?" Griffin said, hoping to keep any story sharing to a minimum.

Two brown paper sacks sat on the lounge table. He reached in and pulled one red-and-white container out after another.

"Griff, you wanna say the blessing?" Declan asked once they'd all fixed their plates.

"Sure." He bowed his head.

"Thank you, Father, for providing for all our needs. For this food we are grateful, and even more so for keeping Finley and me safe today. Thank you for not allowing us to be shot. Amen."

All eyes shifted to him.

Declan arched his brows. "Something you want to tell us?"

The ranger was good. Clearly there was more to him than met the eye. Only someone with a similar skill set could have caught sight of him. He placed the Dragunov in his case—cleaned and ready for next time. And there would be a next time. But first it was time to find out exactly whom he was dealing with.

— 12 —

"Do you think he followed you there?" Parker asked, taking a bite of kung pao chicken.

"But how could he know we'd be there?" Finley asked, pinching her lo mein noodles with her chopsticks. "Unless he was one of the men we spoke to."

"I doubt it's that easy," Griffin said, popping a steamed dumpling in his mouth. Stranger things had happened, but finding Jane Doe's killer at the first shooting range they'd visited seemed far too easy. And he couldn't ignore the feeling that the man had been stalking them ever since they'd uncovered Jane Doe's body.

"Another possibility exists," Parker said. "Someone you talked to could have let him know that you were poking around, asking questions."

"Which would mean one of the men we spoke with knows the killer," Finley said.

"Make a list of everyone you spoke with." Declan pulled a small pad and pen from his shirt pocket and tossed it to Griffin.

"Most only go by their first name or a nick-name."

"Yeah," Finley said, dabbing the soy sauce from her bottom lip.

Such a full, soft lip that he'd love to . . . Griffin straightened. *Get your head in the game.* They were dealing with a killer and he was entranced with Finley. He needed to focus.

"We spoke with a gentleman named Gator today," she said, a smile rounding her lips.

Griffin laughed. "Don't think Gator could ever be accused of such."

Finley smirked. "Well, he was a gentleman with me."

Griffin shook his head. "They all were. You should have seen them. Some serious rough-necks, a former sniper, even a former Navy Seal. All polite and flirtatious as could be."

"They didn't *flirt* with me." She pointed her chopsticks in his direction. "They were too scared with you around."

Parker chuckled. "Jealous sort, are we, Griff?"

He gave Parker a warning glare.

Parker took the hint and slouched back in his chair, kicking his booted feet up on the empty chair opposite him with a playful grin.

"I just meant they clearly respected your presence," Finley said, pushing her chopsticks around in her container. She looked up, her heartfelt gaze locking on him. "So did I."

He swallowed, warmth flooding him. How did she do that with a simple smile? Because her smile was anything but ordinary.

Parker and Declan exchanged bemused glances, but were wise enough to let it drop. The time for silly ribbing had ceased years ago. They were grown men. Though he doubted it'd be that easy. They'd mouth off again. They were just considerate enough to wait until they were out of Finley's presence. Besides, as good as he felt in Finley's presence and at the thought of spending more time with her, he still couldn't go there. Listening to his instincts was dangerous, and even more importantly, he wasn't where he needed to be spiritually to be in a relationship.

God called husbands to love their wives like the church—that he believed he could do—but he couldn't lead his wife while still struggling with his own demons. Until he conquered them, he couldn't move forward. And he certainly wasn't into casual dating, and most definitely not with an amazing woman like Finley Scott. If he pursued her, it'd be with passion and purpose.

"What about your friend Gunny?" Declan asked.

"He tried his best to be charming with Finley at least until we started asking the hard questions." All he'd had to say was *Dragunov* and the man's demeanor shifted. Did Gunny know more than he was saying?

"He probably knows the real names, last names, of the men you spoke with."

"Maybe, but no guarantees. You'd be surprised at the level of anonymity most of these guys manage to keep—pay cash, stick to basic topics —guns, ammo, politics—but I'll ask Gunny tomorrow."

"Tomorrow?" Avery lurched forward in her chair. "You're going *back?*"

"We need to speak with Vern Michaels," Finley said.

Parker shifted. "You're going back too?"

Finley nodded.

He dipped his head in Griffin's direction. "You think that wise?"

Griffin opened his mouth to respond, but Finley cut in before he could get a word out. "I'm going."

He exhaled. As much as he didn't want her out of his sight, perhaps she would be safer at the lab. "It might not—"

"Stop right there. I'm going. Either with you or on my own."

Parker's lips twitched with admiration. "Looks like she's not giving you a choice."

Griffin smiled. "Guess not." And it didn't surprise him in the least. The woman was the definition of determination. He shifted his gaze to Declan. "Any luck on identifying our Jane Doe?"

Declan wiped his mouth and set his empty plate aside. "I quickly expanded our missing persons search, as no Jane Does matched locally." He stood, moving to the whiteboard they'd pulled into the lounge.

Parker lifted his chin. "And?"

"And I've found four possibilities by extending our reach regionally." He pulled out four missing-person flyers and stepped to the whiteboard, pinning them up with thumbtack-size magnets.

Four images of beautiful women, all in their twenties and thirties, all blond, and all missing. Just the sight of them hit Griffin hard in the gut. He kept his gaze fixed fast on the board, careful not to look at Parker.

"First victim is Jennifer Beckham," Declan began. "She's from Chevy Chase. Age twenty-five. Reported missing March sixth by her roommate when she didn't show up for a birthday party. No significant leads reported. Second victim is Karen Miller. Age thirty-five, reported missing February twenty-third by her friend after receiving no word from her for three days. There was a history of domestic violence in the home, but no evidence to hold the husband on. Third victim is Marley Trent. Reported missing on March ninth by a co-worker when she didn't show up to work. No open leads. And last—"

"Wait," Finley interrupted, standing.

Declan arched a brow. "Yes?"

"Is that Marley Trent, as in social justice lawyer Marley Trent?"

Declan glanced back over the information he had. Just the bare essentials. "It says she was a lawyer. Why? Did you know her?"

"Not personally, but definitely by reputation. She's one of Towson University's star alums. She finished her undergrad degree there—well, one of them—but it was before I started on staff. The woman is a legend."

"Why's that?"

"She fights for those who can't fight for themselves."

Griffin smiled at her. "Sounds like someone I know."

She smiled back. "I'd like to think we share or shared a purpose in our work. Both fighting injustice, just in different areas. She was a remarkable woman. I hate to think it's her, but it would be nice to finally know what happened."

"It could be her," Declan said. "But there are four possibilities."

"Right." Finley smoothed her shirt and retook her seat. "Sorry to interrupt."

"No problem at all. If it is Marley Trent, you may be a great asset to us, knowing what you do about the woman. Now . . . where were we . . ." Declan's eyes tracked over the information he had about the woman on the final flyer. "Alexandra Samson. From Westminster. Age thirty-one. Reported missing by her parents March third when they arrived for a visit and found her home broken into and no sign of Alex. She lived alone, and it appears she may have been missing for a couple days before her folks arrived. Detectives on the case looked pretty deeply into a male neighbor but couldn't make anything stick."

"So they are all cold cases?" Griffin loathed the term. They all did.

Declan looked down. "I'm afraid so."

"What's the next step?" Finley asked.

"We check into getting more information about the women—to see if anything matches up with the hat and ring we found on our Jane Doe. I also pulled dentals on all the missing women." Declan grabbed the oversized manila envelopes and handed them to Finley.

"Great. I'll have Dr. Kent do the comparisons," she said. "He's the best odontologist on the east coast. I'll run these up to his office. Sometimes he works late—actually prefers to, I think. I'll also pop in on Shirley. She's the forensic artist I called in. Let me check on her progress. It's possible we may have a rendering of our victim's face tonight."

Declan looked to Parker as Finley ducked out of the room. "What about you? Any progress on your end?"

"Yes." He retrieved a file from the counter, and Avery joined him at the whiteboard, pinning up magnified shots of the trace evidence in question. "Avery spent today combing back over all the shots I took. The first particulates we found definitely were glass. Glass specifically manufactured for cars. GMC vehicles to be precise, but this particular glass was used only from 2005–2008, which narrows things down significantly." He shifted to the next photo. "The second particulate we removed from our victim's baseball hat and Dr. Scott removed from her skull is a plastic used in camera flashes."

"Camera flashes?" Declan asked.

"That's correct. I'm narrowing it down as quickly as I can to locate which particular brands and models it's used in. I should have a manageable list for you in the next twenty-four hours."

"Okay." Griffin sat, hunching forward, resting his hands on his thighs. "Are you saying our victim was shot through a car window *and* a camera flash?"

Parker nodded. "That's what the evidence shows."

Griffin exhaled.

"What?"

"Our sniper is a superior shot. Fifteen hundred meters is select enough, maybe a hundred guys in the world, but through two barriers . . ." He shook his head with a whistle. "We're dealing with an extraordinarily skilled sniper."

Which made the fact he'd had Finley and him in his crosshairs a whole new level of deadly. He looked to Finley as she reentered the room and swallowed. Sticking to her like glue didn't come close. She'd better get ready, because if they didn't ID the vic tonight, he'd be bunking on her couch. Yeah, it might be overkill, but better to be overly cautious than risk anything happening to her.

— 13 —

"Dr. Scott," Declan said, using formal names, as he did when he was getting serious. He recapped what Parker had shared while she was out of the room, and then asked, "Is that concurrent with your findings?"

"Yes. Fragments of glass and what we now know are shards of camera flash were embedded in our victim's skull at the point of impact."

"Which explains why the bullet didn't exit the skull," Griffin said, standing and moving to the whiteboard to examine the gunshot wound more closely.

"Meaning . . . ?" Avery asked.

"Even at a distance of fifteen hundred meters, there should be both entry and exit wounds. I was curious why the bullet embedded in the brain rather than shooting straight through, but if the bullet had to travel through two barriers before hitting the victim's head, that would slow the velocity further, causing the bullet to lodge in her brain."

"Okay, so how does this information help with the case?" Finley asked.

"For one, it tells us what the victim was doing at the time of her death," Declan said. "Taking pictures."

"Or using her camera as a telescopic device," Avery offered.

Declan frowned. "What?"

"If I want to see something that's out of my field of vision more clearly, I'll look through my telephoto lens."

"Excellent point. Okay, so our victim was either watching someone or taking pictures of them," Parker said.

Griffin shifted. "I don't know. . . .That's quite a leap."

Parker stiffened. "How do you figure?"

"If our victim was a tourist at Gettysburg, she might simply have been taking photos of the battlefield."

"True," Declan said. "*If* she was killed at Gettysburg, but I think given the evidence we have, regardless of what our victim was doing at the time of her death, hers was a professional hit with that kind of shot."

"Or some sicko's target practice," Griffin said.

Finley's eyes widened. "What?"

"You cannot be serious?" Avery gaped.

"Sorry to break it to you, but there are monsters in this world." Some way too close to home.

"Somebody would seriously kill another human being for sport?" Finley's face paled with disgust.

"I'd love to tell you it's never happened," Griffin said.

"Why? How? I don't understand."

Because it was beyond comprehension.

"Men get used to killing in war. Snipers are no different. Some of them feed off of it. Being in control. Taking a life with the squeeze of a trigger. I'm not saying that's what we're dealing with, but it's always best to consider every possibility, no matter how improbable."

Professor Warner, their mentor and friend, had instilled the adage into their brains throughout their college years and beyond. *"No matter how improbable, consider every possibility."* It didn't have to be probable to happen, just possible.

"Okay. Let's run both scenarios," Declan said, rubbing his hands together. "Scenario one, our victim was spying on someone, which could be the reason for her death. She saw something she wasn't supposed to."

"That would indicate the person she was spying on knew she was spying and set her up for the kill," Griffin said. "He or she gave her something to watch to hold her attention while the sniper took her out."

"Meaning she was lured to her death," Finley said. "Set up."

Griffin nodded.

"Scenario two, the sniper was simply waiting at a public location hoping for a mark to hit."

"Of the two, the first scenario is the most plausible, but we shouldn't discount the latter. Hopefully between the forensic artist rendering and dentals we should have a match tonight."

Griffin prayed for Finley's safety—and the victim's family's peace of mind—but the thought of no longer needing to be at Finley's side disappointed him on a far deeper level than anticipated. What was it about this woman that entranced him so? Whatever *it* was, it had to be ignored. As soon as he was certain Finley was safe, he was back to Gettysburg and routine. That's where he belonged, regardless of what his gut kept saying.

— 14 —

"Dental results are in, Dr. Scott." Finley looked up several hours later to find another one of the lab techs, Max, standing in front of her with a folder, his jaw tight. They all wanted to find John's and Jane Doe's killer—assuming they were one and the same.

"Thanks." She blinked the drowsiness from her eyes and grasped it, praying it held the answers they needed, though disappointment sifted through her at the thought of not being paired with Griffin any longer. She opened the folder.

Most doctors sent results via the computer, but Dr. Kent was old school. She didn't mind in the least though, considering his level of expertise and his compulsion for working until his desk was cleared each day—as late as that might take.

She looked across the lounge at Griffin. There was something so calming and yet tantalizing about his steadfast presence. "Here comes the moment of truth," she said. Swallowing, she glanced up at the women's faces on the whiteboard. Whose family were they about to bring closure to?

"Results, I hope," Declan said, striding back in the lounge.

"Yes."

"Great. I've got some of my own." He'd set up a command center of sorts in a recently evacuated office down the hall from Finley's while they waited, not wanting to be far away when news came in.

"So do I," Parker said, rejoining the group. He and Avery had been hard at work on the trace evidence.

"Wonderful." They'd be able to give Jane Doe a name and a family closure. She looked at Griffin, anticipation darting through her. She loved this part. Finding the answer. Giving the dead back their identity. It's why she did what she did.

"You first," Declan said, lifting his chin.

With a deep breath, she flipped open and scanned the folder's contents. Shock rippled through her. It couldn't be. "I don't believe it."

Declan shifted. "What is it?"

She handed him the file. "No match."

He frowned. "What do you mean no match?"

"That's what the report says." How could it *not* be one of their victims?

"But victim number three, Marley Trent, drove a 2007 GMC Silver Envoy," Declan said.

"Which matches the glass fragments found on her remains," Parker added.

"Right." Declan's voice held the urgency Finley felt sifting through her. Wanting something so badly, being so close you could grasp it, and yet feeling it slip through your fingers. "Parker, you said you had results as well?"

"I did some tracking on Jane Doe's ring. As you know there was no alma mater on it. Just the phrase *Omnia Pro Patria,* and the emblem of a town."

"And?" Declan pressed.

"And it's the emblem for University of Nevada, Las Vegas."

"Any idea where each of our victims in question attended college?" Griffin asked.

"I can look, but it's a moot point," Declan said. "Dentals didn't match any of them."

"I think I recall reading Marley received her first undergrad degree from UNLV before moving to Towson and completing her pre-professional studies in law. It was part of her alum bio."

"That may be, but she's not our Jane Doe. The dentals didn't match."

"Okay, then you should extend the missing persons search radius," Finley said. Just because they'd struck out with these four women didn't mean they were finished. Jane Doe had a name. They just had to keep digging. She was not letting go of this one.

"I'll hit the drawing board anew," Declan said, handing her back the folder with a sigh.

Shirley Mitchell, the forensic artist she'd called in, entered the room. "Why all the long faces?"

"We thought we'd gotten a positive ID."

"Oh, sorry, but maybe this will help." She set her laptop on the table and stood back. "Your Jane Doe."

Finley moved closer, her gaze fixed on the image. She *knew* that face.

"That's Marley Trent," Declan said, excitement renewed in his voice.

"How is that possible?" Griffin asked.

"There must have been a mistake with the dentals," Parker offered.

"I'll get back in touch with Ms. Trent's dentist and see if he can resend a copy of her films." Declan pulled his cell from his pocket, clearly not realizing the lateness of the hour.

"Better if you personally pick up the films," Parker said.

"What are you thinking?"

"We need to rule out foul play."

Finley frowned. "You think someone intentionally switched the films?"

Parker shrugged. "I'm saying someone might be doing everything they can to make sure their victim isn't identified. It's not out of the realm of possibility that somewhere along the line a switch was made."

"If that's the case," Griffin said, "then what's to say all of Marley's films haven't been switched? They could have hit the dental office. Where's her dentist located?"

"Baltimore," Declan said.

"How long has she been with that dentist?" Griffin asked pointedly.

Declan snapped his fingers. "On it."

Finley watched Declan race from the room. "What just happened?"

Parker smiled. "Griffin just came up with a brilliant idea."

"What now?" she asked.

Griffin exhaled. "We wait."

How many times had he been told that?

"Just wait and be patient. We're working the case."

"Just wait and let us do our jobs. These things take time."

"Just wait for your mark."

"Just wait—it takes time to get over things like this."

He was sick and tired of waiting. Waiting through pain. Waiting for justice. Waiting for God to act.

Where are you in this injustice, Lord?

Aren't you the God of justice? Don't you say those who wait on the Lord will mount on wings of eagles? That we will be more than conquerors?

I've been waiting, Lord, but just when I think I've found some measure of control and peace, all hell breaks loose and I'm reminded of the helplessness in waiting.

How long will you let injustice prevail?

"Hopefully we'll have an ID tomorrow," Parker said, interrupting Griffin's thoughts. Probably for the best. Sometimes he felt sinful for expressing his frustration, but God already knew his heart, knew what he was thinking. Better to be up front than pretend to hide the frustration brewing inside.

He'd been praying for understanding, praying for God's action, but it was cases like this that exposed the bitterness still burrowed inside.

110

How long, Lord?

"In the meantime . . ." Parker stood and stretched. "Everyone take precautions. Someone was very intent on preventing this woman's ID. I can't imagine he'd let up now."

Griffin looked at Finley. "I meant what I said earlier. I don't want you staying alone until an ID is made. I have a guest room, or if you prefer I can bunk on your couch."

A mix of emotions rushed over her face. "Are you sure that's necessary?"

"Yes."

"It's not a bad idea," Parker said, shocking him. "In fact . . ." He looked to Avery. "You should probably stay at my place."

Avery rolled her eyes. "Nice try."

"I'm serious." He held up his hands. "No funny business, I promise. I agree with Griff. You ladies should not be alone until our Jane Doe is identified."

Avery exhaled. "Fine. I'll stay at your place, but any sign of funny business and you're losing digits."

Parker grinned. Clearly he appreciated the lady's style.

They decided to stop by Griffin's place so he could grab a few things on the way to Finley's house. The thought of Griffin spending the night in her guest room was a mix of reassuring and unnerving. She loved the protection aspect, but she hadn't had a man in her home since Brent Howard.

She swallowed the bile burning up her throat at the traumatic memory, trying to ground herself as the room began to spin.

It was a wonder she hadn't moved, but she *refused* to be driven from her home because of *him*.

Griffin unlocked his front door and flipped on the entryway light.

She would have pegged him as the cabin type, especially in the wooded area of Thurmont, but somehow the rustic farmhouse—a two-story, deep greyish-blue home with a gorgeous wraparound front porch she could spend hours reading on—suited him too.

He stepped back, allowing her passage inside. Exquisite, handcrafted pine wainscoting covered the bottom half of the walls from the chair rail to the hardwood floors, the top half painted a crisp white, the ceiling navy blue with track lighting. The effect was stunning. Sailor's rope framed the pictures of the Chesapeake lining the long, narrow entryway—images of ships, shore, sunsets, and crabs. On top of the pictures ran a row of antique oars. Griffin clearly loved the Chesapeake.

An Irish wolfhound, his head level with her rib cage, lumbered forward with a red Kong in his mouth.

"Easy, Winston," Griffin said, and the dog heeded, sitting on his haunches with what she swore was a smile, his tail wagging.

Griffin squatted and ruffled the dog behind his ears, his tail going into hyperdrive.

"Don't let his size scare you. As you can see he's a big softie."

"If you're staying with me, who's taking care of Winston?"

"My neighbor Kristin. She adores him. And he'd probably trade me in an instant for her."

"You're welcome to bring him along."

Griffin cocked his head with a smile. "Really?"

"Yeah, why not?"

"Most people don't want such a large dog in their home."

She shrugged with a smile of her own. "I'm not most people." She didn't mean it in a conceited way. She just didn't fret the small stuff, especially when it came to animals. Besides, after the day they'd had, she wouldn't mind the added level of protection.

"No." Griffin's smile widened. "I suppose you aren't."

She bit the side of her lip, wondering if that was a compliment or an insult. She couldn't always tell with the man. He left her unbalanced, which while intriguing, was also terrifying.

Griffin looked at Winston. "Road trip, buddy?"

Winston raced for his leash hanging on an anchor-shaped peg by the front door.

She cocked her head. "Did he just . . . ?"

"He loves road trips."

So did she. Any kind of trip really, as long as it involved water or mountains, but since the incident she'd been embarrassingly nervous to travel on her own. It angered her that she allowed *him* any lingering control over her, but traveling in the midst of panic attacks was hardly enjoyable. She still forced herself to go, determined not to let one evil man's actions destroy a lifelong love of exploration, but the fact she struggled ticked her off.

Winston nudged his leash off the peg with his nose, the blue strap dropping at his feet, the metal clasp clanging on the wooden floor.

"Hold on, buddy," Griffin said. "I gotta grab a few things first. Come on, let's go out."

With a grunt, Winston left the leash and followed Griffin through the house to the kitchen and out the back door.

Finley followed them. "Nice kitchen," she said

looking around. Vaulted ceiling with wooden beams, glass-front cupboards, weathered hardwood floors.

"Thanks. It's a work in progress."

She took in the ladder propped against the back wall, the can of stain in the corner. "You did this?"

"I'm refurbishing little by little. Sort of a project of mine."

"Refurbishing kitchens?" She never would have pegged him as the renovating sort, though she was quickly coming to realize she didn't have him pegged at all. He was so much more.

"That's a part of it," he said, offering her a drink.

She accepted a glass of OJ and hopped up on the stool. The sweet juice would no doubt give her a renewed burst of energy, which she needed. She was dragging. It'd been a long couple of days.

"I enjoy restoring older homes and then selling them," he said, topping off her glass.

"Cool. So flipping houses?" She took another sip.

"Yeah. Run-down ones with character."

"You give them new life."

He smiled, looking around the rafters. "I suppose you could say that."

Winston pawed the door, and Griffin let him in. He wasted no time in bustling back to his leash.

"I'd better go get my stuff before he starts grunting again."

"Is it done?" he asked over the phone.
   "Almost."
   "See that everything's in place."
   "I understand."
   "I want it set to go tonight."
   He got it. He wasn't an idiot. "We'll own them."
   "Where are they now?"
   "At his place."
   "Together?"
   "Yes."
   "Hmm."
   "What?"
   "This could prove to be an interesting development. If things progress between them on a personal level it may provide the leverage we've been searching for. Continue to focus on them."
   "And the federal agent?"
   "Him, I've got taken care of."

— 16 —

Griffin followed Finley along the cobblestone sidewalk lining Thames Street, the fishy scent of the bay wafting on the cool November breeze, the wind-capped water sloshing the ships docked in the marina edging Fell's Point.

Finley's paid parking slot sat several blocks from her home and the thought of her walking through Fell's Point alone each night terrified him. Not that it was a bad neighborhood, by any means—it'd been beautifully restored and was a Baltimore nighttime hot spot—but it was also only a handful of blocks from the blue light district, and a woman living on her own *anywhere* needed to be vigilant.

He prayed she paid attention to her surroundings, to the people they were passing on the short jaunt past the restaurants lining the block, the Thames Oyster Company being his personal favorite.

His attention gravitated to the dark water, across the harbor to the Canton warehouse district where Parker lived, curious if he could spot his loft. It was a distinct building, though he hadn't been since the day they'd helped Parker move in. It was hard to believe they were all working together again—all but Luke, of course.

Finley stepped around the old-fashioned black lamppost on the corner and banked right onto South Bond Street, stepping to the first house on the left—a traditional brick rowhome, with a small fenced yard jutting out in the triangular shape of the corner it sat on. A knotted sailor's wreath with blue crabs hung on her bright blue door illuminated by a strand of white, sparkling lights woven around. The small light to the right of the door was lit, but the interior of her home was dark. *Not smart*.

"You really should leave some interior lights on too," he said, stepping through the narrow doorway.

"I always leave the entry table lamp on," she said, moving toward it, flipping the hall light as she went. "Must have burnt out."

Winston happily pranced through the bright yellow entry, the walls covered with beautifully framed and mounted postcards. A vast and unique collection from the cursory glance he took. Though he was more interested in the fact no alarm had been triggered upon their entry.

She stepped to the alarm keypad. "That's strange."

"What is?"

"Must not have set my alarm today."

At least she had one.

She dropped her keys in the giant overturned seashell functioning as a bowl on the table and bent, turning the lamp knob. "Nada," she said, straightening. "I'm sure I've got an extra bulb somewhere around here."

Griffin walked the interior of the main floor with Winston thumping beside him while she searched for a bulb, seeking out the best place to set up camp. It was obvious from the weathered steamer trunk functioning as a coffee table, glass jars brimming over with seashells, beach-

118

themed quote boxes lining her mantel, and the eclectic collection of geographically diverse artwork framing her walls that she loved travel and the sea. The latter they had in common, but . . . He didn't mind traveling, but his idea of travel involved weeklong hiking-camping treks, skiing out west, and pushing off the dock and sailing into the sunset. Her travel interests evoked a love of experiencing new cultures, which was very cool.

"Found one," she said, returning a few minutes later with bulb in hand.

"Here." He held out his flattened palm. "I can swap it for you."

"Thanks."

He ducked under the lampshade, wrapping his hand around the existing bulb's base. With a grimace he pulled his hand back, blood on his fingers.

Her eyes widened. "What happened?"

"The bulb was cracked—I busted it."

She reached for his hand. "Let me take a look."

"It's nothing, really."

"We both know I'm looking. No sense arguing."

The lady was right. Arguing with her, while intellectually stimulating, was, in the end, futile. Unless it came to her safety—about that he'd brook no arguments.

Her fingers gently eased back his, and she bent, examining the cuts. "You've got some glass in here. Hang tight while I grab my first-aid kit."

He opened his mouth to argue and then halted at her steadfast expression, daring him to try.

"Okay," he conceded.

Grabbing the first-aid kit, she waved him into the kitchen. "Better light in here."

Her kitchen was a galley style with a small eating nook. A table with two chairs and cushioned window bench filled the tiny space. He could picture her sipping her morning coffee curled up on the bench.

"Let me see your hand," she said, drawing his attention back.

She smelled amazing. What was that? Something floral and tropical, but not overly sweet. Hints of coconut, perhaps.

Cradling his right hand in her left, she started tweezing out the shards of glass. She paused after removing a few and glanced up. "Doing okay?"

Better than okay. Her skin was so soft, her eyes brimming with compassion. He cleared his throat. "Good."

She turned back to the job and had his cuts cleared, cleaned, and bandaged in a matter of minutes, but didn't release her hold.

What was it about Finley that drew him so—other than the obvious? She was beautiful, funny, intelligent, but there was something stronger, something binding that continued to hold him fast.

"Thanks." He released her hand, taking a deliberate step back. He didn't want to give her the wrong impression. As interested as he was, he wasn't the man for her, not now. Not while still battling his guilt, his past, and his mistakes. "Let's get that bulb swapped."

She looked half-disappointed at his pulling back but nodded and followed him back out to the entry, Winston padding behind them.

A towel in hand, Griffin bent to examine the busted bulb, and his gaze tracked upward, landing on something far more dangerous.

Avery watched as Parker unlocked the tall black door wedged like a slit in the brick side of an old cannery warehouse along the docks of Canton.

A merchant ship sat moored on the left side of the building and a trawler on the right. Avery glanced up at the brick front with *Harrison* painted in fading white letters. Other than a small light shining from the third-floor window, the place was dark.

What had she gotten herself into?

She'd been asking herself that ever since she'd answered Parker's ad for a crime-scene photographer, never expecting him to actually hire her. She'd been desperate to pay her bills and remain behind a camera lens, and so she'd gone for it. Much to her shock, he'd hired her after a few moments' questioning and since then continued to walk her through each step of crime-scene photography with patience few people possessed. But she still didn't understand why.

He was one of the best in his field and surely had plenty of other applicants. Far more experienced applicants.

Who was she kidding? She had *zero* crime-scene experience. Before this gig, her only dalliance with crime photography came purely by accident when she'd stumbled upon State Senator Mulroney attempting to rape a woman in the back room at a gallery showing. Fortunately, she'd just retrieved her camera at the request of one of Annapolis's upper crust eager to see a sampling of her recent work—still loaded on the Canon.

Her quick response of snapping off a few shots of the situation before calling for help substantiated the assaulted women's claim over the hometown hero's vehement denials. It'd cost her the business she'd worked so hard to build, right as it had begun to launch. Mulroney's well-connected society wife had seen to that. But Parker, a renowned albeit unconventional investigator, had taken pity on her. She still couldn't figure out why. What was his end game? Everybody had one.

Parker opened the door and flipped a switch illuminating a metal cage freight elevator.

Lifting the grate, he gestured for her to step

inside. He turned and bolted the front door before joining her in the metal box masquerading as an elevator.

He pulled a lever, and the gears, visible on the right, churned to life. Up what she guessed were two levels—it was difficult to tell in the dark—the elevator shook to a stop and what she could only assume was a motion-sensor light flashed on, revealing a small platform. An oversize grey metal door stood on the other side.

"You aren't some sort of serial killer, are you?" she said, trying to ease the knot in her belly with a really bad joke.

He stepped out of the elevator and extended his hand to help her. "If I were, I'd have the perfect cover, wouldn't I?"

She took his hand and stepped off the elevator, thinking the very same thing. But he was just trying to get a rise out of her.

He entered a security code into the panel beside the door and it slid open.

"Fancy."

"Modern conveniences."

"In an old cannery warehouse?"

He shrugged. "I suppose you could say I have somewhat eclectic tastes."

That much she was aware of. Fruit she'd never heard of—star something or other—Nat King Cole records—*actual records*—and a Triumph motor-cycle. His tastes were most definitely eclectic.

"Make yourself at home," he said, strolling inside.

Wow. Floor-to-ceiling windows ran the length of the two-story rear wall overlooking the harbor, the dim lights of Fed Hill glimmering across the dark expanse. She turned, examining the upper level—an open, airy loft enclosed only by a black double rail running from the ladder leading up to it and the front brick wall.

"Mi casa es su casa." He punched another code into the interior panel, and the door closed behind them, and then he lowered a metal bar across its width. "Told you you'd be safe here."

He wasn't lying. "Nice digs." She strolled farther in. "Not what I'd expected."

He glanced at her with that sexy, subtle smile that made her knees go momentarily goofy. "Oh? Do tell."

She shrugged. "Single player such as yourself. I pictured a swanky condo in the heart of Canton, not a secluded warehouse on the fringes."

"I like seclusion."

"You like distraction. Speaking of which, I see no TV." She spun around, searching the open space. "Please tell me you have a TV." She needed it to fall asleep.

"Never fear, Tate." He picked up a remote, aimed it at the console table in front of the sofa, and pressed a button. The top of the console opened, and a flat-screen TV rose up out of it.

124

"Swanky."

"I prefer streamlined. I'm not much for TV, other than baseball games."

"You like baseball?"

"Yep. Was pretty much my whole life growing up."

"You played?" Not that he wasn't athletic, but team sports just didn't seem his style.

"Since I was three."

"Three?"

"Started with T-ball, then all the way through Little League onto our high school varsity team, and then pick-up games in college."

"*Our* high school team?"

He strolled into the kitchen, separated from the living space only by a long island. "Declan, Griffin, myself, and another friend."

She sank onto one of the bar stools. "This friend have a name?"

He poured himself a Coke. "Luke . . . Gallagher." He lifted a can. "Would you care for one?"

"I'm good, thanks, but please tell me somebody delivers pizza in this neighborhood." If the industrial area could be deemed a *neighborhood*.

"Yes. There's a pizza place, but we won't be ordering in."

"Oh?"

"You're a guest in my home, and therefore I'll be making you a homemade meal."

"That's not necessary."

"Believe me," he said, retrieving ingredients. "It is. We've been working together for what . . . three months now, and I've yet to see you eat anything that hasn't come out of a box or bag."

She shrugged, popping a grape from the bowl on the counter into her mouth. "I'm not the cooking sort."

"Well, lucky for us . . ." He twirled a tomato. "I am."

"So you really do cook?"

"I told you I did."

"Most guys just use that as a pick-up line." She hopped from the stool and moved to the table lined with what appeared to be square containers filled with weeds.

"Herbs," he said.

She bent, inhaling the various savory and sweet scents, recognizing only one—mint. It brought back one of the few good memories of her childhood. A mint vine growing in the dirt along the back corner of their rusted trailer. How it got there no one knew, but her mom would fill a glass pitcher with water, drop in a couple tea bags and a sprig of mint, and then set it out on their splintered picnic table for the sun to do its magic. To this day, it was the one homemade thing she could make—sun tea, like her mom.

"Tate?" Parker had ceased moving around the kitchen and was instead leaning against the island watching her.

How long had he been staring at her like that?

"Don't."

"Don't what?"

"I know that look. Stop profiling me." He might work as a forensic scientist, but his undergrad had been in criminal justice, and he'd either taken a profiling concentration or the gift just came naturally. Either way she didn't want him using it on her.

He stepped from the island, moving slowly toward her. "I can't help if my mind wonders."

"We both know where your mind *wanders* to. And . . ." She placed her palm on his chest, halting his advance. "That's *not* happening."

He placed his hand over hers, and she refused to acknowledge the reaction his touch provoked. "Must you always assume the worst of me?"

She yanked her hand away. "Your reputation precedes you."

"Reputation and reality are often two vastly different things."

"You're denying the rumors?" That he was a player who could charm his way into a woman's heart and bed without batting an eye. With his looks and killer Irish accent, it wasn't hard to believe.

He cocked his head, a delicious smile quirking his lips. "Now don't tell me you've been listening to water-cooler gossip? Really, Tate, I didn't think you the type."

To gossip? Absolutely not. To keep her distance from charmers? You bet. "Charm is nothing more than deceit."

He arched a dark brow. "So you find me charming?"

"Clearly you didn't hear what I just said."

"I took in everything you said—spoken and unspoken."

"I told you, stop reading me."

"*Listening.* I'm listening to you."

And she was excruciatingly tempted to ask what he heard, what he learned, but she was terrified he might actually peg her correctly—that she couldn't hide from him. "Then you heard I'm not interested."

His phone rang, and his eyes widened at the number. "Griff?" he asked, answering it. "What? We'll be right there."

Avery frowned. "What's up?"

"Someone broke into and bugged Finley's home."

— 17 —

Finley sat on the couch, trying her best not to freak out as a handful of federal agents swept her home for listening devices. While waiting for Declan and his team to arrive, she and Griffin had quickly conducted their own search, locating two additional bugs in her kitchen and home office.

Her stomach knotted as the realization that a stranger had been in her home *again* burrowed deep inside her burgeoning fear. She stood, pacing, praying the room would stop spinning, that the floating feeling would decrease.

Please don't let me pass out in front of Griffin.

The horrifically embarrassing thought rattled through her, her stomach squeezing the breath from her lungs. What was wrong with her? Why couldn't she be stronger? So a man had been in her home. It sadly happened to lots of folks, and *they* probably didn't completely freak out. If only she were stronger.

"We got two more," Declan said, entering the front room.

Her heart tightened. "Where?"

"Your den."

She swallowed, sensing there was more. "And?"

Declan's gaze darted to Griffin.

Why was he hesitating? What could be any worse?

Declan exhaled. "Your bedroom."

A cold, pulsating wave washed over her. "They put a bug in my bedroom?"

"Not exactly."

She wrapped her arms across her chest, clinging tight.

"What?" Griffin's one word communicated

the raw intensity of emotion surging through her.

"We found this." Declan held up a marble-size device.

She leaned forward, squinting through her narrowing vision. "What is that?"

Griffin released a heated exhale. "A camera."

Nausea catapulted in her gut.

"We found it in a stuffed monkey."

"A keepsake from my trip to Nevis." It sat on the shelf opposite her bed and brought a smile to her face when she woke. She swallowed the acid bubbling up her throat. Someone could have been watching her sleep, wake . . . dress . . . ? The world tilted on its axis, spinning. She blinked, struggling to find purchase.

Griffin placed his hand on her neck, gently lowering her into a chair and then dipping her head. "Deep breaths."

She inhaled rapidly.

"Slower." His firm voice held a world of comfort. "Deeper."

She listened. A handful of breaths later, she sat up, the space no longer spinning. "Thank you."

"We'll get this guy." The steely determination radiating in his eyes said it was a guarantee.

She nodded. Knowing if the man or men responsible for this intrusion had left any trace of their presence behind—a fingerprint, a strand of hair or flake of dandruff—Parker and Avery were the team to find it. Their work at the lab today had been top-notch. The lab . . . "The UPS package," she said as it hit her.

Griffin arched a brow. "What?"

"The missing UPS package. Maybe there was no delivery." If they'd bugged her home, what's to say they hadn't bugged her office too.

"Smart," Declan said. "When they are done here, I'll tell my team and Parker to search the lab."

Griffin glanced at Winston curled up asleep on top of his feet. No wonder they were numb. Tonight had gone differently than planned, but he was so thankful he'd been there for Finley. Thankful they'd discovered the listening devices and the video camera. The thought of someone watching her, spying on her . . .

Rage seared through him. This entire case was crazy. A murdered lab tech, near body snatch, swapped dental records, listening devices . . .

He shook his head. Bugs weren't typically part of a sniper's arsenal. But, then again, they weren't dealing with a typical sniper. They were dealing with an assassin. Which, in and of itself, made Jane Doe's identity all the more intriguing. What was so important about her? Why had she been killed? And, why was it so vital to keep her identity hidden—even to the point of killing John . . . and nearly Finley?

He glanced at her curled up asleep on the couch

beside him. The urge to sweep her up into his embrace was nearly overwhelming.

Parker entered the room with his kit in hand and a sleepy-looking Avery at his side. He rested the black case on the armchair.

"Anything?" Declan asked, joining them.

"What time is it?" Finley asked, her eyes fluttering open. She yawned and pulled to a seated position.

"A little after two."

Everyone else had left except the five of them. Parker and Avery inspected the house on a meticulous level Griffin had never witnessed before. Impressive didn't come close. Declan, of course, had insisted on staying until the sweep was complete.

"Whoever did this was good, but . . ." Parker began, "we're better."

Griffin stood, stretching his legs, trying to work blood flow back into his feet. Winston just shifted to his side with a sleepy grumble. Good to know he was on watch.

"Whatcha got?" Declan asked.

"A partial shoe print with some residue of lubricant. Best guess, grease, but we'll head back to the lab and start processing. Along with joining the Feds in searching the lab. Will keep you posted."

Declan followed them out, leaving just him and a drowsy Finley—her hair tousled, her eyes heavy. Man, she was beautiful. Whoever married her would be one lucky man—getting to wake up to such beauty every day. If only . . .

"Is it even worth going to bed?" she asked.

"You need your rest. Besides, we've still got a few hours before we need to head back to the range."

"Okay." She stifled a yawn. "I'll set you and Winston up in the guest room."

"Thanks, but I'll stick here on the couch and . . ." He looked down at his dog sprawled out between the couch and the coffee table, all four paws up in the air. "And clearly Winston is content on the floor."

"Okay . . . but why the couch?"

"I can respond faster to an intruder down here."

"Oh." She bit her bottom lip.

"Not that I anticipate anyone being stupid enough to come back. I just want to take every precaution."

"I understand, and I appreciate it. I'll go grab you some bedding."

She returned a few minutes later with an oversized pillow for Winston and one for him, along with a sheet and blanket.

"Thanks."

Winston woke long enough to circle the pillow, flop down, squish it between his front paws, and burrow his large head into its white, fluffy depths.

Griffin shook his head. "Real manly, bud."

"Aww. He's adorable." She bent, petting him good-night, and then stepped to Griffin.

"Good night."

"Night."

She lifted onto her tiptoes, leaning in.

His breath hitched.

"Thank you," she said, pressing a soft kiss to his cheek.

He struggled to wrangle in the heat flaring through him. "You're welcome," he said, praying that hadn't come out as throaty as it sounded to his ears. He'd practically groaned. This was bad. Very, *very* bad.

Winston whimpered as she exited the room.

He glanced over at his dog. "Believe me—" he exhaled the tautness coiled tight inside, all from a single kiss to the cheek—"I know how you feel."

With apprehension and acid burning a hole in his gut, he placed the call.

"Yes?"

He cleared his throat, knowing he was a dead man. "They found the bugs at her place."

"I'm aware, and I've been anticipating your call."

"The rest are still in play." As far as he knew. He needed to track back to the lab to be certain.

"Is that supposed to make me feel better?"

He swallowed, hard. "No, sir."

"Did you leave anything that could tie back to us?"

"No." The only mistake had been knocking over the lamp when he heard someone approaching the rowhome, but he'd righted it before slipping out the rear and hopping the back fence.

"You'd better be correct."

If not, it'd be his head. Literally.

— 18 —

Griffin pulled into the Red Barn parking lot, his throat tight and muscles coiled. They were sitting ducks anywhere out in the open—or near a window, for that matter—and he loathed the associated vulnerability. The cold, hard truth was, if the sniper watching them yesterday had wanted them dead, they would be.

Father, as much as I want to protect Finley, we both know only you can truly protect her. You are the God of heaven and earth. You are the One who protects us from evil. Please shelter us in the shadow of your wings. Send your army of angels to encamp around us. Help equip us to see this case through and justice done.

"You think he'll be here?" Finley asked, glancing out the truck window.

"Vern or the man watching us?"

She slipped a loose strand of hair behind her ear—even the woman's ear was alluring. He envisioned kissing his way along the curve of her neck up to . . . *Whoa! Time for some cold, crisp air.*

"Both, I suppose," she said.

He took a deep, focusing breath. "Gunny says Vern never misses a shooting time, so unless he's heard about us and has something to hide, he'll be here."

"How would he hear about us?"

"Shooting is a tight community. If any of the guys we spoke with yesterday thought Vern, or anyone else for that matter, should know about us, they'd have contacted them as soon as they left."

"So yesterday's watcher?"

"Could have been tipped off to our presence."

"He could have shot here?"

"It's possible, or he could have simply followed us here. He might have been following us since the news stations first announced our discovery of the body on Little Round Top."

"That's comforting." She exhaled. "But it would mean he might not have anything to do with the range?"

Griffin shook his head.

"You think it's still worthwhile to question Vern Michaels?"

"Yeah. He's the man in the know according to

everyone, which means he knows the shooters in the area, knows their gun preference, and knows if someone likes to shoot or owns our weapon in question."

"But if our killer is simply following us and has no ties here . . . ?"

"Then this may prove to be a dead end, but it's not in vain. If nothing else, we've learned our killer is close. Close enough to respond to us finding Jane Doe's remains quickly and close enough to try and steal her body."

Griffin chose the most concealed spot to park— close to the building's rear and Gunny's motorhome, providing them cover all the way to the front door. *Nearly.*

The last few steps were in the open, and that was unacceptable. He'd use his body to shield Finley from any possible threat, any sniper's scope.

Griffin scanned the perimeter from the cover of the motorhome, while Finley remained sheltered inside the truck. No sign or inner sense of someone watching.

Maybe the man knew he'd screwed up, had drawn too much heat. He had to know they were on to him, perhaps not his identity, but most certainly his presence.

With a steadying breath, he opened the door and indicated for Finley to come. They moved quickly for the door and he exhaled a giant *whoosh* of relief once they were safely inside.

"You're back," Gunny said, irritation ringing in his voice.

He understood the man didn't want them harassing his clientele and they'd be as quick and noninvasive as they could with Vern Michaels, but the fact was a woman was dead, a sniper was tracking them, and they needed answers.

"Told you we'd be," he said striding down the ammo aisle toward the man, Finley at his side. "Vern Michaels here?"

"Yeah, but he's not going to react well to your questions."

"Why not? I heard he likes to talk guns."

"With other shooters. Not law enforcement or whatever she is." Gunny lifted his chin in Finley's direction. So he had done some digging.

"Forensic anthropologist," she said.

"Whatever. As charming as you are, lady, Vern isn't the sort to betray confidences."

"Confidences? Interesting choice of words." Griffin leaned against the counter, resting his forearms on the glass. "You make it sound like Vern definitely knows something."

"Guess that's for you and your lady friend to find out. Vern's on lane three."

"Thanks."

"You may not want to thank me yet."

He paused. "Why's that?"

"Vern's not exactly what you'd call cordial."

Finley rocked back on her heels with a slight grin in Griffin's direction. "You two should get along great."

Gunny actually chuckled. Amazing how Finley had that effect. Even on the hardest of men.

He had a reputation of his own and he preferred it that way, but somehow, in some inexplicable way, Finley had seen past all that.

"A word of advice?" Gunny said.

"Yeah?"

"Don't tick him off. You don't want to see Vern mad."

"Great . . ." *This ought to be fun.* He opened the door, unsure of what to expect as he and Finley made their way to lane three.

Vern Michaels was six-three, two hundred and thirty pounds, with burly tattooed arms and a thick neck.

Griffin sat back and watched him hit the bull's-eye three hundred yards out with his Mosin.

"That weapon," he said while Vern dropped the empty mag and pulled the plugs from his ears, "is the precursor to our killer's Dragunov."

"Really?"

"I don't know anything about a killer," Vern said, turning to face them, "but Griffin is right. Dragunovs are basically new generation Mosins."

"I didn't realize we've met," Griffin said at the man's use of his name.

"We haven't, but your reputation precedes you."

Griffin wasn't sure if that was a good or bad thing, considering the information they needed.

"Finley Scott," she said, stepping up onto the shooting platform as Vern lowered the gun into his case.

Griffin waited to see how Vern would react. He hadn't invited them into his space, and after Gunny's warning . . . But if anyone could ease a man's hardened defenses, it was the charming Finley Scott.

Vern's assessing gaze raked over her as he shook her hand. "Vern Michaels." He looked past her at Griffin, lifting his chin. "I heard you two were asking questions about a certain gun here yesterday."

"That's right." Word did travel fast.

"We were really hoping to ask you a few questions," she said.

He shut his gun case. "Why me?"

"Word is you're the guy in the know," Griffin said.

"So what is it a U.S. gold medalist in the 600 meter rifle event and a forensic doc want to know about the Dragunov?"

Finley turned to Griffin, surprised.

He shrugged. It wasn't something he touted.

"We want to know who owns one around here. Who shoots one?"

"Why?"

"A woman was killed," Finley said.

Vern's gaze narrowed. "So you are looking for a killer?"

Griffin nodded, intrigued Vern Michaels had done some research of his own, finding out who they were before they showed up. No doubt he'd been tipped off to their arrival just as the killer perhaps had.

"You think he's local?" Vern asked. It was a question every shooter hated. None wanted to think there was a gun for hire in their backyard.

"He could be. Any names come to mind?"

"How good a shot are we talking?"

"Fifteen hundred meters through more than one barrier."

Vern whistled. "Well, that certainly narrows down the pool."

"Bring any names to mind?"

"I know a couple guys who could pull off that distance, but they're not for hire. The ones who are, they're a different breed, and they certainly don't go around advertising it."

"What about the Dragunov?" Maybe if they focused on the weapon rather than pressing Vern for names.

"Haven't seen one at this range."

"What about other ranges in the area, the region?" Finley asked, clearly refusing to leave empty-handed.

Griffin bit back a smile. He admired her persistence.

Vern mulled it over, his lips pinching, his gaze fixed on Finley.

"Please," she said. "We're just trying to bring a killer to justice."

He relented. "I suppose I could ask around. Seems I recall a friend telling me about a cool semi-automatic he saw."

"This friend have a name?"

"Not one I'm going to share, but I'll give him a call. See what details he can recall. If I think I've learned anything helpful, I'll be in touch."

"Thank you so much." Finley handed him her card.

"Any word of a shooter visiting town?" Griffin asked, wanting to be completely thorough, searching every option.

"When are we talking?"

"Last winter. March, most likely."

"I'll check."

Clearly that prospect sat better with him, and Griffin understood. A killer in their backyard was infuriating and unsettling.

Minutes later they were back in the parking lot. "Well, he was a teddy bear." Finley tugged off her gloves as Griffin started the engine and turned up the heat.

He chuckled.

"What?"

"Pretty positive Vern Michaels has never been referred to as a teddy bear before."

"Men can be strong and tender too. It's the combo that's enticing in the right man."

He wondered what other qualities she found enticing in the right man.

"You still think it could be someone local or regional?"

Griffin shifted into drive. "If it is, he's done a good job keeping his profession a secret."

"Sniper?" she asked, her brows pinching.

He shook his head. "Assassin."

"So you're an Olympic gold medalist?"

He exhaled. "Yeah." For a skill he'd failed at.

Finley entered her office at Towson University. Griffin wouldn't be pleased she'd left the lab on her own after their visit to the gun range early this morning, but she needed to grab some papers to grade over break along with a book on bone density analysis.

Besides, they were all waiting on Dr. Kent to give them their next step. She prayed the dentals would match Marley Trent so her mysterious disappearance nearly eight months ago could finally be laid to rest and her family brought some amount of closure—even though that closure would bring with it a terrible finality and the realization their daughter had been killed in cold blood, no doubt with a cold shot.

As Griffin had explained to her on the drive back from the range to her lab, a cold shot was the first shot out of a sniper's rifle. No practice, no warm-up. Just a "cold" shot. The term added an extra sense of brutality, lack of all compassion, just as the term *in cold blood* did.

She strolled down the nearly empty university corridors. Most students were home with their families for fall break. She pulled her keys out to unlock her office when Dr. Leonard Cooper rounded the corner.

"Finley." Her colleague and friend, Dr. Cooper, smiled. "I didn't expect to see you in here over break."

"I needed to grab a research book along with some papers."

"Working a new case?"

"Yes, and it's a doozy." She stepped into her office and he followed. "I may need to call on your expertise at some point." He ran the pre-law department and had a vast background in criminal justice, focusing on the sociological and psychological effects of crime on its victims and society. He was a distinguished member of their academic community, a tenured professor on the board, and someone who'd become a close friend since her attack. It was no wonder he'd been so proud of Marley Trent's accomplishments. She was fighting causes he was personally and professionally passionate about.

"Of course. I'm always happy to help," he said as she dropped her purse on her desk, quickly wondering if this office had been tapped too. She should mention that possibility to Parker. He could run a sweep.

"This case wouldn't have anything to do with the body discovered at Gettysburg, would it?" Leonard asked as she retrieved the pile of papers sitting on her desk. "I know your dig is up there. I wondered if you got called in."

"Yes. You saw it on the news?" She stuffed the papers in her bag and stepped to the book-case.

"All over it. Not every day a modern body is found at Gettysburg."

"How'd you know it was modern?"

"Feds wouldn't be involved if it wasn't." Reporters had quickly mentioned Declan by name as head of the investigation.

"It's amazing how quickly news spreads." To the reporters and the killer, or whomever had swapped the dental records. She found the book she was looking for and snagged it off the shelf. "It appears the dental records were compromised before they made it to the lab."

"What?" Leonard's face crimped. "Are you certain?"

"The investigators are looking into it as we speak."

"Who would . . . ?" His face slackened. "Is

there a chance the killer is still involved? I hate to think of you in any danger again."

"Unfortunately," she said, adding the book to her bag, "that's exactly what I think. The killer is trying to prevent Jane Doe's ID."

"Any chance it was a mix-up? That would make me feel a whole lot better."

"It's possible, I suppose, but considering someone tried to steal Jane Doe's remains and killed one of our lab techs in the process, I'd say something more serious is afoot."

His dark brown eyes widened. "*Killed* a lab tech?"

"Leonard, I know this goes without saying, that everything I've shared is confidential." Clearly he knew that.

"Of course, but I do worry about what kind of case you're dealing with."

As did she. She couldn't tell him Marley was a possible match. Not yet. There was no sense upsetting him when Jane Doe might be someone else. Leonard had cherished Marley. Rumor around campus was she'd been his star student, and Finley could see why—they both stood as stalwarts in the battle against injustice.

"Seriously, Finley. Be careful on this one. I don't want to see it turn out—" He cut himself off, but she knew precisely where he was about to go. He cupped her right hand in his. "Just promise me you'll be careful, dear."

"I promise." At least she wasn't alone on this one. She had Griffin. Okay, *had* might be too strong a word, but he'd be there for her until this case was over, and the knowledge brought a measure of peace she hadn't experienced in over a year. "I have faith the right man is on the job."

Declan was clearly adept at his job, but something told her it was Griffin who had a distinct and vital role to play—both in the case and, she was quickly coming to believe, in her life.

Finley walked back to the parking garage, her bag loaded down with papers and books. She'd ended up finding several more that might be helpful. So many more, in fact, her arms were piled high. Good thing she thrived on research. Loved it, really.

Her heels clicked along the steps as she made her way to the bottom level, the concrete building sheltering her from the brisk wind. Rounding the final set of steps, she collided with some-one—her heart pounding in her throat at the sudden impact.

She looked up to find a poor woman drenched with coffee—all over her tan coat.

Relief and embarrassment replaced her momentary fear. "I'm so sorry. Was lost in my thoughts, I guess."

"No," the woman said, brushing off her coat.

"I wasn't paying attention. Hey," she said, smiling, "you're Dr. Scott, right?"

"Yes."

"I'm hoping to take your 304 class next semester."

"Oh. Unfortunately it's already full, but I've got a wait list going. What's your name?"

"My name?"

"Yes."

"Oh, sorry, Megan."

"Well, Megan, if you head over to registration and ask for Teri, she'll get you on the wait list. Tell her I sent you."

"Great. Thanks. I'll head over there now." She turned in the wrong direction.

"Registration is that way," Finley said, discomfort mounting.

"Oh, right." Was the woman feigning embarrassment? "It's my first semester, and I still get all turned around." Her gaze flashed past Finley and she swore panic set in the woman's eyes.

"First semester . . . Are you a freshman? 304 is for upperclassmen only."

"I'm a transfer student."

That didn't sound right. "That's funny. I don't remember approving a transfer student named Megan for my program."

"Oh, I'm not officially in your program. Just interested in the class," she said, backing away. "Heard it was awesome."

Now something was really wrong. "I haven't taught it before."

"Then I must be thinking of something else." She hurried her step, moving toward the quad. "Thanks for your time. I really gotta go." She turned and bolted.

"Hey," Finley called, but the woman rounded the corner and was gone. Griffin would be livid if she followed the woman—but something was off, and she wanted to know what.

Her phone chimed. *Great.* Shifting the heavy weight of the books to one arm and shoulder, she managed to fish out her phone and glance at the number.

She picked it up. "Hello, Dr. Kent. I hope you have good news for me?"

"If you're looking for a match, then I do. Dental records confirm your victim is Marley Trent."

Griffin sat across the table from Declan at Jimmy's—their favorite short-order diner in Fell's Point. Declan had retrieved Marley Trent's dentals from her childhood-through-college dentist in Ocean City, where her father still lived, dropped them off at the lab, and twisted Griffin's arm into joining him for lunch while they waited, yet again.

His and Finley's early morning visit with Vern Michaels at the range had gone well, Vern no less enamored with Finley than all the men had been. It had taken a little finagling and some "Finley charm" to get Vern to open up even a smidge, but in the end, he'd promised to ask around.

Griffin bit into his Crabs Benedict—a Jimmy's specialty—the creamy sauce slipping down his lip. He took another bite, then wiped his mouth. He was waiting for Declan to bring up Parker. A lunch between them never went by without Declan's attempt to fix matters. But sometimes things were frayed beyond fixing.

Declan took a sip of his Coke and lifted his chin. "It's nice working together again."

And here we go . . . "I'm just in to make sure Finley's safe until an ID is made." After that it made no sense for someone to come after her. "Speaking of ID . . . how long do you expect the tooth doc to take?"

Declan glanced at his watch. "Anytime now. Hoping it'll confirm Marley Trent as the victim so I can dive into the case. Although . . ."

Griffin arched a brow. "Although . . . ?"

"When her name came up as a possible match, I got a visit from my boss."

"That was quick, but you did say he wasn't fond of cold cases." Griffin ignored how much that irritated him.

"I think there's more to it. When I mentioned I was running to Marley Trent's hometown for dentals, he reacted in a way that . . ." He dabbed his fry in ketchup.

"That . . . ?"

150

"It seemed like he's familiar with her or her case, and not a fan."

"Was he one of the officers on record?"

"No, but he would have been supervising them, just as he is with me."

"You think they dropped the ball on Marley's case?"

"I don't know. It was like her name alone irritated him." His cell rang. "Hang on." He lifted the phone to his ear. "Agent Grey. Oh. Hey, Finley. Uh-huh. Okay. Thanks."

Griffin waited with anxious interest. "Well?"

"We got our vic."

"Marley Trent?"

He nodded. "Marley Trent."

"I am guessing your boss will be thrilled. So what's your first move?"

"I'll go talk with the man who reported her missing. Work her timeline from there."

"Good luck."

Declan stood and lifted the check off the table.

Griffin reached for it. "I got it."

Declan tucked it in his shirt pocket. "You can get the next one." He paused, turning back to Griffin. "Why don't you come with me?"

He frowned. "To interview the co-worker? Why?" While still law enforcement, he certainly wasn't a Fed.

"Because my boss said I'd be on my own for the cold case."

"But you've positively ID'd the vic."

"Which I doubt will change anything. Give me five while I make a call."

Griffin agreed and strolled across the cobblestone street to the harbor, his gaze shifting to Finley's place only a couple blocks away. Waking up at her place had felt incredible, but now that Marley Trent had been ID'd, the danger to her would cease. It wasn't like she was a threat to the killer or still pursuing the case.

"Told you," Declan said, joining him at the water's edge.

"Huh?"

"Talked to O'Neil—my boss—and I'm on my own for this one, so come with. Not only can I use another set of eyes and ears, but your ability to read people is uncanny."

Exactly what he used to think, but he was two for two and both were dead. He slid his sunglasses on, the sun bright, the sky blue, and the air frigidly crisp. Wind gusts sheered across the water as they returned to their vehicle. "What'd you do to tick off this O'Neil?"

Declan smiled. "Just being myself."

Griffin popped a piece of gum in his mouth as he opened his door. "That'll do it."

"We've got a big problem."

"I'm listening."

"They ID'd her."

"How? I took care of the dentals."

"It seems they figured that out and circum-vented the problem by pulling her earlier records."

A string of expletives spewed over the line. "It's only a matter of time then."

"What do you want me to do?"

"Let me run containment scenarios and I'll be back in touch."

"We could sweep them all."

"It'll draw too much attention. I'll figure out the right nerve to hit."

"In the meantime?"

"Keep on them."

— 19 —

Finley took a deep breath, knowing what she had to do and knowing the heartache this would bring Leonard. She dumped her stuff in her car and headed for his office, finding him at his desk.

He looked up with a smile. "Finley. Did you forget something?"

"Actually . . ." Exhaling, she entered the room, closing the door behind her. "I'm afraid I have some difficult news."

He took off his reading glasses, propping his elbows on the book he was reading. "Oh?"

"I just received a call from Dr. Kent. We've

made a positive ID. The remains we found belong to Marley Trent."

Leonard slumped back in his leather armchair, his eyes widening. "Marley? Are you certain?"

"I'm afraid so."

He shook his head, his dark hair closely cropped. "After all this time I feared the worst, but there was still a small part of me holding out hope . . . Wait a minute . . ." He sat forward. "It was Marley's body they tried to steal? Her body they killed the tech over?"

"Yes."

"Someone didn't want her identified. First they tried to make her disappear and now they are trying to impede the investigation. I'm so glad the FBI is taking this seriously."

"Well . . ." She'd overheard Declan telling Parker last night that his boss was not a fan of cold cases, period.

"Well, what?"

"I got the impression this isn't going to be a high-priority case." Though, now that they had identified the victim, maybe that would change matters.

"They tried to shut her up in life. Now I bet you they try and do the same in her death." He got to his feet, rounding the desk. "Well, I won't stand for it. Promise me you'll stick with this until Marley's killer is caught and brought to justice."

"I'll do whatever I can, but I'm not law enforcement."

"No, but you know how to work a case, and you're familiar with Marley's work. She dedicated her life to fighting injustice. Just as you do, giving the dead a voice and families closure." He bent, looking her square in the eyes. "Don't let the ultimate injustice happen to Marley. Don't let her killer go free."

"Yes, sir." She'd stick with this case to the end, even if it meant stepping out of her traditional bounds and inserting herself into the investigation. Just as she had on Jessica Flores' case.

Her stomach flipped.

She'd nearly died pursuing Jessica's killer. In the end, he'd pursued *her*.

Please, Father, don't let that happen with Marley's case.

But she feared in her gut it might prove far more dangerous.

Griffin followed Declan across the footbridge leading to the Global Justice Mission's headquarters, which were based inside Baltimore's World Trade Center.

The area used to be part of his rookie patrol back in the day.

The Inner Harbor had changed a lot since then. More stores. More restaurants. More crime.

The crabby scent of the harbor imbued the air, making him instantly feel at home.

He walked the familiar brick path, leading to

the building sharing an unforgettable name with the site of New York City's 9/11 disaster.

They strode beneath the flags flapping in the brisk November wind, the halyard clanging against the metal post, and entered through the glass doors, moving slowly through security and taking the elevator to the fifth floor, where Global Justice Mission was located.

A doorbell and speaker sat to the right of the double wooden doors.

Griffin glanced up at the security camera angled down at them. "What do you know about this place?"

"Global Justice Mission is a nongovernmental organization that works primarily overseas to combat human rights injustice." Declan pressed the bell.

"May I help you?" a woman's voice asked over the intercom.

"Special Agent Declan Grey." He held his badge up toward the camera. "And my colleague Chief McCray. We need to speak with Paul Geller."

"Just a moment, please."

The door buzzed, and Declan grabbed the handle and pulled. A large counter stood before them, with GJM written in bold black letters across the grey wall behind.

"Special Agent Grey." A tall brunette stepped around the counter to greet them. "Our Director of Public Relations, Emily Wilcox, will be right with you."

"Great, but we need to speak with Paul Geller."

"Emily can assist you with whatever you require." Glancing to their right, she gestured toward the petite blonde headed their way.

"Ms. Wilcox?" Declan asked.

"Agent Grey, is it?" She shook his hand.

"Yes, and this is my colleague Chief Griffin McCray."

She shook his hand in turn.

"We need to speak with Paul Geller." Declan was beginning to sound like a broken record.

"May I ask what this is in reference to?"

"Marley Trent's murder."

Emily swallowed. "Marley *was* murdered?"

"I'm afraid so."

"When she disappeared we all feared the worst after months with no word, but . . ." She inhaled and released it slowly. "This will be especially hard on Paul."

"Why is that?"

"You'll see."

They waited in the small conference room while Emily got Paul.

A wiry man, average height, with buzz-cut red hair. He wore a navy blue sweater and grey trousers. "It took you long enough," he said storming in.

Declan's shoulders broadened. "I beg your pardon?"

"It took you long enough to finally realize Marley had been murdered."

"Why's that?"

"Because the week she disappeared I told your man who killed her."

— 20 —

"You know who killed Marley Trent?" Declan asked, his tone calm and even.

Griffin studied the man while he responded to Declan's questions—his movements, posture, where his gaze darted.

"Of course."

"And you told the agent who questioned you back in March following Marley's disappearance that she was dead?"

"Yes." Paul paced impatiently.

"How did you know she was dead?" They'd just discovered her body.

"Because it was the only thing that made sense."

The man was clearly agitated.

Griffin leaned forward. "Why was that the only thing that made sense?"

"Because Marley lived for this job. She'd never just take off. The notion's preposterous. I told them she was dead, but they didn't listen. Clearly I was right. Emily said she was murdered?"

158

"That's correct."

He sat down, running his hand over his thinning hair.

Griffin looked to Declan and he nodded, giving him the go-ahead to take over.

Griffin shifted forward. "You seem awfully distraught, Mr. Geller."

"Of course I'm distraught. Marley was an amazing lady."

"You seem to have taken her death particularly hard."

"I'm not the only one."

"What do you mean?"

"Marley's intern, Rachel Lester, was so upset upon learning about Marley's disappearance she left that very day."

"Left her job?"

"Yes."

"Any idea where we can find Miss Lester?"

"She rented a place over on Pratt Street, I believe," Emily said, speaking for the first time since Paul entered the office. "I'll see if I can't locate her address when we're finished here."

"Thanks." Declan jotted down the name.

"Let's get back to you and Marley," Griffin said, feeling there was more there. A strange, perhaps, but certainly deeper connection than was typically seen between co-workers.

Paul narrowed his tear-tinged eyes. "What are you asking?"

"Were you and Ms. Trent involved?"

"We were close."

"Romantically close?"

"We were on our way there. Marley had a lot on her plate, but she was worth the wait."

Sounded like Paul was way more interested in her than she was in him. Perhaps the *involvement* was one sided. "Any idea if Marley reciprocated your feelings?"

Defiance stirred in Paul's eyes. "What do either of our feelings have to do with her murder? You two are just like the others—not interested in who killed Marley or why."

"Okay," Declan said. "Who killed Marley?"

"Mark Perera."

Griffin knew the name. He sifted through his memory. "Former U.S. Joint Chief of Staff General Mark Perera?" Surely it couldn't be the same man.

Paul looked at them as if they were idiots. "Yes!"

Griffin looked at Declan, aching to share Perera's sniper background, but now was not the time.

"Mr. Geller. Please take a deep breath and start at the beginning," Declan said, always more diplomatic than Griffin chose to be.

Paul released a breath in a steady stream. "Fine." He shook his long fingers out. "Marley was working the Perera case at the time of her disappearance."

160

"What Perera case?"

Paul's jaw flickered. "You don't know?" He shook his head. "Of course you don't know. Marley was the one fighting to bring it to light, but he got to her before she could."

"Bring what to light?" What had a man like Mark Perera done to warrant GJM's attention?

"The fact that he's molesting underage girls in Cambodia and running a highly lucrative sex tourism business for all his perverted American comrades."

Griffin couldn't resist jumping in. "Hold on a moment. You're saying a decorated war hero"— the man had been a sniper in 'Nam—"with an exemplary career, who went on to become joint chief of staff for four years before retiring from the Corp with distinction and then becoming U.S. ambassador to Cambodia, is running a sex tourism business?"

"Yes."

"And . . . do you have proof of this?" It was a serious accusation against a very powerful man.

"Marley was compiling it, but after she was killed, the most pertinent files disappeared. That's how I knew he'd done it or hired someone to."

"Wait a second," Declan said. "If Perera is committing these heinous crimes in Cambodia, wouldn't he have to stand trial there?"

"Trials there are a joke. Last guy that got caught doing what Perera is got two years. Man molested

161

numerous young girls and got two years. No, Marley and her contact in GJM's Cambodian office were working under the Protection Act to get Perera extradited back here to stand trial."

"Wouldn't that be something for ICE to deal with?"

Declan was right. A case like Paul was suggesting would be handled by the U.S. Department of Homeland Security Immigration and Customs Enforcement.

"That's exactly who Marley was trying to convince of Perera's guilt. Pushing them to pursue his extradition so he could face trial here."

"Why Marley?" How had she gotten involved in this?

"Marley was working with her friend Tanner Shaw, who ran the aftercare program over there."

"Aftercare?"

"Yes. After the girls are rescued, we don't just put them back out on the street. We give them shelter, training for a vocation, and so on. Tanner worked with a lot of Perera's victims and called Marley. The two went to college together. Tanner knew she needed Marley's help on the U.S. end.

"Tanner disappeared not long after Marley. Hence why the case fell apart. The two key players and the critical files are gone. We still have the investigators Tanner worked with on her end, and we can try to rebuild the case on this end, but we'll basically be starting from scratch."

"And no one's heard from Tanner Shaw?"

"No, but I imagine she was scared—and maybe was killed too. After three years running the after-care program in Cambodia she passed it off to a co-worker. Left work that day and never returned."

"Did someone file a missing persons report?"

"Her co-workers from the field office did."

"And?"

"No sign of her."

So they had two connected missing persons, albeit one was way out of their jurisdiction except for the fact she was an American citizen according to Paul. One had been found dead. Griffin feared for the other's safety—if she wasn't already in the ground.

"We'll need what information you have on Tanner Shaw," Declan said.

"I thought you were here to talk about Marley?"

"We are, but if another GJM employee is missing—one working the same case at the time of her disappearance—it's highly likely the disappearances are linked. Solving one helps solve the other."

"I'll also get you whatever we have on Tanner," Emily said, excusing herself.

"Thanks."

"Now," Paul said as Emily shut the door, "can we get back to Marley?"

"Of course," Declan said.

Griffin stiffened. Apparently Tanner's disappearance didn't bother him in the least.

"What can you tell us about Marley's role here at GJM?"

"She was GJM's head legal counsel."

"Can you elaborate on what that role entails?"

"Sure. Marley was GJM's lawyer, meaning it was her job to make certain everything GJM undertakes is impeccable and aboveboard from a legal and ethical standard. She represented the board and counseled GJM's lawyers located at field offices around the world on the most prudent ways to conduct legal investigations in their given country."

"I know you mentioned some of Marley's files were missing."

"The critical ones."

"Yes. I need you to compile a list of what is known to be missing. And we'll need access to the remainder of her files."

"The detective in charge of her missing persons case took the remaining files as evidence. We've been in a legal battle to get them released back to us, but it's all a bunch of red tape at this point."

"Okay," Declan said. "What about her personal effects?"

"I have most of those."

Griffin tried to maintain a neutral expression. Why on earth did Marley's co-worker have her personal effects?

"Don't personal effects typically go to the next of kin?" Declan asked.

"Her next of kin is her dad. He lives down in Ocean City. I sent down what he could handle and then stored the rest."

"What he could handle?" Griffin asked.

"He's got a ton of health issues. Beginning stages of dementia. Heart issues. I can't recall all the details. I just know Marley went down every weekend to be with him. She tried to get him to move up here, but he insisted on staying in his own home, so Marley hired a live-in nurse. Anyway, I sent down the few things he asked for and some stuff I thought he'd like—pictures of them, mementos, that sort of thing."

"And the rest . . . you said you stored. Where?"

"In my spare bedroom."

Griffin looked at Declan, wondering how he could remain so nonreactionary. Paul was keeping a dead woman's things, a woman who by his own admission was just a friend, in his home? *Creepy*.

— 21 —

"We're going to need to go through her personal belongings," Declan informed Paul.

Paul's jaw tightened. "What for? I told you who killed her."

165

"Procedure."

He exhaled, his hands balling in his lap. "Fine. You can swing by my place after work. I'm on the early-bird schedule. Home by four."

"We'll be there."

We? Griffin shifted in his chair. Apparently Declan wanted him along for the day, which was fine as long as he was back to escort Finley home.

"Now, when was the last time you saw Marley?" Declan asked.

"March fifth," Paul said without hesitation.

"Wow. You have a good memory." And a quick response. Most people would have taken time to think and most likely generalized by saying the beginning of March.

"Trust me, when someone you love disappears, you remember the last moments you had with them."

Griffin didn't need to be told that. He lived it—daily.

Declan scrolled through his phone calendar. "March fifth was a Thursday."

"Yes."

"Then what happened?"

"I called the police when she didn't show for work Monday."

"Monday?" Griffin narrowed his eyes. "She didn't work Fridays?"

"Normally she did. She'd taken that Friday off as a personal day."

"Do you know why?" Declan asked.

"I assumed to have a long weekend with her dad, but she must have planned it as a surprise, because when she didn't show up for work Monday my first call was to him to see when she'd left. He said she hadn't been there all weekend. That's when I knew."

"So you think she was taken or killed before she reached her dad's?"

"It's the only thing that makes sense."

"What time did she leave on Thursday?"

"Five, maybe five-thirty."

Declan jotted down the information as Griffin continued to question.

"I thought you worked the early-bird shift?"

"I do. Started this summer. Prior to that I was nine-to-five."

"And Marley?"

"The same, though she always stayed late. . . . Come to think of it, that night she seemed particularly anxious to get going."

"Sounds like you were one of the last people— if not *the* last—to see Marley Trent alive."

"Other than her killer," Paul said.

"Right."

"Did you walk her out?"

"Yes. We were both parked in the garage."

"Did you see her get into her car?"

"Yes."

"A 2007 GMC Envoy?"

"Y . . . esss," he said, drawing out the word as his brows pinched. "I'm sorry. I don't understand where you are going with these questions."

"We're trying to establish exactly—or as closely as we can—when she was taken."

"Oh." His face paled. "You think he could have been waiting in the garage?"

"It's possible." Perhaps in the backseat of her car. "Did you see her pull out of the garage?"

"Yes."

"Any chance you remember which way she went?"

"Right."

"Again, good memory." Though again it was creepy how quickly and distinctly he responded. As if he had often tracked Marley Trent's moves.

"Marley lived left," he continued. "Another reason I assumed she was heading elsewhere. She typically turned right when headed to her dad's, but there are a number of ways to get to Route 97."

Again, creepy. "Did you notice any other cars pulling out around the same time?"

"No, but I wasn't really paying attention." He sat back with a physical shiver. "To think Perera might have been there. Waiting for her. Following her."

"It's just a theory at this point." In fact, Griffin was starting to consider Paul more a possible suspect than Perera just from his actions and answers. He couldn't wait until he and Declan could get outside and have time to discuss the creepy co-worker. Perhaps Paul was so determined to pin the murder on Perera because he'd killed Marley himself?

"I'll just be glad when that man is behind bars where he belongs," Paul said.

"I'm curious," Griffin said, reclining slightly into the hard-backed chair. "How would that work?"

"What do you mean?"

"Perera, at least according to the latest news article I read on him, decided to retire in Cambodia when his ambassadorship was finished."

"Yes."

"So extradition would be required?" Declan said.

"Yes, which like I said, is what Marley was working with the ICE agent and Cambodian police to try and facilitate."

Declan cocked his head. "But I didn't see an ICE agent listed in Marley's missing persons file. Do you have his or her name?"

"His. Last name was . . . Rosario or maybe Rodriquez. I'm sorry. That information was part of the files that were stolen."

"Okay," Declan said, leaning forward. "Let's shift gears for a moment."

Paul crossed his leg, smoothing out the crease in his trousers. "All right."

"Any idea what Marley might have been doing up in Gettysburg the weekend she went missing?"

"What?" Paul frowned. "Why would you think . . . ?" His pale faced turned ashen. "Oh no. Was the body found at the battlefield Marley's?"

Griffin nodded. "I'm afraid so."

Paul braced his head in his hand. "I have no idea. Gettysburg is a completely different direction out of Baltimore than the eastern shore." He looked up, fresh tears in his eyes. "Do you think he buried her there because of the military connection?"

"At this point we are just speculating, but Perera"—if he was their man—"served in 'Nam. A far stretch to a Civil War battlefield."

"What about Marley?" Declan asked. "Any chance she was a history buff?"

Good thought. Maybe the lady had taken or planned on taking a mini-vacation.

"No." Paul shook his head. "Not really her thing. I have no clue why she'd be up there."

"Thanks for your time, Mr. Geller," Declan said, standing. "I believe that's it for now. We'll see you at your place after work."

"Fine." His tone did nothing to mask his irritation at their perceived intrusion.

Declan tapped Griffin's shoulder as they headed back out the way they'd entered. "We need to stop in Emily's office and get that contact information." He gestured to the door on the right.

They found her on the phone at her desk.

She waved them in and gestured for them to take a seat. Her office was compact, the walls bare, her desk covered with files, her shelves with books. Griffin surveyed some of the titles—*The Locust Effect, International Human Rights,* and a number of biblical commentaries.

"Yes," Emily responded over the headset. "Have him call me as soon as he gets in. Thanks." She hung up and looked at them. "So, how can I help?"

Declan began, "What can you tell us about Tanner Shaw?"

"As Paul mentioned, Tanner ran the aftercare program in conjunction with our Cambodian field office."

"And she was assisting Marley with the Perera case?"

"They were both vital to it."

"How so?"

"Working with his victims, Tanner saw the damage Perera caused firsthand. Tanner's the one who prompted GJM to look into Perera. Helped them build a case. But for that she needed Marley's expertise. The two worked together. Tanner on location and Marley here trying to convince ICE to press Cambodian authorities to extradite Perera to stand trial in the U.S."

"Has anything like that ever happened

before?" Seemed like a long shot. A very worthwhile one, but a long shot all the same.

"Yes, as a matter of fact. In 2007, a retired U.S. Marine captain, Michael Pepe, was successfully extradited to the U.S. He was tried and convicted for violent sexual assault of underage Cambodian girls and is currently serving 210 years in federal prison."

"And no one has seen this Tanner Shaw since Marley's disappearance?"

"Not that I'm aware of. Field agents investigated, but with no luck."

"Any chance she fled of her own accord?" Griffin asked.

"It's possible, but I doubt she'd just go into hiding and let the case she'd worked so hard on drop."

"Unless she feared for her life," Griffin said.

"Either way she's missing, and so are the files."

"Which brings us to Rachel Lester," Declan said.

Emily's brows pinched. "I don't really understand the interest in Rachel."

"Paul said she was so distraught over Marley's disappearance, she left her internship."

"That's correct. She was no longer interested in working with GJM."

"Any chance she took the missing Perera files with her when she left?"

Emily sat back, crossing her legs. "What exactly are you implying?"

"If Perera is behind Marley's death and the stolen files, perhaps he had a mole in place. Someone to keep tabs on Marley and take the necessary information to prosecute him with her when she left."

"I just don't see it. Rachel was a sweet girl. She seemed genuinely upset at Marley's disappearance."

"Or perhaps she was scared too." There were so many options, so many pieces to track down before they discovered the truth and how the puzzle all fit together.

"Perhaps."

"Do you have that address for Rachel?" Declan asked.

She retrieved it from her computer, jotted it down, and handed them the paper. "Give me your card and I'll have the head of the Cambodian field office get in touch when he's able. He's better equipped to answer your questions about Tanner."

"Thanks." Declan folded the slip of paper and tucked it in his pocket, handing Emily his card in exchange.

"One more thing before we go," Griffin said, standing.

"Yes?"

"Paul and Marley?"

"I think I know where you're going with this."

"Oh?"

She indicated for him to shut the door. He did and turned to face her, curious where this was going.

"I wouldn't want Paul's feelings to be hurt, especially considering . . ." She tapped her fingers on her desk. "Paul clearly had deep feelings for Marley."

"And Marley?"

"Was friendly with Paul, but in a kind, polite, friend-slash-co-worker way."

So the affection wasn't reciprocated, which made Paul having Marley's things all the creepier.

"Did Marley have anyone else in her life? The missing persons file didn't indicate anyone special."

"She was really focused on her work. Consumed with the job, especially at the end. But . . . there was this one guy."

"Yes?" Griffin pressed.

"I don't know the level of relationship they had, but she lit up whenever she mentioned him."

"This guy have a name?"

"Ben, I think."

"Any chance you recall her mentioning his| last name?"

"No. Sorry. But he lives in Ocean City."

"Like her dad?"

"Yes. I think she spent time with him while she was down there on weekends visiting her dad."

So there was another man in the picture. "Did Paul know about Ben?"

"I'm not sure. If he did, he didn't let on."

"Paul was borderline obsessed with Marley," Declan said as he and Griff walked down the ramp of the Pier V garage.

Griffin slid his sunglasses on, a glare coming off the water. "Hold the borderline."

"And Marley didn't reciprocate his affection."

"If he learned about Ben, it might have thrown him over the edge." Griffin had seen people crack over far less back in his BPD days. Between 75 and 90 percent of hostage situations involved domestic violence. "Though I highly doubt Paul possesses the necessary sniper skills."

"Yeah. Hardly appears the type."

Griffin arched a brow.

"Trust me." Declan unlocked the Expedition. "It was a compliment."

They climbed inside, and Griffin buckled in. "He could have hired someone."

"I'll get a warrant to check his financials."

"And in the meantime?"

"Let's hit Marley's last-known residence."

— 22 —

Patricia poked her head around the door of Finley's office. "Special Agent Brad Lewis is on line one."

Of course Brad would introduce himself as Special Agent. Like she wouldn't know her ex-boyfriend by name. Fortunately they'd parted on good terms. He'd understood the traumatic event with Brent Howard had left scars, and she hadn't been in any place to be in a serious relationship. She wondered when that had shifted. Now the thought of the possibility of her and Griffin in a relationship only brought interest, not fear of intimacy, of vulnerability. While she hated the helplessness she still felt when it came to Brent Howard, she didn't fear it in Griffin's presence, and that was a remarkable change.

Shifting her focus, she answered the phone. "Hey, Brad. Thanks for calling me back." He was the first in a long line of calls she'd placed.

"Hey, Fin. Anything for you."

"So you have some news?"

"Some, but . . ." He lowered his voice. "I gotta tell you, I generated a lot of irritation and called in a ton of favors on this one."

"I can't tell you how deeply I appreciate it."

"The lawyer, Marley Trent, wasn't exactly a friend to the Bureau."

"What do you mean?"

"I mean she was always butting heads with them, pushing them to get involved in one of her cases or threatening to sue if she felt a case was being overlooked."

"Overseas cases?" The FBI had select and extremely specific international privileges.

"Yes."

"Ever bring you guys a case on a former high-ranking general?"

"I never got that far. Walls came down faster than I could get past a serious chew out. Sorry, Fin. I did the best I could."

"Thanks for trying."

"Word of advice?"

"Sure."

"This doesn't sound like the type of case you should be digging into. I mean, after . . ." He hesitated. "I just worry about you."

The thought of this case turning into another situation like Brent Howard . . .

She swallowed the fear that invoked.

Marley's last apartment was a small studio over Beatrice Wilkinson's garage on the Severn River in Severna Park south of Baltimore—less than a half-hour from their hometown of Chesapeake Harbor. Being near home brought so many memories to the surface for Griffin. He visited fairly often, and every time he did, it was impossible to escape the past—at least as far as Jenna and Parker were concerned.

"We appreciate you letting us take a look," Declan said to Marley's landlady, climbing the stairs in front of Griffin.

"No trouble at all," Beatrice said with a smile over her shoulder.

"How long did Marley live here?"

"Four years."

Griffin looked over the property situated on a small hill overlooking the Severn River, tall weeping willows, devoid of leaves, lining the space between Beatrice's place and the next property over.

Marley's front porch overlooked the water, and a weathered blue Adirondack chair sat in the corner. Griffin pictured her sitting there, enjoying the sunset before her life had been cut short.

Please, Father, let us find her killer. Don't let this become another shelved cold case.

As they entered the apartment, the sun's rays streamed through the colorful cross suncatcher in the front bay window, casting beams of green, blue, and purple across the cream carpet.

"And no one has rented it since Marley?" Declan asked.

Beatrice clutched her floral housecoat over

her chest. "I just haven't had the heart to rent it out yet."

"You and Marley were close?" Griffin ventured.

"I wouldn't say close. She used to go to my church before she needed to start spending weekends with her dad. But I liked her."

Griffin strolled through the small space—twenty-by-twenty all told, he'd wager. A galley kitchen flanked the south wall, a bed the north, with a silver curtain rod with seashell-patterned curtains in shades of jade and turquoise separating the bedroom from the living space.

"I don't need the income from renting," Beatrice said, looking around. "I just do it when I think someone can really use the space. Marley was a good girl. I liked having her around. When she was here, that is. That girl was work, work, work."

Declan looked around. "Is the furniture yours?"

"Yes. Marley didn't exactly have a lot when she moved in. I keep the place furnished for my renters. Well, all three that I've had since Earl built the place back in '06."

"When you say she didn't have a lot . . . do you mean she was short on funds?" Griffin asked.

Beatrice shook her grey head. "Time and desire. Both she gave solely to work, with the exception of her dad, of course. Such a sweet daughter."

"What about Marley's personal effects?"

"I planned to pack up her things and ship them to her dad, but Marley's friend Paul said he'd take care of it for me."

He took care of it all right—keeping most for himself, it appeared.

"You know Paul?" Declan asked.

"Sure. Sweet young man. Worked with Marley."

"He come by often?"

"Occasionally."

"You ever get the impression he and Marley were romantically involved?"

"He wanted to be. It was written all over that poor boy's lovesick face, but Marley? Nuh-uh. She liked Paul, but it was clear, at least to me, only as a friend."

"Did Marley get a lot of visitors?"

"Marley?" She chuckled with a swish of her freckled hand. "Oh, my no. That girl was all about her job. Dedicating her life to others to the point she really had no life of her own."

"Do you recall the last time you saw her?"

"It was a Thursday morning. I remember because I host Bible study here on Thursdays, and Marley always greeted the ladies on her way out."

"When was this? Do you remember the month?"

"Yes. Beginning of March. She'd given me her rent check a few days prior. It was the last one." Tears misted in Beatrice's pale blue eyes.

"So she didn't come home from work that night?"

"No, but she had an overnight bag with her when she left for work."

"She did?"

Beatrice nodded.

"Did she say where she was headed?"

"No. I assumed her dad's."

"Thank you for your time." Declan handed her his card. "In case you think of anything else."

"You got it, young man. I'm so thankful Marley can have a proper burial now."

"Beautiful lady," Avery said over Finley's shoulder.

"Yes, she was." Finley compared Shirley's rendering to Marley's missing persons photo, astounded by the likeness but taking note of the subtle differences.

Avery leaned against the counter. "Always shocks me that someone can take another's life."

Avery was new to crime scene investigation according to Parker, but Finley would never have guessed it. She had adapted readily to the work. Finley just prayed she never adapted to the loss—never became complacent about the death they investigated day after day.

She'd never understand how one human being could murder another, and yet the heinous act went back to the first couple's children—Cain and Abel. Brother killing brother. It was unthinkable, and yet Gettysburg was littered with familial casualties. The cycle never ended, because of sin. Because of evil.

Avery linked her arms across her chest. "What do you think happened to her?"

"You mean *why* was she killed?" They already knew *how*—gunshot wound to the head.

"Yeah. I mean, do you think she was spying on someone? Saw something she wasn't meant to?"

"It's too early to speculate." But she'd spent the last hour placing calls. Anything and everything she could do to keep her promise to Leonard and the vow she'd made to Marley—to bring her killer to justice. If last fall had gone differently, *she* could have easily been a Jane Doe dug up years from now, and she hoped people would have done their best to bring her killer to justice. Marley deserved no less.

Avery smiled. "You sound like Griffin."

She supposed that was because they both approached things in a methodical manner. Seeing results, but not latching on to one until every possible option had been pursued.

"There's something I'm curious about," Avery said. "Something I wanted to run by you."

Finley glanced over, her curiosity piqued. "Sure."

"What's with the tension and barbs between Parker and Griffin?"

She'd been wondering the very same thing. "No clue." She took a seat at the workbench and invited Avery to pull up a seat.

Avery settled into the chair. "You want to hear my theory?"

"You sound like Parker," Finley teased. "Brimming with possibilities."

"Can't help it—my mind is always spinning."

"So what has it spinning about Griffin and Parker?"

"They used to all be close—Declan, Parker, Griffin, and the fourth guy they mentioned— Luke. I saw him in a couple pictures at Parker's. I think something difficult happened and it fractured them."

"Difficult as in . . . ?"

"I don't know, but I'm guessing it has to do with Luke."

"Have you asked Parker?" She always found honesty to be the best policy.

"Yes, I did."

"And?"

"And he quickly changed the subject."

"Interesting . . . but probably not the mystery we should be focusing our time on." She glanced back at Marley's picture.

"You're right." Avery got to her feet. "My mind tends to track on all kinds of things, but she's where our full focus should be. How long until Declan and Griffin get back?"

"I told Griffin I'd wrap up around six-thirty or seven." She was anxious to see him, to be in his comforting and engaging presence.

It was difficult to relax knowing someone had invaded her home again—and, as it turned out, her office too. Sweeping the lab they'd found more listening devices. She glanced at the line of small rectangular windows high on the room's outside wall and shivered. On top of it all, she couldn't shake the feeling of being constantly watched.

— 23 —

Griffin and Declan made a stop by Rachel Lester's last known address on their way up to Paul Geller's place in Aberdeen. She lived off Pratt Street, but not the nicer end. Her apartment was above a shabby laundromat. The entrance was located at the rear of the building, and a gentleman who reminded Griffin of a run-down Donnie Wahlberg sat on a folding chair on the crumbling concrete porch.

He lifted his chin. "What you two want?"

"We're looking for Rachel Lester."

"And you are?"

"Federal Agent Grey and Chief McCray."

"FBI and the po-po." He spit out a mouthful of sunflower seeds. "What'd Rach do this time?"

"This time?"

"Rach is always skirting trouble. Figured that's why she took off."

"Took off?"

"Yeah. Probably been eight, nine months since I've seen her around."

Same time Marley disappeared.

"Any idea why she took off?"

He popped more sunflower seeds in his mouth. "Nope."

A small tan dog yapped in the fenced yard next door.

"Shut up, Rex," the man yelled, but the dog continued. He stood and leaned over the crumbling stone porch wall. "I said shut it."

With a whimper the dog quieted.

"Any idea where she went?" Declan asked.

The sun beat down on Griffin's back, warming him despite the chill in the air.

"Nope." He retook his seat.

"And what was your relationship with her, Mr. . . . ?"

He laughed. "I'd hardly call it a relationship. We hooked up now and again."

"You lived in the same building, Mr. . . . ?" Declan asked.

"Ted Stavros, and, nah, she was bunking at my place."

Declan glanced over his sunglasses at Griffin, then back to the man. "Living together sounds more serious than hooking up."

"Dude, she couldn't afford her rent. What was I gonna do? Kick her to the curb?" He wiped his nose and checked out a woman walking by. He yanked up his jeans and sucked in his gut as he replied, his eyes still fixed on the girl. "I ain't that kind of guy."

Yeah, Griff thought, it was quite clear what kind of guy Ted was.

"Does Rachel have family nearby? Could she be staying with them?"

"Nah. Her family is out west, I think, and they aren't close."

Not sounding like the passionate, dedicated people they'd witnessed interning at GJM.

"Why'd she want to work at GJM?"

"Beats me."

"She never said?"

"Nah-uh. You'd have to ask her."

They'd also want to chat with Emily at GJM and see how Rachel presented herself during her initial interview and conducted herself through-out her internship.

Ted's description of the girl was very different than the brief description Emily had given. Better not to judge until all the information was in.

The question forming in Griffin's mind was, had she run because she was scared or because she'd been Perera's mole? And, more importantly, where was she now?

A man like Perera, according to the picture Paul painted, didn't leave loose ends. If Rachel had worked for Perera, she would most certainly have been considered a loose end.

●●●

Before leaving the city they made a quick swing back by GJM. Paul had just left for the day when they arrived, but their chat with Emily could be important and wouldn't take long. It was worth the short side trip.

"Gentlemen. Didn't expect to see you again so soon." Emily closed the folder she'd been working out of. "What can I do for you?"

"Rachel Lester."

"What about her?"

"Who interviewed her when she applied for the internship?"

"A number of us did."

"But you were among them?"

"Yes." Her thinly arched brows furrowed.

"What was your impression of her?"

"I don't understand this line of questioning. I thought you were looking for *Marley's* killer."

"Please," Declan said. "It may prove quite helpful."

"All right." She exhaled. "As I recall, Rachel seemed quite nervous that day."

"Like she had something to hide?"

"Like she really wanted the position." She narrowed her eyes. "I think I see where this is going."

"And where's that?"

"Rachel's past."

"Her past?"

"Yes. As a Christian organization, we ask people where they are with their faith."

"And Rachel?"

"Had recently come to Christ. She said she'd made mistakes in her past, but she'd given her life to Jesus and wanted to serve Him in every area of her life."

"And you believed her?"

"She gave me no reason to doubt her."

"Did you run a background check? Finger-prints?"

"Of course, due to the sensitive nature of our work."

"And no record?"

"No."

At least not adult, but Griffin figured her juvie record told a very different story.

Emily folded her hands on the desktop. "Why are you focusing on Rachel?"

"Were you aware she was living with a man at the time of her disappearance?" Declan asked.

"Yes. She told me she was having a hard time financially and was staying on his couch. I was trying to help her find a roommate among her fellow interns, but I'd hardly call leaving an internship disappearing."

"The man she was living with said he hasn't seen her since March."

"Oh, dear. I'm sorry to hear that. I thought she just didn't feel comfortable staying after Marley disappeared. Is there anything I or the organization can do?"

"Give us whatever you have on her."

"Of course, and please keep me posted. This is extremely disconcerting."

As they headed for Declan's vehicle, Declan asked, "What do you think?"

"I don't know." Griffin's gut said Rachel was in trouble or already dead, but, then again, his gut couldn't be trusted in high-pressure situations.

— 24 —

The scent of Old Bay seasoning, a Maryland staple, wafted down the hall of Paul Geller's condo building in Aberdeen—forty-five minutes north-east of Baltimore. His condo sat on the shores of an inlet to the Chesapeake Bay, a community beachfront picnic area visible from the hall windows they passed between condo doors.

"Number 203," Declan said.

"Up on the left," Griffin noted, hoping Paul didn't give them any resistance. The man was emotion-driven, which made him unpredictable.

Declan hovered his fist over the door. "Here goes nothing." He knocked.

Paul answered, dressed in running attire. "Great. You're here. I can still make my four-twenty run."

"It may take longer than that," Declan said, stepping inside. "We need to go through Marley's belongings."

"I've saved you the trouble." He retrieved a file box from his coffee table. "I've gathered anything you might consider pertinent." He handed Declan the box.

"While I appreciate your efforts, Mr. Geller, my colleague and I need to see all of Marley's things—not just what you feel is pertinent."

"Is that really necessary?"

Griffin shifted his stance, wondering what Paul was hiding.

"If you'd like I can have a warrant and team here within the hour to conduct a full-scale search of your premises."

Paul's lips thinned. "That won't be necessary. Follow me."

Declan set the box back on the coffee table, taking in the leather sectional, the large-screen HDTV, and custom cherry bookshelves lining the walls—masterful workmanship. They followed Paul down the hall, noting the pictures of Marley lining them. Some she was posing for, others held an unsettling feel of voyeurism. No wonder he didn't want them traipsing through his home.

He paused outside of a room, his head bent, his hand on the knob. "Are you sure this is necessary?"

Seriously. What was the man hiding?

"Positive. Would you prefer we get a warrant?"

Paul ground his jaw. "No," he said, "that won't be necessary." Releasing a deep exhale, he opened the door.

Griffin forced his feet to stay rooted in place, the urge to stagger tugging his legs.

Before them was an exact replica of Marley's studio bedroom, right down to the silver curtain rod and seashell curtains in front of the bed.

Griffin took mental inventory of the room's contents. The dresser was slightly different but painted to appear the same. A cross suncatcher hung in the window, though composed of a more primary color palette. The difficulty would be determining exactly which items had actually belonged to Marley and which ones Paul had so carefully replicated.

Paul stood uncomfortably, shifting his weight from one foot to the other while Griffin and Declan examined the contents of Marley's re-created room.

"It would be helpful if you could point out what items of Marley's you brought into the room," Declan said.

Paul swiped his nose. "What do you mean?"

Griffin wondered how tactful Declan would handle this one.

"I'm assuming everything in the room didn't belong to Marley. Her landlady mentioned the place Marley rented was furnished, so I'm assuming some of this belongs to you?"

Well done. He let Paul know they'd seen Marley's place without fully pointing out the massive creep-out factor.

"I see," Paul said, stepping in the room. "The jewelry on the dresser is hers." He cleared his throat. "The clothes inside."

He'd kept her clothes? Griffin's skin itched.

Declan stepped to the closet and opened the door to reveal what Griffin could only assume was Marley's wardrobe. What depth of sicko were they dealing with?

"Wow!" Griffin said, sticking Paul's offered file box on Declan's backseat, curiosity nipping at him. He'd probably riffle through it on the drive back to the lab. What had Paul deemed important, or had he simply given them what he was willing to part with?

"No joke," Declan said, glancing in the rearview mirror at Paul's waterfront condo complex. "If he were a sniper . . ."

"I know." They'd have their man. "How long will it take to go through his financials?" His condo's location and furnishings definitely spoke of a comfortable livelihood.

"Probably a couple days."

Unable to resist the niggling curiosity, Griffin grabbed the box from the backseat and balanced it on his lap. "Let's see what we got." He lifted the lid and sifted through the contents.

A handful of personal files, older bill statements, letters, clipped articles, nothing to tie to Perera—at least not anything apparent.

He pulled out a handful of notebooks in various shapes and sizes, flipping through them.

"Looks like an eclectic combination of a diary, to-do lists, notes from conversations, shopping lists . . ." He flipped pages, intrigued by the different shades of ink she used, even the variance in handwriting styles.

"Guess she preferred old school," Declan said.

"Guess so."

He tried to follow the doodles, attempting to track the woman's train of thought as her notes shifted from a handful of linear sentences at the top of each page to numerous patches of script and winding trails along the side edges, some even zigzagging and wrapping around the top, forcing him to turn the notebook upside down.

"You're gonna have fun with this project." He could only imagine left-brained, linear-thinking Declan trying to follow Marley's creative flow.

"Au contraire. You, my good man, get this one."

"Funny." Griffin stuffed the notebooks back into the box.

"I'm serious."

"Why on earth would you put me on this?"

"One, as I told you, my boss has made it painfully apparent I'm on my own for this. Two, you're currently on leave, so you've got time. And three, and most importantly, you get people."

The ultimate irony. Declan was right. As much as Griffin loved solitude and privacy, God had gifted him with the ability to read people—though at times he definitely didn't view it as a gift. And twice in his life the gift had flat-out failed him when he needed it most.

"What about Parker?" he asked. God had gifted Parker in that same area. Though Parker, of course, tended more toward the philosophical while *he* was all about the tactile.

"He's got his hands full in the lab. Besides, he's a profiler—focused on what motivates people. You, on the other hand, are a natural detective—able to see the small pieces of a person's life and then put the puzzle together to form a whole. You see the details, and that's what we need."

Truth was, if Griffin hadn't been so set on SWAT, he'd have enjoyed being a detective.

Even Kate had tried to hire him on when she'd left the Bureau to start her private investigator business. Speaking of Kate and being able to read people . . . "Heard from Kate lately?"

Declan glanced over at him, wariness flickering in his eyes.

Kate was Luke's girl, had been since the first

day on campus at the University of Maryland. She'd lived in their dorm, one floor up. Luke had taken one look at her knockout smile and offered to help move her in. They'd been inseparable since, right up to Luke's disappearance nearly seven years ago.

Sadly, Declan had fallen for Kate just as quickly, but it appeared no matter how much time passed she'd always be Luke's girl, and Declan knew it. In all the years since Luke's disappearance, Declan had never made a move. Oh, he'd kept in close contact with Kate. Helped her on her quest to find Luke—who they both believed was still alive and off on some heroic adventure. But he was just as certain that Luke wouldn't just leave them like that. No way.

"Last week," Declan finally said, knowing Griff could read him too.

"How's she doing?"

"Business is keeping her on her toes."

Kate thrived off adrenaline. "Bet she loves that."

"Yeah."

Like he loved her.

Griffin felt for the guy. It couldn't be easy being in love with a woman whose heart still belonged to someone else, especially when that someone else was one of his best friends, and even further complicated by the fact that he'd been missing for years.

"Have you thought about bringing her in on this one?" Kate possessed a unique and impressive skill set. Part bloodhound, part ninja.

She could provide great insight, and Declan came to life whenever she was around, though Griffin knew he beat himself up on the inside every day for it. Even though Luke had been gone for years, the fact remained a guy didn't move in on another guy's girl—or sister, for that matter. At least *Declan* got that.

Declan tapped the steering wheel. "I've thought of it."

"And?" Her presence clearly brought him a mixture of pleasure and pain.

"Maybe I'll give her a call."

It'd be good to see Kate again. It'd been months since he'd seen her. Last time was Fourth of July weekend in Chesapeake Harbor.

"Good, then maybe she can handle this." He dropped the box back onto the rear seat of Declan's Expedition.

Declan flashed a smug smile. "Sorry, friend. Getting inside Marley Trent's head is all yours."

So they took her things.

If only he'd considered the co-worker earlier.

That'd been his mistake.

He'd hit her office and home, but somebody had already been there. Items were missing—home files picked through. He'd assumed the cops had confiscated them as evidence and simply missed what he feared, but apparently the co-worker had slipped in first.

But why? He clearly was obsessed with the woman. That much was apparent now. But how had he known she was dead—that she wasn't coming back—before anyone else figured it out?

— 25 —

Declan lifted his chin toward the Gunpowder pull-off a quarter of a mile ahead on the left. "How about it?"

Griffin glanced at his watch. Finley said she wouldn't wrap up at the lab for a couple more hours.

"Sure. We've got time for a quick hike."

Declan switched on his blinker and pulled into the trailhead lot. "Excellent."

"We've got a situation."

"What's wrong now?"

"They took stuff from the co-worker's place."

"What *kind* of stuff?"

"A file box for one."

"I thought you said our girl in-house got all the pertinent files?"

"She did."

"Then why the hesitation in your voice?"

Because she waited until after he'd shot her to let him know she hadn't taken everything they needed. It irritated him that the crazy broad had died with a smug smile on her face.

"This has gone on long enough. I'm taking over."

"I got this. They just pulled off into a trailhead. It's the perfect opportunity."

"Then pull the bloody trigger. Just make it look like an accident. I don't want any more heat. Then take care of the woman. She's poking her nose where it doesn't belong."

Only one other car sat in the dirt lot, the newer trailhead still not known by most, or they simply preferred the paved lot a quarter of a mile down the road. Either way Griffin wasn't complaining. He liked having the place nearly to themselves.

The early evening air was crisp as he stepped from Declan's vehicle, the sun already sinking in the pink-hued sky. Nothing like a brisk day for a brisk hike.

Declan tossed him a water bottle from his knapsack stashed in the rear of the Expedition and they set off on foot, leaves crunching beneath their boots as they entered the woods.

The Gunpowder River was swift and fairly high, thanks to the recent rain, the water rushing around and surging over rocks and boulders. They banked right at the first trail fork, heading up the steep incline, away from the road, the faint sound of cars disappearing in the distance, all worldly distractions diminishing with each step further up and further in.

He tracked them, careful to keep his distance, waiting for the right vantage point. They were absorbed in conversation, no doubt discussing what they'd found at the co-worker's.

The co-worker.

He shook his head.

Who'd have figured?

The two friends wrapped around the switch-back, heading for the upper falls.

Perfect. He smiled.

The cascading water would help muffle the sound.

"You and Parker seem to be getting along well," Declan said.

Every. Single. Time.

With a sharp inhale, Griffin offered his sternest scowl in reply, hoping Declan would leave it at that. And for a moment he did, but then came that soft shake of his head that signaled more was coming.

"At some point . . ." he said, rounding the large oak at the top of the rise.

Griffin balled his hands tight. "At some point, what?"

"Never mind. You're right. Much better to spend your life punishing him right along with yourself." Declan started down the winding narrow path toward the falls.

"That's ridiculous."

Declan glanced back over his shoulder. "Is it?"

"This conversation is over."

"Wow." He scoffed. "That's a new one."

"You're in rare form today."

Declan shrugged. "Just stating the obvious. This has gone on long enough."

"How about we try something different?"

"Such as?"

"Shut it and walk."

"And that's different for you, how?" Declan smirked, pausing as they reached the river's edge.

As Declan analyzed the best path of rocks to cross over, Griffin lifted his chin, toying with the idea of just dunking his smart-aleck behind straight in. "Ya gonna take all day, sunshine?"

"Somebody's all riled up." Declan took the first stride across.

What did he expect after making an off-the-cuff comment like that? Griffin wasn't punishing Parker—at least not any more than he deserved.

Declan nearly slipped on the large rock in the middle, but caught himself.

"Nice balance." Griff chuckled.

"I'm still standing, aren't I?" Declan smiled smugly.

A shot pierced the air, echoing along the curve of the ravine.

Hunting season.

Declan's eyes widened. His hand clutched his shoulder as he fell back.

Griffin rushed forward.

A second report echoed as something blistering whizzed along his right ear. Lunging, he ducked into a sideways roll, drawing his weapon as he collided with a large rock square in the center of his back, his legs sloshing in the frigid water. Lurching his upper body forward, he steadied his arm and fired in the direction the shots had originated from.

Movement shifted through the trees.

He squinted.

A man raced up the ravine, trees sheltering him partially from view.

Turning, Griffin grasped for Declan.

Grabbing hold of his shirt, he yanked upward as Declan struggled for purchase on the slippery rocks. Struggling to shore, Griffin leaned him against a broad tree trunk, shielding him from the hill above.

He quickly assessed. Declan had been shot in the right shoulder, blood seeping through his soaked jacket.

"Go," Declan said. "I'm fine."

"You're not fine."

"He's getting away. Go. I'll call for backup."

Griffin tossed him his phone and then sped up the hill, using trees for cover as he surveyed the terrain.

He spotted the man at ten o'clock, racing in the opposite direction at a fast clip.

The dimming sky shadowed him a time or two from Griffin's sight.

Griffin increased his pace, rushing around trees, bobbing as the man spotted him and fired, the bullet wedging in the trunk mere centimeters from his head.

The man was a good shot. Better than good.

Pressing flush against a tree, Griffin forced his breath to steady. Leaning around, he sighted in, tracked the man, and fired.

The man staggered.

He fired again.

The man's knees buckled, and he dropped to them. Clutching his chest, he swayed, then slumped fully onto his side.

With weapon drawn, Griffin rushed to stand over him. He'd hit him twice in the chest, but he was still breathing and conscious.

Good. Because he wanted answers.

Declan lay on the stretcher in the first of two ambulances to arrive on scene. Griffin, along with the paramedics and two state troopers, had carried both men out of the woods and back to the trailhead lot.

Griffin climbed in the rear of the ambulance with Declan, his heart thudding. He'd lost too many . . .

He squeezed his eyes shut. He couldn't lose Declan.

Please, Father, give the doctor skilled hands. Don't take Declan away. I can't lose another . . .

He exhaled a shaky breath.

Please, Father. Not again.

"We've managed to stop the bleeding, at least externally," the paramedic said, "but we need to get him to the hospital and into surgery ASAP. I'm pretty sure the bullet penetrated the subclavian artery."

Declan looked up at Griffin, his eyes groggy, his head lolling. "What are you doing?"

"Going with you to the hospital."

"No. Ride with the suspect. You need to question him now, just in case he doesn't pull through. He didn't look good."

Declan was right. They needed answers, and chances were good he wouldn't pull through, but . . .

"I'll be fine." Declan's gaze shifted upward. "I'm in good hands, remember?"

Just as Jenna had been. . . .

With great apprehension, he finally did as Declan asked, climbing out of one ambulance and into the other.

The suspect's pain-etched face scrunched as

Griffin hunkered down beside his stretcher. Clearly he knew what was coming.

Though given the hardened scowl on his paling face, Griffin had the distinct impression he wouldn't be giving up anything easily.

They pulled onto Route 1 headed south for the beltway and University of Maryland Medical Center.

Griffin tugged his phone from his pocket, Declan's blood still on it, needing to call the last person in the world he wanted to.

— 26 —

Parker nodded, his words strangled as shock tracked through him. *Declan shot.*

"Park, did you hear me?" Griffin asked more urgently.

He cleared his throat. "Yeah. We'll head right out."

"Bring Finley."

"Got it." Parker hung up, shock numbing his limbs.

"What is it?" Finley asked, gently touching his shoulder.

He turned, the room spinning in the opposite direction. "Declan's been shot."

"What?" Her face paled.

"Griffin's with him. They're en route to the U of M Medical Center."

"Is Declan going to be okay?" The pitch of her voice increased. "Is Griffin okay?"

"I don't know, and yes, Griffin is fine."

"I'm coming too," Avery said, grabbing her keys. "I'll drive."

A thousand thoughts, fears, and memories flooded Parker's mind. *How can this be happening? Not again.*

The paramedic finished prepping the shooter and moved to sit up in the passenger seat, the sirens wailing as they merged onto I-95. The driver shifted to the radio, alerting the ER staff to the incoming patients' trauma status.

Griffin shifted closer, and the man rolled his bald head, looking away. Leaning in, Griffin deepened his voice. "You can look wherever you want, but I *am* going to get answers out of you." He planted his hand next to the man's ribs, making his steadfast presence painfully clear. "Why take us out? The ID has already been made. What are you so worried we'll find?"

The man remained silent.

"We know who had Marley killed." Or so they'd been told.

"You know nothing."

"I know *you're* no longer a threat to us."

The man rolled his head, his cold eyes locked

on Griffin. "Perhaps for the time being." A sardonic smile formed on his bluing lips. "But I'm not the one you need to worry about."

"Are you talking about Perera?"

He remained silent, and something gnawed at Griffin. Not his threat. He'd been threatened before, but there was something about the man that nagged at him. He replayed the afternoon's events in mind. The steps, the shots . . .

The man was left-handed. Majority of snipers were right-eye dominant, meaning they shot with their right hand regardless of hand dominance, but this guy—he'd shot left-handed, and that made him unique. If they showed his picture at the shooting ranges, surely a left-handed sniper whose weapon of choice was a Dragunov would stand out in people's minds.

Sniper.

There was that nudge again. That niggle in his gut saying something wasn't right.

If this man was the sniper who'd killed Marley, then surely he'd have killed Declan first shot. He'd made a good shot, but not the perfect shot he'd expect from Marley's killer.

What if this wasn't her killer? Had Perera killed Marley himself? If so, where was Perera now?

He leaned over the man, grasping his shirt as panic seared through him. "Who are you working with?"

The man chuckled up blood. "The devil."

"Where is he?"

"Closer than you think."

Finley climbed in her car and shut the door before swallowing a handful of deep, unsteady breaths.

Declan had been shot. Griffin had been with him. What if Declan didn't pull through? What if Griffin had been the one shot? Feelings she hadn't wanted to acknowledge burst uncontrollably through her, trembling through her limbs with searing anxiety.

She lifted her jangling keys, willing her hand to settle so she could slide them into the ignition, when movement in her rearview mirror caught her eye.

"Hello, Dr. Scott," the man said from the backseat.

She froze.

His gun settled against her headrest, the muzzle flush with the back of her skull.

"Wh-who . . . are you?"

"General Perera. But you, my dear, may call me Mark."

— 27 —

Griffin dialed Parker, his chest clamped tight. *No. No. No.*

Parker finally answered on the fifth and final ring.

"Where are you guys?"

"The hospital."

Thank you, Jesus.

"How's Declan? What's your ETA?"

"Fifteen. Let me talk to Finley." He needed to hear her voice. To know she was safe.

"She's not here yet."

"What?" Adrenaline gushed through him, his muscles taut, twitching to move. "You just said you're at the hospital." Only a matter of blocks from the lab.

"Yeah. Me and Avery. Finley wanted to take her own car."

He gripped the phone, fury boiling over. Couldn't Parker protect anyone he loved? "I told you to *bring* her."

"Yeah. To the hospital. She's on her way."

He was going to kill him.

The man he'd shot chuckled with a cough. "Told you I'm not the one you need to worry about."

"Griff?" Parker said. "What's going on? How's Declan?"

"Parker! Find. Finley. Now!"

Hanging up on Parker, he dialed the precinct nearly adjacent to the lab, sending units over ASAP.

Agitation and alarm tap-danced through him as Finley's phone went to voicemail *again.*

"Told you," the man said, more blood gurgling up and streaming down his dimpled chin as they banked right onto MLK Boulevard.

"Five minutes out," the paramedic said, moving to the man's side.

Griffin balled his fists. If Finley didn't answer it'd be the longest, most grueling five minutes of his entire life.

Lunging forward, he grabbed the man by the collar. "What does your boss want with Finley?"

The corner of his lip quirked into a half smile. "He's going for the jugular."

"Meaning?"

"Meaning your partner is effectively out. Without you the case won't move forward. Marley Trent was nothing but a thorn in the Bureau's side. Everyone else will just let her case silently die."

"How do you know . . . Never mind." His boss clearly had a wide reach.

"You're it, mate. To stop you, he's going after what you treasure."

Finley.

Finley's gaze darted to the door, her body drenched with a cold sweat. "How'd you get in here?"

"We don't have time for such details." He glanced at his watch. "I give them three minutes."

"Give who?"

"The police. Come now, Dr. Scott, you're a brilliant woman. Act like it."

"You killed Marley Trent."

"No. Actually, I did not. Which is why I'm here."

"You're lying."

"No. I'm not."

"I'm sorry, but do you really think, given the circumstances, I'm going to believe you?"

"It's your choice, but if you want to live I suggest you hear me out."

She swallowed, the muzzle of his gun flush with her skull. "Don't imagine I have much of a choice."

"No. I don't suppose you do."

Sirens wailing, the ambulance pulled up to the hospital. Griffin didn't wait for it to stop, jumping out as it slowed. Racing past the waiting para-medics, he sprinted down the freshly scrubbed hall, his shoes squeaking as he rounded the corner to the waiting area, relief staggering him at the sight of Finley sitting on one of the chairs.

It all became crystal clear—his love for her.

Despite himself, he'd fallen head over heart in love with the woman.

Rushing toward her, he dropped to his knees in front of her, engulfing her in his arms.

She collapsed into his hold.

Thank you, Jesus, doesn't even come close to the heart-rending depth of gratitude over-whelming me right now, Lord. Thank you.

He reveled in the feel of her, of *them*. He lifted his head pressing a kiss to her forehead before cupping her face in his hands and smoothing the damp hair from her brow. "Are you okay?"

She nodded, her trembling easing.

"What happened?"

"Perera was waiting in my car for me."

"I'm so sorry, Griff," Parker said behind him.

He rose and turned with a swing, his fist colliding with Parker's face.

Avery jumped between them. "What are you doing?"

Parker clamped his hand on Avery's shoulder. "It's okay, love. I deserved it."

Griffin shook his hand, trying to shake off the fury. "You were supposed to protect her. Just like you were supposed to protect Jenna!"

Parker swallowed the knife to the gut he'd intended it to be, and horrific guilt washed over Griffin. His gut was letting him down again. Why should *he* feel guilty? Parker screwed up *again,* and it could have cost Finley her life.

"Looks like you two wasted no time in going for each other's throats," Kate said, strolling in. She pulled a tissue from her bag and handed it to Parker. "Right hook?"

Parker nodded, dabbing at the blood streaming down his nose.

"He's always packed a killer hook."

"Katie." Griffin pressed a kiss to the top of her blond head, his fury settling. "You heard?"

"Parker called."

At least he'd done something right.

Kate looked over her shoulder. "Dec's family is right behind me, so I suggest you two rein this in."

— 28 —

After seeing Declan's, Griffin's, and Parker's parents into the waiting room and sharing a group prayer, the five of them stepped back outside to finish their earlier conversation. The sky was black, the cloud cover thick. Rain misted, but they huddled under the eaves.

Finley studied the two blond women flanking Parker—Kate, as she'd been introduced by Parker, and Avery. Both tall and slender but athletic in build—runners, she guessed, and both tough. They eyed each other warily, as if sizing one another up.

Parker's nose was swollen, both eyes blackening.

"What happened?" Griffin asked Finley, clearly wanting the rest of the story. But she feared saying anything that might reignite the fire smoldering barely beneath the surface between him and Parker. Who was Jenna?

"Perera wanted to talk," she said.

Kate cocked her head, her shoulder-length blond hair slipping over her right shoulder "Talk?"

"What did he say?" Griffin asked, his voice tight.

"He said someone else killed Marley Trent and set him up."

"Well, that's awfully convenient," Parker said.

"He admitted he considered killing Marley, but someone beat him to it."

Kate's eyes narrowed. "You sound like you actually believe him."

"Well, I'm not just going to take his word for it, but it's curious."

"What is?" Parker asked.

"If he's lying, why bother coming to me and trying to convince me of his innocence?"

Griffin swallowed, his Adam's apple bobbing. "He may have had other motives."

"Like trying to get us to waste our time looking elsewhere," Parker said.

"To what purpose?" she asked. "If he's guilty, the evidence will track back to him."

"If?" Parker said. "Come on, Finley. Don't tell me you actually believe the man?"

"He admitted his intent to kill Marley."

Kate rolled her eyes. "Well, that's big of him."

"He claims someone beat him to it."

"So does this *'someone,'*" Parker said with air quotes, "have a name?"

"He said that's where we come in."

"He expects us to overlook the evidence pointing to him and go in search of another suspect?"

Finley looked at Griffin. "I'm not saying I believe him, but what if he's telling the truth?"

Parker shook his head. "How can you even entertain the idea? Declan's in surgery now because of Perera's man."

"So the man works for Perera?"

"Admitted as much," Griffin said. "Referred to him as the devil."

Parker leaned against the doorframe. "Charming."

"Where is he now? The man? Please tell me he's in custody?" Finley asked.

"Griffin got him. He's in surgery too." Parker looked to Griffin. "Good job, by the way."

Griffin nodded.

Kate turned to Finley and asked, "And Perera?"

"We spotted squad car lights and then everything went black. Next thing I know Parker is waking me up and Perera is nowhere to be seen. We got here only minutes before you arrived."

• • •

Three hours later the surgeon emerged. The entire waiting room, consisting of nearly their entire hometown of Chesapeake Harbor, stood.

The surgeon removed his cap with a sigh and Griffin's breath hitched.

"He's going to be okay. Not overnight. He's going to require recovery time, but he'll pull through."

"When can we see him?" Declan's mom asked, her tearstained cheeks still pale, her eyes and nose red.

"Immediate family can see him now, for a minute. He's in ICU. Tomorrow, hopefully, he'll be moved to the recovery ward, and you can all see him."

Relief surged through Griffin.

"Oh, and the other man you came in with . . ." The surgeon lifted his chin at Griffin.

Part of him wanted the man dead for shooting Declan—the other part wanted him alive to stretch over the racks. "Yes?"

"He wasn't so lucky," the surgeon said. "Died an hour ago."

Griffin nodded. "Thanks for letting us know. Can we take a look at his personal belongings?"

"You'll have to talk to the hospital administrator. There's a protocol to follow when we hand items over to the authorities. They'll be given to the officer in charge of the investigation."

"Declan is in charge of the investigation."

"I'm afraid not anymore."

The man had gotten what he wanted. Declan out of commission. Marley Trent's case swept away. Well, not if he had anything to say about it.

Kate rested a hand on his shoulder. "You should get Finley home. She's had a long day. Declan's out of harm's way, and we can't see him until morning."

"Kate's right." He rested his hand on Finley's back. "Let me get you home." But his home. His turf. Perera had declared war.

— 29 —

They retrieved Winston from Finley's and headed back to Griffin's place in Thurmont.

Finley battled the fear threatening to swallow her whole. Men had been spying on her in *her* home. Perera had been waiting in *her* car. She felt nothing of hers was safe, and it was a terrible realization.

Griffin carried the overnight bag she'd packed into the house. "Would you like something to eat before bed?"

She wasn't hungry, but she had no desire to sleep. To be alone in a room, in the dark. It was pitiful, but she couldn't stop shaking.

"Maybe a cup of decaf or tea, if you have it."

"Pretty sure I have both. My dad likes decaf and my mom tea, so I keep them on hand."

Finley rubbed her forehead. "I'll take tea, then."

"Why don't you get settled in the family room? I'll make your tea and start a fire."

"Thanks." That sounded wonderful. Griffin. Warmth. Protection.

Thank you, Lord, for keeping me safe tonight. Things could have gone in a far different direction. Please bring healing to Declan and to whatever is causing such pain between Griffin and Parker.

She kicked off her shoes and sat on the brown leather sofa, curling her legs beneath her.

Griffin returned with two steaming mugs in hand. "Tea for you. I wasn't sure what you liked, so I went with something called Swiss Apple."

"Oh, I love that tea. From Tea Forte?"

He shrugged. "No idea. Just what my mom brought up last time she came. I don't think she's a big fan of the generic black tea I buy."

Finley didn't blame her, especially when awesome teas like Tea Forte existed. "Thanks." She cupped the mug, inhaling the crisp scent of apples with a hint of cinnamon. "This is great."

He set his coffee mug on the table, started a fire, and joined her on the couch. "Crazy day."

"We've had quite a few." The shooting range,

the listening devices in her home, and then tonight.

He reached out and cupped her hand. "But we've made it through *together*."

She smiled up at him, at his gesture of affection, and her heart swelled. There was so much she wanted to know about this man. Her heart was already there, but her mind needed time to catch up. At least that's what the sensible part of her screamed. "Can I ask you something?"

He reclined on an exhale, clearly knowing what was coming. "Yeah. You want to know about Jenna?"

She nodded.

He pulled out his wallet and handed her a picture of a teenage girl with long brown hair, bright blue eyes, and a fabulous smile. "She's beautiful."

"Yeah, she was." Griffin swallowed.

"Was?"

His bottom lip pulled into his mouth slightly and he looked past her with a shaky exhale, then fixed his stalwart gaze back on her. "My sister, Jenna, was murdered her senior year of high school."

"Oh, Griffin." She clutched his hand tighter. "I'm so sorry."

"It was years ago, but sometimes, most times, it's still raw."

"I can't imagine the toll that kind of loss takes."

He took the picture back and slipped it in his shirt pocket. "Collaterally."

"What?"

"That kind of loss. The way it happened. It was like shrapnel spewing in a hundred wounding directions all at once."

"We don't have to talk about this." She shouldn't have pushed. She'd give anything to erase the pain on his face. She should have let it be.

"No. I'd like you to know about Jenna."

She lifted her mug to her lips, pausing before taking a sip. "I'd love to know about her."

"She was bright, outgoing, and had the best sense of humor."

Finley settled in deeper to the comfy couch cushions. "Tell me more."

"She was an O's fanatic. Never missed a home game. Was addicted to Gobstoppers—always had boxes everywhere—and she loved people." He inhaled sharply. "She had the most giving heart."

"I'm so sorry."

"Like I said, it was a long time ago."

As much as she was longing to understand how Parker tied into it all, they'd both endured enough trauma for one night, so she changed the subject at Griffin's silence.

"I had a strange encounter on campus today."

His brows arched. "Oh?"

"Yeah. I went in to grab a few things I needed and I bumped into a woman. She stumbled when I asked her name and didn't seem to know what she was talking about."

"You think she was lying to you about who she was?"

"Yeah, I do."

His thumb traced circles along her palm, sending the good kind of goose bumps fluttering along her skin.

"You cold?"

A soft smile curled on her lips as her toes followed suit. "No. I'm good."

He returned the smile, his eyes holding fast to hers. "When I thought . . ."

"I know." She nodded. Her first thoughts had been of him, fearing she might never get to see him, to tell him . . .

Cupping her face, he swooped in. Her lips parted, and he pressed his to hers—tender at first, then growing passionate in intensity.

After a moment he pulled back, but only so far as to rest his forehead against hers.

"I should get you to bed."

She jolted.

He laughed. "Sorry. That came out way wrong. I meant it's getting late, you've had a long, hard day . . . You should get to bed—in my guest room."

Of course that's what he meant, because he was

a stand-up guy, and she treasured him for it. "Thanks, but I'd like to stay with you awhile longer, if that's okay."

He smiled. "You'll get no argument from me."

She leaned into his hold, snuggling against him on the couch, her heart soaring, despite the fright she'd endured.

"This woman you ran into . . . any idea who she might have been? Any chance it was Rachel Lester?" he asked.

She frowned. "Who?"

"Marley's intern I was telling you about on the ride home."

"Oh, right. I have no idea. What does Rachel look like?"

"Five foot four, roughly one hundred and twenty pounds, long dark hair."

"It could have been."

"I've got her picture in the file box in Declan's car. . . . Shoot."

"What's wrong?"

"The state trooper said he'd contacted local police to send a rookie over to drive Declan's car back to the field office, but Marley's stuff is still in the vehicle."

"You think someone would break into his car in front of the field office?"

"Based on the last couple days, I wouldn't put anything past whoever is running this show."

Perera.

"Let me make a call."

He returned a few minutes later.

"You get ahold of someone?"

"Yeah. Kate. She's going to collect the stuff."

"Why Kate? Why not one of Declan's co-workers?"

"At this point I don't know who we can trust."

— 30 —

Parker locked the door and set the alarm behind them once he and Avery were safely in his loft. He was impressed and shocked she'd agreed to stay again, but after the night's events he wasn't giving her a choice.

His nose hurt like crazy, but as he said, he'd deserved it. He never should have left Finley alone, but he had no idea . . .

He shook out his hand. It didn't matter. He shouldn't have left her alone, and he certainly wouldn't be leaving Avery alone until this case was solved—whether she liked it or not.

He'd come to care a great deal for her. He respected her. Enjoyed her company. And was intrigued by the weight of some unknown she carried around—some shame he couldn't fathom the origin of, but he wasn't one to talk. He was drowning in shame and guilt. It was, in part, what propelled him to do all he could to help solve the cases before him, bring justice to the victims, closure to their families, and maybe, just maybe, earn some measure of forgiveness—if there was any to be earned.

"Think it's too late to order a pizza?" Avery asked.

He chuckled despite himself. Where did she put all that food? "Considering it's nearly two in the morning, yeah, I'd say you're out of luck. How about I make you an omelet?"

"Sure." She climbed onto a barstool. "If you're sure you don't mind."

He pulled the eggs and some fresh veggies from the fridge. "I love to cook. Remember?"

She pulled her hair over her shoulder and braided it, slipping the hairband off her wrist and onto the base of the braid. "Mind if I change while you cook?"

"I told you, *mi casa es su casa.*"

"For tonight, at least."

Until this case was solved.

He cracked the eggs, Griffin's call replaying through his head. The utter helplessness and panic of that moment ripping back through him—fearing he was about to lose another friend. It was astonishing how a single sentence could raise demons he'd been battling for years right back to the surface.

Father, forgive me. For Jenna and for nearly getting Finley killed tonight. Help me to be more like Griffin. To be someone people can depend on. I'm so sorry, Father.

Suffocating, crushing agony washed over him.

Avery moved back to the kitchen, Parker not even noticing her approach. So unlike him. She had to ask.

"Who's Jenna?" She had to ask.

He hitched, spatula in hand, shoulders tense.

Whoever she was, he cared a great deal for her. As did Griffin.

He slid her omelet onto the plate he'd set in front of her. "Someone I'd rather not discuss tonight."

"Okay." He hadn't pressed her with his questions. She'd return the courtesy.

He set the frying pan back on the stove, turned off the burner, and started out of the kitchen.

"Aren't you going to eat?"

"Actually, I think I'm going to head to bed. I'm suddenly rather tired."

"Okay."

"Can I get you anything else?"

"No, thanks. I'm good."

"Night, Tate."

"Night, Parker."

Griffin sat in the recliner, the chair angled toward the front door and his gun handy as he settled in for what little remained of the night.

Finley lay asleep on his couch.

He ached to curl up with her, to shelter her in his arms, but he'd be the gentleman she deserved him to be.

Resting his head against the cushioned back, he pulled the navy throw over his lap, doubting he'd find any rest.

He glanced to the front window. The blinds were drawn but he still felt exposed. His gut said someone was out there. Watching. If it wasn't Perera, as the man claimed, then who?

— 31 —

Griffin sat on the edge of the couch, petting Winston as Finley's footfalls echoed down the wooden stairwell of his home. She'd used the guest bathroom to shower and change for the day.

Winston's head lifted, and his tail swished back and forth.

Griff shook his head. Apparently his dog had fallen for the lady as hard as he had. "Go on."

Winston bolted from the room.

"Good morning, Winston." Finley laughed, rounding the corner with the wolfhound on her heels.

Griffin stood. Wearing a casual pair of faded jeans and burgundy sweater, she was simply breathtaking. "How you holding up?"

"I'm good."

"I made some coffee."

"I smelled it. Thanks."

"Were you able to sleep any?" He'd watched her fall asleep, but she'd already been up when he woke at six.

"Yeah. I only woke a few minutes before you. Knowing you were right here . . ." She let her words trail off, slipping her auburn hair behind her ear. "I wanted to talk to you about that."

"About?" His gut clenched. Was she regretting their kiss? It'd been presumptuous and impetuous of him, but the instant he thought he'd lost her, he realized how deeply he cared and how very much he wanted her in his life.

But . . . she knew the truth about him. Maybe that truth of his weakness had finally sunk in and she'd realized he wasn't the man for her. She'd said it wasn't his fault, but he knew in his heart it was. He was the reason Judith Connelly was dead.

Finley stepped in front of him, drawing his attention.

"Sorry," he said. "I was lost in thought."

She gazed up at him with big, beautiful eyes. "I was just wondering when."

His brows furrowed. "When what?"

"When you started having feelings for me."

He smiled. He should have known she wouldn't make this easy on him. "Well, I definitely experienced strong feelings the first time we met."

She exhaled a chuckle. "That much was clear, but not exactly the feelings I'm talking about."

"I know." He took her hand and lowered her to the couch with him. "Our first meeting wasn't exactly . . . *civil*."

She arched her brows.

"Okay. I was . . ."

"Grouchy? Grumpy?" she supplied.

"Okay, let's stop naming dwarves, shall we?"

She laughed. "But there are so many that come to mind."

"You really aren't going to make this easy on me, are you?"

She smirked. "Where's the fun in that?"

He pulled her into his arms and kissed that adorable smirk right off her beautiful face.

Griffin spent the drive to the hospital in prayer while Finley dealt with her overflowing inbox on her phone.

Father, I am in so far over my head. I desperately need you. Please guide me and Finley. Please help me to listen to you and not my gut. Maybe that's been the problem after all. Or . . .

He felt the Lord stirring his heart, and a thought occurred to him he hadn't considered.

Is your Holy Spirit that inner voice?

Had what he'd been calling instinct and his gut actually been the Lord's leading?

But if that's the case, why is Judith Connelly dead?

Because humans make mistakes.

Finley reveled in the feel of Griffin's fingers intertwined with hers as they entered the hospital, praying for good news and the opportunity to see Declan. Griffin needed to see his friend. That much was clear.

They were instructed by the nurse manning the desk that they'd have to wait until Declan was moved from ICU to ward four.

They stepped into the waiting room and found Parker and Avery already there.

Griffin and Parker exchanged a nod.

"Morning," Avery greeted them, her gaze dropping to their clutched hands.

"Morning." Finley smiled.

"I'll go grab us some coffee," Griffin said. "Can I get either of you any?"

"I'd love one," Avery said.

"How do you take it?"

"Black."

"Park?"

"I'm good, thanks."

Griffin nodded and stepped from the room.

Finley took a seat beside Avery, unable to stop smiling.

"Looks like you two had a nice night despite the circumstances," Avery said, nudging her shoulder.

"Yeah, we did." Hearing him share about Jenna, falling asleep with him close by. "He talked about his family."

Parker leaned forward, his dark brows arched. "His family?"

"Yeah."

Parker exhaled. "He told you about Jenna."

Why did Parker look like he was about to pass out? "Yes. He told me she was murdered."

"Oh, how awful," Avery said.

"Awful doesn't even come close," Parker said, his gaze drifting right through them.

"Growing up together, you must have known her," Finley said, choosing her words carefully. Griffin seemed to hold Parker responsible for some aspect of Jenna's death, but she couldn't fathom what. He certainly hadn't murdered her.

"He knew her *extremely* well," Griffin said, standing in the doorway, three coffees in hand. Liquid sloshed over the edge as he dropped the cups on a table next to him.

Parker swallowed.

Finley's gaze darted between the two men. So Griffin's sister *was* the source of the tension between them. But why?

"Jenna and I were in love," Parker said, his voice softer than Finley had ever heard it.

Avery's eyes widened, Finley sure hers were

doing the same as shock surged through her and her mind struggled to put the pieces together.

"Jenna was seventeen." The vein in Griffin's temple flickered.

"She was about to turn eighteen."

"You were twenty-one."

"There's no age requirement on love, and we both know the age difference isn't really what has you riled, so let's get to it if we're really going to do this."

Finley stood as Parker stepped in front of Griffin, mere inches between the men. Griffin's posture poised for a fight. Parker's one of vulnerable defiance. What had she started?

"Overlooking the fact that you were three years older than my kid sister and sneaking around like you had something to hide—which usually indicates you do—the fact is, you're the reason Jenna's dead."

Parker's hands coiled tight into fists at his side. "You think I don't know that? That I don't live with that agonizing regret every single breath of my life?"

"Then why'd you do it?"

"Because I was in love and we wanted to see each other. How could I have known she'd be in any danger?"

"Asking her to sneak out of the safety of her home at midnight to meet you at a park a quarter of a mile away? You didn't stop to think she'd be walking alone—late at night in a secluded area?"

"We met there all the time."

"And clearly the killer knew that."

"We don't know that. Police never determined if the killer had targeted her or if it was a completely random act."

"Whether he targeted her or not doesn't matter. The fact is, she's dead because you weren't man enough to tell me you were seeing her. Couldn't court her the way she deserved." Griffin's vein throbbed in his left temple, his fists tight, his face red.

"I would give my life in her place a thousand times over, and you know it."

Griffin's fists unclenched, and he took a step back. "This isn't getting us anywhere. I'm going to check on Declan."

Finley followed him out of the room, her heart breaking for both men.

Parker lowered himself back into the chair, his hands shaking with anger or pain, Avery couldn't tell.

She rested a hand on his knee. "Wanna talk about it?"

He looked at her like *"What do you think?"*

"I get it. I've never been accused of being the sharing type either." It was much easier—or at least that's what she kept trying to convince herself—to keep things close to the vest, heavy as that vest sometimes became. "But it's painfully obvious you need to unload."

"Griffin's right." He raked a shaky hand through his dark brown hair. "It's my fault Jenna's dead."

"You could have never known someone would murder her on the way to the park."

Parker released an agonizing exhale. "He didn't murder her straight out."

Avery's stomach dropped. "What?"

Tears of rage flooded Parker's soulful eyes. "He abducted her, tortur . . . ed her. Ra . . ." His voice choked, tears falling. He squeezed his eyes shut. "Raped her and then dumped her body in the bay days later."

Dear God. She reached out and engulfed Parker in her arms. He resisted her embrace, but she refused to let go, and finally he gave in to her hold.

"Griffin," Finley said.

"I'd rather not talk about it now."

"The nurse said we needed to wait a few more minutes. Declan's resting."

"I'll be quiet. I just want to see for myself he's okay."

He lifted his chin at the cop manning the door, knowing Barney from his days on the force.

He held the door open for Finley, and she slipped inside. They moved past the curtain and found a nurse at Declan's side.

The nurse looked up with frightened eyes.

"Hey," Finley said. "You're the lady from campus."

"All done in here," she said, scurrying past them.

"Wait!" Griffin called, but she bolted from the room.

Was she Rachel Lester? He hadn't gotten a good enough look. But it'd make sense if Perera sent his mole in to finish Declan off. "I'll be back," he hollered to Finley, bursting into the hall after the woman.

He caught sight of her as she raced through the ward's double doors and took off in pursuit, pushing past the nursing cart in his way.

She wove around chairs, flying through the outer seating area.

Heading for the stairs.

She disappeared into the stairwell a fraction of a second before him.

Grasping the cold metal rail he frantically glanced up and down, finally spotting her rounding the landing below.

He swung around the rail, darting down the stairs, taking several with each stride.

She exited on the garage level, the chilly exhaust-filled air assailing him as he maintained pursuit.

She darted between vehicles and he lost visual. She'd dropped somewhere.

He moved along the car line, stepping back to glance under the row of vehicles, working to not compromise his position.

Nothing.

He followed the row, looking between each car. Two vehicles from the end, he caught a swipe of movement.

Gotcha.

He lunged around the front of the vehicle, snagging her around the waist as she attempted to dart past him.

"Let me go!" She struggled in his arms.

"Not until you tell me who you are and what you were doing in my friend's room."

A couple entered the garage and froze at the sight of them.

"It's okay, folks. I'm a cop apprehending a suspect," he said.

She fought his hold. "I'm hardly a suspect."

"Then who are you?"

"My name is Tanner Shaw."

— 32 —

Declan groaned, drawing Finley's attention. She'd been anxiously pacing his room waiting for Griffin to return. Where was he, and who *was* that woman?

Declan's eyes opened. He blinked and struggled to sit forward.

"Easy there." She rushed to his side.

"Hey, Finley," he said groggily.

"Hey, yourself." She helped him to an upright position, propping pillows behind his back for support. "I can't tell you how happy I am to see you awake."

He stretched, his movements stiff and punctuated. "How long have I been out?"

"Just overnight."

"Overnight?" He lurched forward, and she braced a restraining hand on his shoulder.

"Whoa there."

"What happened with the man? What have I missed?"

Finley filled him in.

"Tanner Shaw?" Griffin released her and took a step back. "We were led to believe you were dead."

She straightened the light blue scrubs she'd most likely pilfered. "That's good. Hopefully the men hunting me believe that too."

"Perera's men?"

Relief eased the muscles pinched in her face. "So you know?"

"I have a feeling we only know the tip of the iceberg."

"You're working Marley's case?"

"Yes." He explained the circumstances.

"Then we need to talk." She rubbed her arms,

the long-sleeve white cotton shirt layered beneath her scrubs sliding up and down with the movement. "But not here."

Finley sighed with relief when Griffin's text finally came through. "Said he's fine. Talking with the woman now. Be up soon."

"Great." Declan stretched out farther this time, his movements easing, the color returning to his face. "Sounds like we've got a bit of time. You've done a great job updating me on the case—now, tell me what else is going on?"

"Like what?"

"Something is bothering you outside of the case. I can read it on your face."

She touched her cheek. Was she that obvious? Or was he simply that good?

He patted the bed and she sat down beside him. "I'm worried about Parker and Griffin."

Declan exhaled. "I worry about them too, but they've been making some big strides lately."

She bit the inside of her cheek. "I fear I may have undone all that and made it far worse."

Declan frowned. "What happened?"

"They had a blowout about Jenna."

"They actually *talked* about Jenna with each other?"

"Talk is probably not the most apt description."

Declan pinched the bridge of his nose. "No.

I'm sure it's not. When it comes to Jenna, tensions run high."

"That's an understatement." She stood up. "I realize Griffin's devastated by the death of his sister, and if she hadn't left her house that night, maybe it never would have happened, but what's to say the killer wouldn't have waited and grabbed her another time?"

"We'll never know. Her murderer was never caught."

Her lips gaped open. "What?"

"Jenna's body was found washed up on shore at the edge of town a week after she disappeared. He'd done horrible things to her."

Finley squeezed her eyes shut.

"But they never caught the guy?"

No wonder they all hated the term *cold case*.

"Parker wasn't trying to harm Jenna. He clearly loved her," Finley said a moment later. It was painfully apparent in the crushing sorrow etched across his face at the mention of her name. "Surely Griffin sees that?"

"They way it was handled didn't help."

"What do you mean?"

"It was a secret."

"Parker and Jenna?"

"They'd been seeing each other for months and managed to keep it from Griffin—who was Parker's best friend."

"Griffin and Parker were best friends?"

"Yeah. We all four hung out and were close, but Parker and Griffin were tight."

"Why didn't Parker tell him?"

"Because Jenna begged him not to."

"He told you that?"

He shook his head. "Jenna did."

Her eyes widened. "You knew?"

"I caught them at the park one night. Was there with a date and . . ." He shrugged. "Jenna begged me not to tell Griffin just as she'd begged Parker not to."

"Why?"

"You see how protective Griffin is of those he loves."

"Yes."

"With Jenna . . . Maybe because it was just the two of them. Maybe because Jenna was sick when she was little."

"Sick with what?"

"Guillain-Barre syndrome. She had a horrible reaction to a vaccination. Spent weeks in Kennedy Krieger. After that, Griffin became ultra-protective of her. She pulled through and had no real lasting repercussions, but I think nearly losing her forged a special protective bond between them."

"Who else knew about them? Parker and Jenna?"

"Griff's mom, Kay. And that was a huge point of contention between her, Griff, and Griffin's dad after Jenna's disappearance. Everything imploded that night."

"And now?"

"It's better."

"But?" She could sense there was more in his hesitant tone.

"Some wounds time doesn't heal."

<h1 style="text-align:center">— 33 —</h1>

"But you all went to the same college," Finley said, still trying to put the pieces together.

"But we had Luke. He was always the peace-keeper. Somehow he was able to keep Parker and Griffin from coming to blows—until he disappeared."

"Luke disappeared? Griffin mentioned he was gone, but I had no idea . . . what happened?"

"That remains a great source of debate and further fracture in Griffin and Parker's relation-ship."

"Why?"

"Because Parker's convinced Luke left of his own accord. And I tend to agree, but I hope it was for a good reason we just don't understand."

"And Griffin?"

"Convinced that Luke would never abandon his friends."

"Sounds like Griffin." His loyalty ran deep.

"What about Kate? Griffin said she was Luke's girlfriend?"

"Still very much in love with him." He swallowed. "And dedicating most of her time between clients to figuring out what happened."

"She thinks he's still alive?"

"She's convinced."

"And you?"

"Try to help her out with resources when she thinks she's found a lead."

"Do you think he's still alive?"

"I don't know. If he is, I can't fathom why he hasn't been in touch."

The door opened, and Griffin popped his head in the room.

"You're awake." He smiled at Declan. "Your doctor is on the way in to check on you. Finley, could I grab you for a minute?"

"Sure."

Declan frowned. "What's going on?"

The doctor stepped around Griffin, entering.

"I'll fill you all in when we return."

Finley's brows furrowed at the sight of the woman Griffin had chased from the room. She stood just behind him, her gaze darting warily up and down the hall.

"Let's find someplace we can talk while Declan's busy with the doc."

Finley followed Griffin and the mysterious woman down the hall to an empty room where the woman explained who she was and how she'd gotten there. Her story was so amazing and insightful, nearly an hour passed before Finley bothered glancing at the clock. "We should head back to Declan's room. I'm sure he and everyone else heading over will want to hear this."

Parker watched Griffin, Finley, and a tall brunette enter Declan's room a few strides in front of them.

"You look good," Griffin said to Declan as Parker pushed the door open.

"Feeling much better."

It was so good to hear Declan's voice sounding strong.

"And," Declan continued, "incredibly curious who this lovely lady is."

Parker shifted his gaze to the brunette, equally curious.

"This is Tanner Shaw."

"Tanner Shaw?" He said, drawing all eyes to the doorway. "I thought you were missing and presumed dead."

"I was," Tanner said.

"You look quite alive to me." He stepped inside, allowing Avery and her balloon bouquet passage in.

Tanner dipped her head. "And you two are?"

"Parker Mitchell. This is Avery Tate, and this . . ." He looked back at the door. "Where did she get to? She wasn't far behind."

"Who?" Finley asked.

"Kate," he said with a smile as she entered.

"Kate." Declan sat up, smoothing his hair. "What are you doing here?"

"Parker called." She strode over and kissed his forehead. "You doing okay?"

"Much better." He smiled.

Of course. Parker sighed. Declan was always better when Kate was in the room. *Poor, lovesick fool.*

Griffin took point, explaining to Tanner who everyone was and how the team fit together— and managed to do so without ever making direct eye contact with him. *So they were back to this.*

"Tanner was just explaining everything from the start," Declan said.

"Wonderful." Parker moved in and found a comfortable place to hold up the wall. Griffin stood, offering Avery his chair.

"Thanks." She tied the balloons to Declan's bedrail and moved to sit.

"Kate, I'll find you a chair," Griffin offered.

"I'm good." She plunked down on the end of Declan's bed.

"Miss Shaw, I believe you have a captive audience," Parker said.

She stared at him, trying to get a handle on him, no doubt. He'd seen the attempt at assessment before. Question was, what angle was she coming from? Hopefully by the time she was finished talking, he'd know everything he needed to about Tanner Shaw.

"As I was saying." She looked back to the group. "I first became acquainted with Perera's vile *enterprise,* as he calls it, while working in the aftercare program with one of his victims. A fifteen-year-old girl named Selma."

"So it's true?" Avery asked. "He really was running a sex tourism business?"

"*Is* running. At the time when I had to flee, I'd already worked with a handful of his victims we'd managed to rescue, but there are scores more."

She continued in detail with how the operation ran, how they managed to rescue the girls they did, and where the investigation stood when she'd brought it to Marley.

"Cambodian police were beyond hesitant to pursue any kind of case against a former U.S. ambassador with critical ties in the region."

"What kind of ties?" Declan asked.

"China and the U.S. are competing for influence in Cambodia. The U.S. initiated defense cooperation with Cambodia in 2006, and over the next seven years the U.S. became Cambodia's major defense-cooperation partner. China, however, has stepped up its defense cooperation in a development that many analysts see as an attempt to supplant the United States.

"Perera was sent there to see that doesn't happen. Even after officially retiring his ambassadorship, he chose to remain in the 'land he loved.' " She said those words with disgust and punctuated with air quotes. "The fact is he remained to take advantage of the vulnerable girls for his twisted pleasure and that of his American friends. But at the same time he continues to consult as a liaison between the U.S. and Cambodia, so he's still a valuable asset to the U.S. government."

"When you say 'his American friends,' what sort of people are you talking about?" Kate asked.

"Perera's client list is believed to contain at least one U.S. senator, a federal judge, and a three-star general. Not to mention the scores of his former military buddies. What they do to these girls is barbaric."

Outrage burned through Parker.

"How does he get away with it?" Avery stiffened. "Why isn't this all over the news?"

Parker loved Avery's fire, loved her innocence. She hadn't been tainted by the job yet, and he prayed she never would. It seemed neither had Finley, strangely enough.

"Because he's a very powerful man with immense connections and funds," Tanner said. "He's gotten rich off the molestation of Cambodian minors."

Avery paled. "I think I'm going to throw up."

"Trust me, I know the feeling—which is why I contacted Marley. She was just as enraged as I was and began working with me to compile an extradition case to present to the Office of U.S. Immigration and Customs Enforcement."

"And?" Griffin asked.

"Marley got pushback."

"Bureaucracy," Griffin said, his lips thin.

Parker shared his disgust.

"I don't understand," Avery said.

"Marley didn't know if the ICE agent she was working with was being paid off, threatened, or just pressured to look the other way, but he told Marley there wasn't enough there for him to move forward. He told her to let the case drop."

"I'm guessing, based on what we've learned about Marley, she refused," Finley said.

"She fought even harder, and then she disappeared along with most of her evidence against Perera."

"And you?" Kate asked.

"Knew I was next. I'd already had one close call. A car accident I highly suspect was no accident. I knew it was only a matter of time, and I wasn't going to let them get away with disposing of my friend, so I left, making my way along an underground transport system I'd learned about. I was determined to help find Marley, but after I arrived I saw on the news you already had."

"Why didn't you come to us straightaway?" Declan asked.

"I tried to approach Dr. Scott at the university, but I caught sight of him."

"Him?"

"Perera's right-hand man. Simon Reuben."

"If he's the man with the spider tattoo on his neck, he's dead," Declan said. "Griffin took him out after Simon put me here."

"That's great, but I'm sure Perera will have him replaced immediately. He may be in Cambodia, but his reach is long."

"He's here," Finley said.

Tanner's eyes widened. "Perera?" Fear filled her face.

"Was waiting for me in my car," Finley explained. "Wanted to talk."

"Talk?" Tanner's brows pinched. "About what?"

"Claims he didn't kill Marley, that he's being set up."

"Please." She gaped at Finley and then Griffin. "Wait. You don't for a second believe him, do you?"

— 34 —

"We found it odd," Griffin said in answer to Tanner's question. "Why bother coming to Finley if he's guilty?"

Parker sloughed off his jacket. The temperature

outside was dropping, but in Declan's hospital room it was quickly heating up.

"Because he wanted to throw you off. He's guilty, and I have the evidence to prove it," Tanner said.

"You have evidence he killed Marley?"

"I have evidence of his nasty business, which provides the perfect motivation for Marley's murder."

"I thought it disappeared with Marley?"

"Hers, yes, but I kept some copies as a safeguard."

"Where are they?"

"Someplace safe."

"We need to get them. There might be something in there we can use to pin Marley's murder on him."

"And what are you going to do with them?"

"Give them to the necessary authorities."

She shook her head. "Perera has ties. I don't know who can be trusted. He had the ICE agent in his pocket—who knows who else? I'd take them to GJM, but it's not safe either. If Marley's files were stolen from there, who's to say mine won't be too?"

"Bring them to me, and we'll get them in the right hands," Declan said.

"No offense," Tanner said, "but it doesn't look like you're out of his reach either."

"So what do you want to do?" Griffin asked.

"Figure out who I can trust, and in the meantime find the evidence needed to prove Perera either killed Marley or had her killed."

Parker pushed off the wall. "Then ragtag as we may be, we're your new team."

A knock rapped on the door, and Tanner jumped.

Parker rested a hand on her shoulder. "Easy, love."

With gun in hand, Griffin opened the door. "Hey, Mac." He stepped back and let the man enter. "It's okay."

"MacDonald Harris," Parker said. "It's been a while. You still with the BPD?"

"Yep. Surprised our paths haven't crossed."

"I'm selective in the cases I work." It was the benefit of being an independent contractor. He worked with professionals he trusted. Detectives who were ethical and capable.

"I heard that." He set an evidence box on Declan's tray table.

"What's this?" Parker lifted his chin.

"Marley Trent's personal effects."

Parker looked to Griffin.

Griffin shrugged. "With Declan out of commission, we were stuck."

"Hence why I called Kate," Parker said to Declan.

"I also called an old friend to see if the police still had any of Marley's effects in evidence,"

Griffin said. "Mac confirmed her effects hadn't been released back to the family."

"Aren't you supposed to release them after everything's been processed and not deemed essential to any ongoing investigation?" Finley said.

"Yes." Mac nodded.

"So whatever's in that box was deemed important?" she asked.

Mac shook his head. "No."

Her eyes narrowed. "I don't follow."

"When Griff called, I took a look. Turns out it had been mis-shelved."

"Convenient." Parker shook his head with a frustrated smile.

"Told you he had ties." Tanner crossed her arms over her chest.

"You can't possibly think . . . ?" Avery said.

"The men on his client list stand to lose a lot if the truth ever comes out. They're here in the States. Some less than an hour away in D.C."

"Okay." Parker held up his hands. "For argument's sake, let's say it was purposely misshelved."

"I told Griffin it was there, but without a proper signature for release no way I could give it to him," Mac said.

"So when Declan woke," Finley said, "I caught him up to speed."

"And I made some calls while I was waiting for

249

you guys to return," Declan said. "First to Mac."

"As lead agent on Ms. Trent's case, this evidence belongs to you." Mac handed Declan a release form to sign. "Oh, and I got you the number of the cop who picked up Simon Reuben's personal effects."

"Simon Reuben?"

"The man Griffin shot. He mentioned you wanted access to Reuben's belongings."

"How did you know his name? He had no identification on him that we could find."

"They fingerprinted him and ran it. He popped. Former military. Looks like he's been out of the service and the country for a number of years."

"Let me guess. Cambodia?"

"No idea. You can call Frank—the cop who collected his things and put them into evidence—but all he had on him was a burner cell."

"Thanks." He handed the clipboard back to Mac.

"Happy to help, and I gotta say it's nice to see you all together again, minus the circumstances, of course."

"Sounds like you have another call to make," Parker said after Mac left. "I'll see if Frank will release the burner cell to me, and we'll let Kate take a look."

"How'd it go with your other calls?"

"Finally got financials on Paul and Marley," Declan said.

"And?"

"Paul apparently is quite wealthy. Came from a well-off family. He certainly could have afforded to hire someone. There appears to be no large transfers in his account history, but we can dig deeper. Kate"—Declan looked to her—"can I put you on combing through his accounts? Make sure nothing was missed. No offshore accounts."

"Of course."

"One other thing. Looks like he rented a storage unit shortly after Marley's death."

"You have the address?"

"I did, but when I called to follow up, they said he closed it months ago."

"So he no longer has one or he moved the stuff?"

"If he moved it, he's paying cash."

"Which indicated he has something to hide."

"On it," Kate said.

"And Marley?" Griffin asked.

"Marley didn't use credit cards or even debit cards," Tanner said. "She was old school. Cash and checks. Said it made it easier to balance her checkbook."

Parker quipped. "Do they even still have those? Checkbooks?" Everything was online these days.

"Old-school financials fits with her notebook collection," Griffin said. "Which . . ." He glanced at Kate. "Did you bring it?"

"Yes. It's in my trunk. I'll grab it for you when you're ready to head out."

"Smart," Declan said. "You thought to grab it."

"Not until late last night, but, thankfully, it was still in your Expedition."

"Probably because the man who would have taken it was taken out, thanks to Griff," Parker said.

"If only I'd had time with Perera," Griff said, his gaze fixing on Finley.

Parker shared the sentiment, if not the skill set.

"Let's see what's in this box, shall we?" Declan said, lifting the lid. "One laptop." He handed it directly to Kate, who was their resident computer guru. "One calendar." He pulled out the eight-by-ten flip-over calendar.

"Wow. She really was old school. I bet I find . . ." Parker stepped to the box and shuffled through the contents. "Yes!" He held up the small book. "An address book." He flipped through the pages, feeling a sense of nostalgia. His mother still kept one.

"So if she only pays with cash, it will be virtually impossible to figure out where Marley was headed when she left work that Thursday," Griffin said.

Silence filled the room as everyone seemed to be thinking what Parker was—that with little to go on, they would be searching for a needle in a haystack.

"Did your being shot do anything to change

252

your boss's mind about the importance of finding Marley's killer?" Finley asked. "Is he willing now to put more agents on the case?"

"On the contrary, he insists Griffin killed Marley's killer."

Tanner jumped up from her chair. "But he's just Perera's right-hand man."

"That may be, but he's sticking with the assumption Simon Reuben was working alone. It makes his life so much easier—Marley's case is wrapped up, and he can forget about it. Besides, there's something else going on."

"What do you mean something else?" Parker asked.

"I don't know, but I got the feeling he was happy I was out of the office for a while. Don't know if there's a big case he doesn't want me intruding on or if he's just mad I pressed Marley's case, but he was very clear in his insistence I take a good amount of time off."

"So we're really it?" Finley said. "We're the only ones who care about finding Marley's killer?"

Declan nodded. "I'm afraid so."

"Okay, so what's our next move?" she asked.

Griffin stood. "You and I will finish reading through Marley's notebooks tonight, and tomorrow we'll head down to Ocean City to talk with Marley's father. I'll also follow up with Vern Michaels. I never heard back from him about snipers in the area."

"Is that unexpected?" Declan asked.

"Nah, he was probably just humoring us and never intended to ask around, but it's certainly worth a follow-up call."

"I'll go through the laptop and financials," Kate said, already tapping away on the keyboard.

"Our resident hacker," Parker explained to Tanner and Avery with the reverence Kate's impressive skills deserved.

"Park, I'll need you and Avery to head to Gettysburg in the morning," Declan said.

"Okay. What specifically are we looking for?"

"I think we need to start with the assumption Marley was killed in the Gettysburg area, since that's where her body was found. We may find out otherwise down the road, but it's a place to start. Her landlady said she took an overnight bag with her when she left for work. Stands to reason she may have spent a night up there. Griffin and Finley can find out if she had plans to visit her father when they talk with him tomorrow."

"And I'll go through her calendar and address book, since I'm stuck in this bed for a few more days." Declan sighed. "I'll also make some follow-up calls. I checked into the ICE agent Marley contacted. His name is Gabriel Rosario, and he's been reassigned to Houston since April."

"Convenient timing. Not long after Marley's death."

"He hasn't returned my call, but I'm good at tracking people down."

"Speaking about tracking people down . . . What about Tanner?" Parker said.

Tanner looked at him curiously. "What about me?"

"Perera's in town. If he discovers you are here, you said yourself you're dead. You need to stay with one of us."

"She can hang with me," Kate offered.

"Probably the safest place," Declan said. "Perera has no idea of Kate's involvement in the case, and besides, we all know Kate's the toughest of the group."

None of the men argued.

He watched the group file out of the hospital. There were two new players.

Women. He needed to track down their identities, see if they were a threat that needed to be dealt with.

— 35 —

The next morning was warmer than it had been for a while, the high expected to reach the low fifties. The sun had actually broken through the grey blanket that typically hovered over Baltimore from October until April, and there was a hint

255

of blue sky as they crossed the last bridge into Ocean City. Seagulls swooped across the sky, disappearing into the horizon over the ocean.

Finley cracked her window, letting the sea air seep in and soothe her soul. The sea always filled her with such peace.

Maybe today would be the day they finally got some concrete answers rather than more questions.

"There," Finley said, pointing at the duplex bungalow one block off the ocean. "55B."

Down a block Griffin found an open section of street parking.

"It's nice Marley was so close with her dad, coming down most weekends to see him," Finley said as they climbed the front porch steps, a weathered swing creaking in the wind. She turned to find another on the adjoining porch.

"The file said her mom passed when Marley was nine."

"So her dad raised her alone?" she asked, turning back to Mr. Trent's place.

"Appears that way." Griffin opened the storm door and knocked.

The interior door opened, and a woman with curly blond hair that bounced just at her shoulders, brown eyes, and a friendly smile greeted them. "Yes?"

"Hello, ma'am," Griffin began.

"Ma'am." She smiled, all tickled. "Well, aren't

you the gentleman, but you know us ladies under a certain age prefer *miss*."

"Oh." Griffin looked embarrassed for the second time since Finley had met him—his cheeks actually flushing slightly. "Sorry. I didn't mean—"

"No worries. I'm Sammie." She took pity on his bumbling.

"Griffin." He nodded with a smile. "And this is Finley."

"Finley? That's a unique name. I like it."

"Thanks."

She stepped back, inviting them inside. "My name is actually Sammie Jo. My mother was a die-hard *Dynasty* fan. Gotta laugh at the ludicrousness of being named after a nighttime soap opera character or it'd make me want to cry. I know it's ridiculous, but that's Mama. Follow me. Mr. Trent's expecting you."

She led them around the corner to a cozy front room. The furniture was straight out of the '80s and more Floridian than Chesapeake in style— white rattan furniture with palm-patterned cushions in mint and peach shades, but all impeccably maintained. Framed pictures lined the white mantel. Images of Marley as a kid. Most in front of the ocean or by a pool, her wearing a bright smile and colorful ribbons.

"She was half mermaid," an elderly voice crackled behind them. Finley turned as the man entered. His shoulders and upper back hunched and slightly curved to the right, decreasing his probable five-ten frame by several inches. He had salt-and-pepper hair, an aquiline nose, pale skin, and drooping jowls. His soft blue shirt was mostly covered by a well-loved grey cardigan sweater with leather buttons. He pushed his walker across the room toward them.

"Mr. Trent." Griffin extended his hand. "We appreciate your taking the time to speak with us."

"Time. Ha! Got plenty of that these days. Not able to do much—not with Little Miss Bossy around."

"I heard that," Sammie's southern twang echoed from the adjacent room.

"Of course you did," he called back with a grin. "She drives a hard line, but she means well. Please, have a seat." He lowered into the mint green La-Z-Boy as Griffin and Finley took a seat on the sofa.

Mr. Trent set his walker to the side and reclined, the non-skid soles of his grey slippers peeking up at them—a smiley-face sticker on the center of the right and a hang-loose sticker on the left.

Finley smiled. She was happy to see he still had a sense of humor. It was easy to lose with age and loss. "Sounds like Sammie takes good care of you."

"Marley found her for me. Marley always excelled at finding good people. She could read them easily."

"We are terribly sorry for your loss," Griffin said.

"Do either of you have children?"

"No," Finley said, wondering what kind of dad Griffin would be. She smiled to herself. A really great one, she bet.

"Trust me, they never stop being your child." He looked at the picture of Marley and him on his side table.

It looked recent. Sometime in the last few years of her life.

Tears pooled in his eyes. "She'll always be my little girl."

Finley blinked back the tears stinging her eyes. She hated having to bring Marley's death back to the surface for the poor man. She moved to his chair and sank into a squat, covering his hand with hers. "We're so very sorry."

He nodded, sniffing back tears. "Thank you."

Sammie entered, compassion and concern evident on her round face. "Thought y'all might like some tea."

"Thanks," Finley said as they each took a cup.

Mr. Trent took a sip and puckered his lips. "Sammie, why is mine unsweet?"

"Because the doctor said you have to watch your sugar, among other things."

He shook his head, setting the glass aside. "Unsweet tea. Really? What's the point?"

"Mr. Trent—" Griffin began.

"Nonsense. Please, call me Arthur."

"Arthur." Griffin nodded. "I couldn't help but notice the cross suncatcher on your front window."

Finley turned, taking in the yellow, orange, and red hues of the suncatcher.

"By any chance did Marley collect suncatchers?" Griffin asked.

"Yes she did. That"—he pointed with a slightly crooked finger—"was her favorite. Said it reminded her of the sun and beach. She loved both dearly. Part mermaid, like I said."

He winked and Finley noted the purple tint to the whites of his eyes. Combined with the spine curvature . . . So Marley had inherited the genetic disorder osteogenesis imperfecta from her dad.

"I'm sorry. Am I interrupting?" A man about Griffin's age and stature stood in the doorway balancing two paper buckets of what smelled like vinegar and potatoes in one hand and a drink tray in the other.

"Ben." Arthur lit, his wrinkled face smiling. "Come in."

"Hey, Art. I brought you Thrasher's."

Arthur beamed. "You spoil me."

"Yes, he does," Sammie said, planting her hands on her hips.

Arthur blinked. "You wouldn't deny an old man his Thrasher's now, would you?"

Sammie rolled her eyes. "Those puppy-dog eyes are only going to work for so long."

Arthur smiled and reached into the bucket with a smile.

Finley looked at Griffin. "Thrasher's?"

"Iconic O.C. right in your hands. Hand-cut fries with malt vinegar and salt," Ben said, sitting down and digging into his own bucket. "I'm sorry. Would you like some?" He extended the bucket.

"I'm good, but thanks," Finley said.

"I'll be sure to grab a bucket before we leave," Griffin said. "I'm Griffin McCray, by the way, and this is Finley Scott."

"Nice to meet you. I'm Ben Douglas, Art's neighbor. I hope you don't mind if I eat. They are best warm."

Griffin waved him on as Arthur popped a fry in his mouth.

Sammie stood next to Ben, her Looney Tunes scrubs a stark contrast to his understated tan sweater.

Ben waved a fry in her direction. "Come on, you know you wanna have one."

"I'm good, but you won't be if Arthur's sodium levels are off the charts at his next exam."

Ben quickly postured a mischievous schoolboy repentance smile. "Yes, ma'am."

"That time I'll take the *ma'am*." She winked at Griffin before exiting the room.

"They are the ones who found Marley," Arthur said out of the blue between bites.

Ben stilled. "Oh?"

"I'm afraid so," Griffin said, sitting forward. "You knew Marley?"

"Yes."

"Were you close?"

He looked at Arthur and then back to them.

Griffin took the hint and got to his feet. "Ben, any chance you'd be willing to show us around the place while Arthur finishes his fries? Marley's old room, that sort of thing."

Ben wiped his hands on his napkin. "Sure." He set his tan-and-blue bucket aside and stood. "We'll be back, Art."

"Take your time. I'll work on these." He popped another fry in his mouth with a smile.

"Thanks," Ben said as they exited the room and started upstairs. "Arthur's memory is spotty, and I don't know how much Marley told him about our relationship."

"It's uncomfortable talking about a relationship with your girl's parents," Griffin said.

Ben exhaled. "Right."

Finley smiled at Griffin's choice of affectionate phrase. She wondered if he would or perhaps already did view her as *his girl*.

"I'm afraid I don't know how much help I'll be," he said, reaching the top landing. "I don't really know anything about that part of Marley's life."

"Which part would that be?" Griffin asked as

he led them to the curtained, glass-paned door at the end of the hall.

"Her work."

"Why do you assume her death was related to her work?"

Finley looked at Griffin, curious about his question. They all knew or at least assumed Marley's death was related to her work.

"Because her whole life revolved around her work. And . . ." He glanced back at the stairs. "Arthur. She loved her dad very much."

Finley could tell he cared a great deal about the man too. She bet that would make Marley very happy to know her dad was still being cared for and lovingly looked after.

"When the police came . . . When Marley first went missing they asked us a bunch of questions about her personal life, but we told them that, other than her weekends here, she didn't really have a personal life. Everything she did was about fighting for those who couldn't fight for themselves."

"Sounds like you admired her." And was at the same time frustrated or concerned by her consuming drive for work.

"Of course I did. She took on bullies for a living. How could I not admire her?" He rubbed his neck. "But in the end I fear it's what got her killed. Are you any closer to catching her killer?"

"We've got a number of leads."

"Well, that's a start. Last investigator seemed like he was just going through the motions."

"I give you my word we aren't," Griffin said. "We are doing everything we can to find Marley's killer."

"I appreciate that. She was a remarkable woman." He exhaled and shook his head, as if struggling to refocus on them and the present.

"So tell us about you and Marley," Griffin said as Ben opened the door they'd been standing in front of.

Marley's room. Finley looked at the window, noting the pearl dove suncatcher, wondering how Griffin knew Marley had collected them.

"There isn't much to tell." Ben looked around the room, his eyes reddening.

"I know this is painful, and I'm sorry," she said. "But anything you can tell us may help."

"Yeah." Ben pinched the bridge of his nose, taking a moment to compose himself before looking up and adjusting his glasses.

"How long did you know Marley?" Griffin asked.

"Since I moved in next door to Arthur summer before last. I saw her coming every weekend to visit, and one time we got to talking on the front porch." He glanced down with a hint of a smile. "Truth is, I waited out on that porch all day, hoping she'd pop out, as she tended to do." He looked up, his smile widening. "She was more amazing than I ever could have imagined."

"And then?" Griffin asked, his voice lower. He hated pressing. Finley could read it on his face, but he had a job to do. They both did. To find Marley's killer.

"And then we became friends."

"Just friends?"

"I like to think we were on our way to becoming more."

Just as Paul had believed.

"Meaning?"

"We kissed the weekend before she disappeared. When she called to say she wouldn't be coming down the following weekend, I thought maybe it was because I'd scared her off. Moved too fast."

"I highly doubt you were the reason," Finley said, probably overstepping her bounds, but if anything she said could bring him comfort . . . "Griffin said he was told she lit up when she spoke of you."

He looked at Griffin, his eyes welling with hope. "Is that true?"

She prayed Griffin understood why she'd shared what he'd told her. Ben deserved to know.

"Yes," Griffin said. "I was told by a woman Marley worked with that she lit up whenever she spoke of you."

Ben swiped his nose, sniffed, and then cleared this throat. "Thank you for that."

Griffin nodded and looked at Finley. She exhaled in relief. He understood.

"I hate to keep pressing . . ." he said.

"But you are trying to find Marley's killer." Ben nodded. "I understand."

"Do you have any idea why she was found up at Gettysburg?"

"None whatsoever."

"She didn't mention she was headed there?"

"No. Just said she needed to take care of something but that she'd be down the following weekend and was really looking forward to spending some time together."

He stepped to the window, running a finger along the suncatcher's edge. "It was the last time I heard her voice." He looked up, trying to shake off the heartache, but was doing a terrible job. Sorrow was etched on the lines of his face.

"Stained glass," he said. "She loved suncatchers. I didn't understand it. Her love for them. I mean it's colored glass, but she said when the sun flooded in and the colorful rays bounced off the dim interior, it reminded her how God brings beauty and light to the darkest places. And that all the broken pieces of different and uniquely shaped glass making up one beautiful image reminded her how God brings beauty out of brokenness and uses the smallest of pieces to make up a whole. Despite her job, despite the ugliness she saw and her own struggles, she trusted God in the dark places."

"That's beautiful," Finley said. What an amazing reminder of God's faithfulness.

"That's Marley," he said. "Seeing the possible, believing God could perform miracles and make the broken whole."

"And do you believe that?" she asked, stepping toward him.

"Finley," Griffin said, his tone hushed, his eyes widening. Now she'd really overstepped her bounds.

Ben held up his hand. "It's fine. Yes, I used to believe, but then . . ."

"Marley disappeared."

He nodded, swallowing, his Adam's apple bobbing in his narrow throat.

"Don't let the darkness win," Griffin said, surprising them both.

"What?" Ben's brow furrowed.

"Someone may have taken her life, but it doesn't erase the person she was—is. She's alive in heaven. And if she shared all of that with you, it's because she wanted you to know it. Don't discount the truth of her words just because she's no longer here."

— 36 —

"Are you coming back?" Arthur's voice trailed up through the heating vent.

Ben smiled. "We'll be right down," he called back through the vent.

As they made their way downstairs, Arthur said, "I was starting to think you weren't coming back."

"Sorry, Arthur. We got to talking," Ben said.

"Would it be all right if we asked you a few questions about Marley?" Griffin asked with the utmost respect.

Arthur nodded.

"As you know, Marley was found at Gettysburg. Do you have any idea what she was doing up there?"

"No."

They had to be missing something. "Had she visited it before?"

"We went up last fall," Ben said.

"Oh?"

"Yeah, for the Gettysburg Address Remembrance parade. They had reenactments going on that day too. I thought it'd be a fun thing to see."

"And Marley?"

"Went along to humor me. History's really not her thing, but we had a great time until . . ."

Griffin's voice deepened. "Until?"

Ben shook his head. "I'd forgotten all about it, but something spooked Marley that day."

"What do you mean 'spooked'?"

"She saw something or someone that startled her."

"Did you ask her about it?"

"Yeah. She said it was nothing, but the rest of the day she kept looking around. It was like she'd seen a ghost."

"Did she ever bring it up again?"

"No. Never spoke about it. I figured it was nothing. Forgot about it."

"Did she go back up there?"

"Not that I'm aware of, but I guess she must have. I mean, you found her there."

Griffin looked to Finley. Now they were getting somewhere.

"Any idea why she'd bring a camera with her? I mean if, like you said, she wasn't into history."

Had she been looking for someone? Had she been taking pictures of them? Was that what had gotten her killed?

"She brought that thing with her everywhere," Arthur said.

"The camera?" Finley asked.

"Yes. It was her aunt's. She gave it to Marley when she started with GJM."

"Were Marley and her aunt close?"

"Like this." Arthur linked his gnarled fingers.

"After Sally—Marley's mom—passed," he explained, "Marley and Sally's brother's wife, Andrea, became close. I did the best I could, but Marley was only nine when her mom died. A girl needs a woman in her life, and Andrea tried to help fill the gap."

"We should speak with Andrea," Griffin said. "She may be able to offer some further insights." Especially if they were that close.

"I'm afraid Andrea passed last year. Lung cancer."

"Smoker?" Finley automatically asked. It was the usual cause.

"No. Chemical weapons during the war."

She hadn't seen that coming. "Which war?"

"Bosnian. Andrea was from Sarajevo. Jim met her when she immigrated after the war."

"She must have had some stories to tell," Finley said. "I can't imagine living in the midst of something like that." She'd helped identify victims of mass graves in the Sudan the spring before last. It was something she'd never forget. She couldn't imagine actually living through something like that.

"I believe she played a significant role in spurring Marley to become a social justice lawyer," Arthur said.

"Because of the injustices her aunt witnessed?" Finley asked.

"Not just witnessed. Photographed. Andrea was

frustrated by the world's lack of action while genocide was happening right in front of her. General Rativik used chemical weapons as well as traditional ones. So she began photographing his atrocities. She passed them on to a CNN war correspondent and they went viral."

"Wow. So she fought back against injustice just like Marley spent her life doing," Finley said, highly impressed.

"Yes." Arthur smiled with pride. "They were two extraordinary women."

"And this camera Andrea gave her . . . ?" Griffin asked, tracking back.

"Wasn't among Marley's possessions, according to her friend Paul who collected her things and shipped the majority of them down here," Ben said.

Because it had been with her at the time of her death.

"Can you describe the camera?" Griffin asked.

"Sure, but why?" Ben asked.

"We think she had it with her at the time of her death."

"Why would you think that? I mean, she had it on her most of the time, but you sound certain she had it with her?"

"There was evidence she did," Finley said without going into detail.

"Okay," Ben said.

Finley was thankful he didn't press. She didn't

want to have to explain that camera fragments had been embedded in Marley's skull.

"It was a Canon EOS-1."

They'd pass the info along to Avery and let her research it.

"As for the rest of Marley's belongings . . ." Finley began. They deserved to know what Paul had done. "You said you'd received the majority of Marley's belongings from Paul?"

"Yes."

Griffin rubbed the back of his neck. "I'm sorry to say Paul didn't send you the majority."

"What he sent seemed like too little, but he said he donated a good portion, and that seemed like what Marley would have wanted."

"I'm afraid that's not true."

Ben shook his head. "I don't understand."

Griffin explained.

"Well, that's disturbing."

"I don't want that man having Marley Bear's things," Arthur said, wringing his hands.

"Don't worry. We'll see everything is delivered to you. I will see to it personally," Griffin promised.

Arthur's shoulders relaxed. "Thank you."

"Thank you, both. You've been very helpful," Griffin said.

"Here's my card." Finley handed it to them.

"My cell is on the back," Griffin said, handing them his. "Call if you need anything."

He sat two tables back, watching them eat their fries as the stupid birds squawked and circled overhead. *Blasted birds.* He was trying to calculate his next move. One to counter Perera's. And they bloody wouldn't shut up.

It had been a bold move showing up in the woman's car. Brilliant, really. Cunning.

He was clearly a worthy adversary.

Highly connected.

But he wasn't going to win this one.

Taking a sip of his soda, he studied Ranger McCray and the woman he clearly loved, planning the pain he was about to inflict.

— 37 —

It took Parker and Avery a handful of hours and hotels before someone recognized Marley's photograph.

"Yeah. I remember her," the friendly lady who'd introduced herself as Linda Jo said.

"Do you remember when you saw her? Ballpark time period?"

"Ah . . . had to have been last winter. Toward the end of it."

"March, by chance?"

"I'd say that sounds about right. We don't get a ton of folks during that time of year so those that do come tend to stick better. I remember things were slow the night she checked in, so we chatted for a while. Sweet lady."

"Any chance you remember what you talked about?"

"Oh, sheesh. Like I said, it's been a while. . . . Most folks visiting like to learn all they can about the battlefield, history of the area, that sort of thing."

"But Marley was different?" Parker asked, sensing it in her tone. "Marley Trent." He held her picture up.

"That's funny." She shook her head, her brown curls bobbing. "It seems like she gave me a different name, but then again, it's been a while."

Unless Marley used an alias.

"So her questions were different than most tourists'?" Avery asked.

"Yeah. Like I said, folks generally like to talk about history of the battlefield, but she seemed more interested in the reenactments, if I recall right."

"Reenactments?" Parker said.

"We're famous for our three-day battle reenactment. We're booked out years in advance. She asked so many questions, I figured she was actually interested in participating, so I'm pretty sure I gave her Bob's contact info."

"Bob?"

"Bob Wade. Coordinates the entire reenact-ment. Oh, I mean he has help, lots of it. All of us locals pitch in, but he's the head honcho. Nobody participates without Bob knowing about it."

"And did she talk to Bob?"

"No idea."

"Could we have Bob's number?"

"I don't see why not." She looked it up and gave Parker the number, which he directly entered into his cell, knowing he'd be dialing it the minute they stepped out of Linda Jo's lobby.

"Any chance you remember how many nights she was here for? Do you keep records that far back?"

"Of course I do. What do you think, this is the Stone Age?" She slipped on her reading glasses and stepped to her computer. She typed and scrolled and then looked up. "Here she is." Her face soured. "She did give me a different name—Andrea Douglas. Hmm. Well, whatever her name is, it says she stayed two nights, but as I recall she only stayed one night."

"Oh?"

"Yep. Saw her, or rather her gentleman friend, carrying out her things Friday night. I remember thinking it was odd to pay in advance for two nights and to only stay one."

Parker tried to contain his excitement, and he could see Avery was struggling to do the same. "Her gentleman friend?"

"Yes. I saw Andrea's car pull up. Went out to say hi and found him instead. He waved back. Friendly sort. Handsome from what little I could see, but that wasn't much. It was dark. He went into the room and came out carrying Andrea's things a little while later. I was surprised he didn't drop the key off, but maybe he didn't think to. A lot of hotels let you leave those key card things in the room."

"Can you describe him?"

"Like I said, I didn't see him clearly. He was tall, broad, sturdy. Well-built sort."

"Hair color?"

"Can't say that I saw. He might have been wearing a hat."

"And his face? Eye color?"

"Handsome, but couldn't tell you eye color. Again—"

"It was too dark."

"He had a nice smile. I'm sorry I can't give you more."

"It's okay. You've been a great help, but could we go back just a step? You said you saw him carry Andrea's things out. Did you see Andrea leave with him?"

"Well, no, but a call came in just after I saw him put the bag in her trunk. I just assumed she stepped out after him. Her car pulled out while I was still on the call."

"Could we see the room she stayed in?"

"Sure, but a lot of other folks have used it since."

"It'd still be helpful."

"Sure. As long as it's not rented out." She looked back at her computer. "Room 112." She glanced back at the key cubby. "You're in luck. It's vacant." She handed him the key.

He clutched it in his hand. Now they were getting somewhere. "Thanks. We'll bring it back when we're done."

"All right." She linked her arms across her chest. "I don't like to pry, but what's this all about, anyway? She in some kind of trouble?"

"Afraid not. She was murdered."

"Murdered?"

"Last March."

"You don't mean . . ." Her eyes widened. "Please tell me that wasn't her body you all dug up at the battlefield?"

Avery nodded. "I'm afraid so."

"Oh dear. You two take all the time you need."

"Thank you."

They stepped outside. "I think we finally hit our stride. If anyone can find a trace of her, it's us. But even if we find nothing, we've got a timeline and our first witness sighting of our man."

Parker placed a call directly to Bob Wade, but it went straight to voicemail, so he left a message.

They entered Room 112. It was small but clean. Done in Civil War fashion.

"You really think it's possible to find something after so much time and"—Avery scoped out the room—"people moving through."

"In my line of work," Parker said, opening his kit and pulling on a pair of gloves, "I've discovered time cements things in place. It moves forward but a person's life print, as I like to call it, remains."

Avery pulled out her camera, a skeptical frown on her face. "Life print?"

Parker walked the perimeter of the room, inspecting every nook and crevice. "The residual effect of a person's life that continues on both physically and emotionally in the lives of those they loved."

"I'm not sure I follow," Avery said, snapping the first of what would be numerous pictures.

"Take Marley, for instance. Her physical remains told us a lot about her. Hair color, stature, gender . . . Each detail helps paint a picture of the woman she was, then you add in the trace evidence and personal effects—her class ring, baseball hat . . ." He started his work-up of the room in earnest, talking as he went. "Then you look at the effect she had on people and the picture becomes richer. We know Marley was an idealistic fighter. She was passionate and she loathed bullies. We all leave these life prints behind when we go."

Parker stood back and studied the room—the

beds, the dresser, even the ceiling, and then dropped to his knees and began searching underneath and around all the pieces of furniture.

Avery frowned. "What are you looking for?"

"Someplace Marley might have stashed something if she felt threatened."

"You think she knew they were after her?"

"She used an alias to rent the room and paid cash. Seems like she feared someone was tracking her, or she could have just been being cautious. Tracking down someone so dangerous had to be unnerving."

"And exciting."

He arched a brow. Another reason he liked Avery.

Reaching into the extremely shallow space beneath the nightstand, he stretched all the way up against the back wall. His fingers trailed over something bristly. "Hey, I think I've got something." He wriggled, having to lie fully on the floor and scooch the item out with his fingers. "A hairbrush. I don't know if it's hers, but we can hope."

"It's definitely unique," Avery said.

Parker examined the antique brush. "Heavy handle, probably gold tone over silver, filigree design."

"Interesting floral print on the back."

"I'm guessing from the sixties."

"I didn't realize you were such a hairbrush expert."

"You'd be surprised the items I have to examine in my line of work."

"Why do you think she'd hide a hairbrush?" Avery asked, flashing a picture of it.

"I doubt she stashed it. More likely she dropped it accidently or knocked it off the nightstand while turning off the alarm." Parker pointed to the clock at the back edge of the nightstand. "I knock all kinds of things off my nightstand when I'm hitting Snooze. Half the time I forget to pick them up upon waking. The point is *if* the man Linda Jo saw collected Marley's things, he'd have no idea to check behind or under the nightstand."

"And it's certainly not something Marley would leave behind. Looks too personal. Too special."

"Exactly. So if it is Marley's, it only further testifies to the fact someone else checked her out."

— 38 —

Avery settled in for the drive back from Gettysburg, surprised how much pleasure she derived from spending time with Parker. She typically preferred solitude, as she surmised Parker did, but somehow together . . .

She exhaled. That was a nonstarter. Not only did she have zero interest in any type of personal relationship, but he was clearly still hanging on to his love for Jenna McCray.

An incoming call from Griffin came through. Parker answered via Bluetooth. "Hey, Griff," he said over the speakers so Avery could hear the conversation, which she greatly appreciated. For not having any investigation experience before coming to work for Parker, she felt somehow oddly at home in the realm.

"Hey, guys. Got you on speaker," Griff said.

"Us too," Parker said.

"How'd it go?" Avery asked.

"Really well. We got a few leads," Finley said. "And one right up your alley, Avery."

Her brows pinched. "Oh?"

"Marley's camera. We know the exact model. It was a Canon EOS-1, which belonged to her aunt, Andrea."

"Andrea," Avery said, looking at Parker.

"Is that name significant to you?" Griffin asked.

"It's the name Marley registered at the hotel in Gettysburg under—Andrea Douglas."

"Douglas was Ben's last name," Finley said.

"Who's Ben?" Avery asked.

"Marley's friend," Griffin said.

"Her friend Ben or her *friend* Ben," Parker's voice dropped as his brows hiked.

"Ugh." Avery sighed in disgust. "Unlike *you,* some men and women are actually able to be just friends."

"Acquaintances, perhaps," he acquiesced, "but close friends with no other feelings involved, no way." He winked at her, then shifted his focus back to the conversation. "So which is it, Griff?"

"They were more than friends, or quickly getting there," he said.

Parker looked over, smiling triumphantly. "Told you, love."

She shook her head with a grunt, ignoring the pleasure the affectionate moniker filled her with, which was ridiculous. It had no meaning behind it, other than the fact that Parker could be a serious flirt.

"Was there anything wonky or suspicious with this Ben?" Parker asked.

"Not that I could tell," Griffin said, "but he did mention something interesting. The two of them visited Gettysburg last November for the Gettysburg Address reenactment ceremonies, and Marley saw someone or something that spooked her."

"Perera?" Avery asked.

"Very possibly."

"But if so, why not mention it to Ben?"

"Who knows?" Griffin said. "Maybe she wasn't sure. She kept looking around as if she was trying to figure something out."

"Well, it finally gives us a Gettysburg tie. Loose as it may be."

"Speaking of which, how did your day go? Sounds like you found her hotel?"

"Yes. The Gettysburg Inn. She registered for two nights, but the inn owner said she only stayed one." Parker went on to explain the full details.

"Let us know the results on the hair samples as soon as you get them," Finley said.

"If it's a match, it'll provide concrete, physical proof Marley was there," Griffin said.

"Doesn't the hotel owner identifying her photograph accomplish that?" Avery asked.

"In court the defense could argue it'd been too long, the lady might be mistaken, there are a lot of people who might look similar, and so on. She registered under a false name and paid cash, which doesn't provide any concrete link," Griffin said.

"Then let's pray the hair's a match," Avery said.

Parker glanced sideways at her. Yes, it was her first use of the word prayer. Her faith was her faith. Not something she shared with others. Not anymore.

"So, the aunt's camera . . . ?" she asked, shifting the conversation back to where they'd begun.

"Right," Finley said. "Apparently her aunt was a photographer whose images of General Rativik's atrocities in Sarajevo become famous— revealing to the world the depths of his depravity."

"Wow." Those had to be some powerful

photographs. "I'll look into the aunt and the camera model."

"Thanks," Griffin said.

Perera greeted his man outside the airport. With Simon's death, he needed someone else he could trust, and Stephen Daniels was it.

"How was the flight?" He'd come from Cambodia.

"Long."

"And everything back home?" Cambodia was home now. The source of his business, his income, and, most importantly, his pleasure.

"Running smoothly."

"Good to hear." He'd exerted great time and effort surrounding himself with the right men. Men who could be trusted. Men loyal to him. Men who didn't question. Just did their job. Mercenaries were the perfect workhorses. Soldiers for money, who did the job and did it well.

"How are things here?"

"Not as smooth as I would like." He pulled out of the airport and onto I-195.

"Have you identified our opponent?"

"Not yet." He was a ghost. Much like the men he surrounded himself with. But everyone had a past. If he just dug deep enough. "He's a worthy adversary. If I didn't have to kill him, I'd love to hire him."

"And the marks?"

"I think the doc actually listened."

Daniels arched his brows. "She believed you?"

"Don't make it sound so unfathomable. I can tell the truth." His lips curled. "Just takes a little more practice."

"And?"

"They are going to need some more persuasion."

Parker watched Avery work at his kitchen island, realizing he didn't want this case to end. Oh, he wanted to see Perera behind bars, and whomever else may be involved, but he didn't want this time with Avery staying at his place to end. It was a startling realization, one he didn't think possible, and one he didn't fully understand. But there was something about Avery Tate . . .

He leaned against the wooden beam, sipping his coffee. She'd slipped past his guard. The first stirring of serious feelings for a woman he'd experienced in eight years and it was exhilaratingly terrifying. He hadn't even seen it coming. Oh, he'd known there was something about Avery the moment they met, but he thought it respect. He hadn't even dared consider the possibility . . .

"Bingo," she said with a snap.

"You found it?" he asked.

She spun around with a jump. "You scared me."

"Sorry. You were so intent on your work, I didn't want to interrupt."

She smoothed her long hair. "How long have you been standing there?"

He smiled. "A few minutes." He loved watching her work. Such passion and intensity for whatever she did.

One day he would learn her story. Well, he already knew the facts. Before working with anyone he did his research, but he longed for her to share *her* story, her life. He wanted to be more than colleagues. Perhaps she was right. A man and a woman could be real friends. He already knew it to be true. They were all friends with Kate, and only two out of the four of them loved her in a romantic way. It had just been too easy and far too fun to get a rise out of Avery on the topic.

"Remind me to look over my shoulder every now and then," she said, focusing back on her work.

"You seem to be doing that all on your own, love. The question . . ." he said, stepping behind her and dipping his head over her shoulder to look at the screen, "is why?"

She tapped—rather, thumbed—the keys. "Because I don't like people sneaking up on me."

"That happen often?"

"With you around, it seems to."

It was more than that, but he wouldn't press. Instead, he indicated the screen. "What did you find?"

"The camera Marley had with her at the time

of her death. I just purchased one off eBay. Not the same as having hers, but it'll let me see its capabilities and let you take it apart."

He squeezed her shoulder. "Nice job, Tate."

"Thanks. I was curious . . ."

"Three words I adore."

She smiled. "You are so weird."

He lifted his brows. "If you only knew . . ."

"I'll pass. Thanks."

"You say that, but I see the curiosity sparking in your eyes."

"What you see is indifference."

"Keep telling yourself that and you'll miss out on all the fun."

"I've had my share of fun. It's overrated."

"Is that so?"

"Can we get back to work already?" She blew out an air of frustration.

"Of course." He fixed his most serious expression. "You said you're curious . . ."

"Right. I did some digging on Marley's aunt. Andrea Trent, maiden name Dugonja. Finley mentioned Andrea's background as a photographer during the Bosnian War. I looked up her work. Pretty powerful stuff." She clicked on the tab and an image popped up of a man, woman, and child dead on a crosswalk with blood pooled around them.

She clicked through image after atrocious image. "No wonder Marley was so inspired by her aunt's work. Not only did she bring the reality of the brutality of the war to light, her photographs exposed the role General Rativik played in war crimes, rapes, and genocide. Some say he was as bad if not more so than Mladic."

"I don't remember a General Rativik standing trial." Mladic certainly had.

"He didn't. It says he was killed in an explo=sion not long before the war ended." She closed her laptop, stood and stretched, running her fingers through her hair and grasping two fistfuls with a grunt. "Aggg. I don't understand."

"What?"

"*People*. How they can do things like this to one another."

"I'm afraid there are monsters in this world."

"Not monsters. Evil."

"Yes." He stepped toward her. "Evil."

She exhaled, for once actually letting down her stringent guard. "It terrifies me."

"That's good."

"Why on earth is that good?"

"Because it means you're still tender despite the horrific things that happen in this world."

She planted her hands on her hips—slender but shapely in the black yoga pants. "And how is that a good thing?"

"Trust me, love." He lifted her chin with his finger, hoping she saw the depth of sincerity he felt in saying this. "It's a gift."

Her shoulders dropped. "It doesn't feel like one."

"You remind me of her."

"Who?"

"Jenna."

"Really?"

"She was tenderhearted too." It made the horror of what happened to her all the more unbearable.

Her gaze bore into his. "You *really* loved her."

"Yes."

She bit her thumbnail.

"That's a terrible habit."

"So is yours of changing the subject."

He looked back over his shoulder with a smile as he moved for the kitchen. "Some would call it a gift."

"Griffin's wrong, you know. It wasn't your fault."

He opened the fridge and peered inside.

"You know that, right?"

He hung his head. If only it were that simple.

— 39 —

Finley settled by Griffin on the pile of pillows he'd dumped in front of his fireplace for them to lounge on as they scoured Marley's notebooks. It was weird getting inside another person's head so intimately, though she longed to be inside Griffin's. To somehow bring him a measure of peace.

Father, I pray you will equip me to be a source of comfort and strength for Griffin. I've fallen for him, hard. It's awesome but requires vulnerability, which we both know is terrifying for me. Please don't let me screw this up. Don't let me give in to the fear. Help me hold fast to you and the direction you are leading me. And I pray it is toward Griffin.

It was hard to believe they were here, at this place, and it had all come through the discovery of Marley Trent's body. A woman she'd never personally met, but a woman who'd made a permanent imprint on so many lives—hers included.

"How do you think Perera ties to Gettysburg?" It'd been bugging her ever since Perera showed up in the backseat of her car. Not that the man was trustworthy or that she necessarily gave any true credence to what he said, but it had got her thinking.

"I've been trying to figure that one out. We need to find out if Perera or one of his associates made a trip back here the month Marley was killed. She could have spotted him or an associate she recognized in Gettysburg and begun tracking them."

"So you think Perera could have been in the

States from November, when she spotted 'the ghost,' to March, when she was killed?"

"Or he made two trips. I really don't know. We need more information before the pieces start making sense."

"It's so frustrating." Waiting.

"I know, but we're making progress, and that's what keeps a case going." His cell rang. "It's Gunny. I better take this."

She nodded.

"Hey, Gunny. Yeah. I've been trying to reach Vern and—" Griffin's jaw tensed. "What? When? Are you sure? I'm sor—"

Gunny's irate voice blared on the other end, then abruptly ceased.

"Gunny?" He looked at the phone and exhaled.

"Did he hang up on you?"

"Can't say I blame him."

"Why?"

"Vern Michaels is dead."

"What?" Finley asked as waves of shock surged through her.

"Gunny said police found him in his apartment yesterday. Been dead for several days. Suicide."

"You don't think . . . ?"

"Gunny sure does. Said Vern would never kill himself. He'd overcome too much. Someone killed him and staged it to look like suicide."

"Because he barely talked to us?"

"Or because he knew the sniper we're looking

for." Griffin stood, and looked about to throw something. "I'm going to go call Declan." He strode from the room. "I'll be back soon."

Griffin returned to the room fifteen minutes later, rejoining her on the floor.

"Declan said he'd contact the lead officer on Vern's case. Find out who the ME is. Ask some questions."

"I can't believe a man is dead because of us."

"You can't carry that blame. We were doing our job. Trying to find a woman's killer."

"But if our questions led to his death . . ."

"It's terrible, but we didn't pull the trigger. The man who killed Vern is the one to blame."

She bit her lip, feeling led to speak. It wasn't going to be an easy conversation, but when it came to a deep relationship—like the one she hoped she and Griffin were developing—things weren't always easy, and she truly believed he needed to hear this. She only prayed he took it the right way. She wasn't trying to cause more pain. She was trying to help.

Are you sure, Lord? I'm the one who needs to say something?

Couldn't Declan or Kate? Perhaps they already had, and God was clearly laying this on her heart—so heavily on her heart she couldn't ignore Him.

Okay, Lord, here goes nothing.

She linked her fingers through Griffin's,

looking up at him, holding his gaze. "Like the men who killed Judith Connelly and Jenna are the ones responsible."

He inhaled sharply.

"I see the pain you're both drowning in. You from both losses, Parker from Jenna's. What happened in both cases was beyond tragic, but letting what some evil men did hold you captive or destroy your friendship with Parker—destroy a bond I'm sure Jenna treasured between you two—isn't the answer."

Griffin shifted in the recliner, wanting to be on the entry level just in case. Winston grunted at his lack of settling in. If he wasn't settled, the dog wasn't settled.

He punched the pillow under his head, the moonlight splaying across the floor in a squared pattern from the front windowpanes. He watched Finley deep in sleep on the sofa across from him.

"Like the men who killed Judith Connelly and Jenna are the ones responsible."

Finley's words cut like a knife, not because she'd intended harm. He knew that was the last thing she wanted. Her concerned expression the rest of the night proved that.

Rather, it stung because he knew in his heart of hearts it was true. Parker could have never known, never anticipated what would happen when he asked Jenna to meet him that night. He loved Jenna deeply. It was painfully obvious by the way he still tortured himself—refusing to have a serious relationship, to love or let himself be loved. Jenna's death had broken him. And *he'd* only made it worse by continuing to blame his best friend.

Learning Parker had been seeing his baby sister behind his back for months had hit him like a sandblaster. Why couldn't Parker have trusted him enough, respected him enough, to do the honorable thing and tell him the truth? She was his baby sister. He was his best friend. He deserved as much.

He thought he knew Parker so well. Thought he had his back. Thought he could trust him. But Parker had been lying to him, keeping a major secret for months. How could he ever trust him again?

He exhaled, pain compressing his chest on the next inhale.

Father, I'm so conflicted. I know Finley is right. I know she said it out of love. I know I've been punishing Parker for far too long. This bitterness is eating me up. I can't carry it anymore.

He rolled off the couch and dropped to his knees, bowing his head.

I give it all to you—my anger, hurt, pain, sorrow, questioning, doubt, bitterness. Everything wrapped up in Judith's and Jenna's deaths and Parker's deception. Help me to stop being so self-righteous with Parker. I'm clearly the last person who should be.

Please help me, Abba, Father, I'm relying on you.

I can't solve this case or, much more importantly, be the man Finley deserves without your enabling. Please protect us all and direct us to Marley's killer. Let justice be done.

In your Son's name I pray. Amen.

Finley stepped inside her home, dropping her keys and purse on the entryway table. It'd been a long day, but she was so much closer to catching Brent Howard. So close, they finally had a name and an address. Federal agents were swarming his house now.

She kicked off her shoes and headed for the kitchen, passing through the living room when someone grabbed her from behind and pressed something over her mouth.

She woke, bound, a bright light shining in her face.

"Hello, Dr. Scott. I hear you've been looking for me."

She thrashed against the restraints, screaming through the duct tape covering her mouth. "Help me!"

But her voice didn't sound muffled. It was loud, piercing.

"Finley." He jarred her. "Finley."

She bolted upright, sweat drenching her.

Blinking, she saw Griffin.

"Hey." He rubbed her arm. "It's okay. It's all okay."

She shook her head, fearing it'd never be okay, that she'd never be okay again.

Griffin brought her a glass of water. "Feeling any better?"

Chills wracked her body, her clothes still damp. "I think a hot shower will help. Do you mind?"

"Of course not."

She stood and moved to step past.

"Hey." He tugged her arm. "Please don't fear him. I won't let Perera get you. I promise."

She bit her bottom lip. It was time she told him. "It's not Perera."

"You think someone else killed Marley?"

"No. I mean the nightmare wasn't about Perera. It was about Brent Howard."

"Brent Howard . . . I know that name. The man who killed five women from Maryland over the last two decades?"

"Yes."

"I don't understand."

— 40 —

Griffin sat in shock as Finley explained.

"I was called to a body dump site. A grave that time and weather eroded. The woman had something in common with a set of skeletal remains I'd assisted on during my internship period at the ME's office."

Now he remembered the case. "Her ring finger had been cut off."

She nodded. "I worked with the federal agent in charge of the cold case, and through our work together and my remembering the other victim . . ."

"You were able to piece together that it had been the same killer."

"Yes, so I combed through case file after case file on Jane Does going back twenty years, and found three other victims. It was the initial victim's cold case that led us to Howard. When the FBI closed in on him, he came after me."

"What?" How had he not heard about that?

"The Bureau was able to keep my name out of it."

"How?"

"I was dating the agent in charge."

"Oh. I'm glad he was able to do that." That kind of press, that invasion into your life after death touched you . . .

He remembered the reporters swarming when Jenna disappeared and again when her body was found—asking horrid questions, prying into every aspect of their lives. He was so thankful Finley had been spared that. But what hadn't she been spared? What had Howard done to her?

His chest tightened, knowing what Howard had done to his victims before finally cutting off their ring finger and suffocating them.

"We don't have to talk about this if you don't want, but I'm here anytime you do."

She nodded. "Let me take a shower and then we can talk."

Perera watched through binoculars, having to move around to the rear of the ranger's home to get any line of sight, slender as it was. He'd only spotted her because she'd moved upstairs. Something had shaken her. Looked like someone else had already done his job. Now to check on the other two.

Finley padded down Griffin's steps, feeling refreshed if not fully clean. Night terrors always brought the feeling of shame, even though she hadn't done anything wrong. In fact, she'd done everything right and yet she was still paying for Howard's evil.

Please, Father, I know you've never left my side. I know you brought me out of that night alive and whole, despite the anxiety. Please let this fear leave for good. Let me trust in Griffin enough to share, and I pray he's the man I think he is and will react the way I hope he will— with understanding and compassion, not guilt and pity, as Brad did.

She didn't blame Brad. But he'd felt responsible for not anticipating Howard's move. For not protecting his girlfriend. But it wasn't his fault. It was Howard's. She knew that, and told Brad as much, but he never could seem to move past it. She'd always be a reminder of the mistake he felt he'd made.

Much like Griffin struggled with guilt over Judith Connelly's death.

Please, Father, please bring healing to us both.

I will. Through you both, a soft voice echoed in her soul.

Entering the front room, she found Griffin perched on the edge of the couch, Winston curled up at his feet.

Griffin looked up at her, eyes brimming with compassion. "Hey."

She slipped her hair behind her ear and moved toward him. "Hey."

He scooted back on the deep leather sofa, his left arm draped across the cushions. "Why don't you join me?"

She sank into the alcove of his arm, slipping

the edges of her long-sleeve knit top over her hands, balling them inside as she curled closer to Griffin, letting his steadfast strength give her courage.

Taking a deep breath, she began, "Howard wanted to punish me for interfering with his *'course of justice,'* as he called it."

"What kind of sicko views torturing and killing women as justice?"

"The first victim was his fiancée-to-be. At least he thought so, but when he proposed she just laughed. So he decided she deserved to die. Each victim after that had, in his watchful eyes, humiliated a man, cheated on her boyfriend or husband, or rejected a proposal. He scoured the Internet under numerous aliases looking for stories, stalking women at bars to see who was out without her spouse. It was an enterprise to him, and I ruined it all." She took a moment to catch her breath, to slow her breathing. In . . . *one . . . two.* Out . . . *one . . . two . . . three . . . four.*

Griffin wrapped his hand around her shoulder, encircling her with his arm, and despite the horror of what she was sharing, she felt safe, sheltered.

"You don't have to say anything you don't want to." His voice was low, reassuring.

"I know." She slipped her hand from her sleeve and grasped his. "I want to." She took another deep breath and dove into the nightmare. "Howard grabbed me in my house, drugged me. When I woke I was tied to a chair and he was . . ." She bit the side of her cheek. "Touching me, running his knife over me, telling me exactly what he was going to do to me."

Griffin clutched her tighter. How she wished he'd been the one with her that night. Brad had rescued her in the end, but then he'd let her down horribly. She'd felt so alone until now. Though she'd never really been alone.

"When you pass through deep waters, I will be with you."

She loved the verse from Isaiah. Whenever the panic surged, she reminded herself God was with her in the darkest of places and that she *would* pass through.

Griffin waited patiently. Not pressing. Just comforting.

"He wanted to give me a taste of what the end would be like. Wanted to toy with me, so he suffocated me multiple times just to the brink of death and then stopped. He was about to cut my ring finger off when Brad and the team burst in." He'd gotten there just in time and yet far too late.

"Oh, honey." Griffin pressed a kiss to her head. "I'm so sorry you had to go through something so awful. If Howard wasn't already dead, I'd kill him myself."

Frank, one of Brad's team, had taken care of

that when Howard rushed him. At least she knew he could never hurt her again, at least not physically. Mentally, emotionally, the pain he inflicted lingered, but she had hope, she *trusted,* one day the scars would fade and she'd be free. That day was nearer now, and Griffin was a big part of it.

Thank you, Jesus, for bringing me Griffin.

Leaning against his chest, he stroked her hair with gentle lovingness, and she rested in the peace of the moment.

Avery studied Parker as he hovered over his microscope in his lab at the Baltimore Medical Examiner's office. Being an independent contractor, he'd applied to rent lab space, and given his abilities—along with the number of cases he worked with the ME—he was granted the space. Parker's wasn't the typical lab—at least not what Avery pictured when she thought of a crime scene lab—nor was it at all similar to the other labs in the building. The walls were burgundy, the silver cabinets with stylized handles. Droplights provided a softer ambiance than the overhead fluorescent ones, which Parker only turned on when needed.

Rolling silver stools were tucked under the counters and pulled out when needed. While everything was meticulous and sterile, the space felt more like a home than a lab.

She glanced back at Parker, hard at work on the hair sample—the sight so familiar it was nearly laughable. They'd probably be there all night. *Intense* didn't come close to describing the man's work ethic.

— 41 —

Griffin and Finley headed for the hospital in the morning. They'd spent the entire night talking. Finley sharing her experience, doubts, and fears she'd struggled with during the last year. Griffin sharing what God had laid on his heart about Parker and the forgiveness he finally needed to extend. He wasn't exactly eager to see Parker. It was never easy eating crow, and he owed him a whopper of an apology.

He held Finley's slender hand in his, so thankful she trusted him enough to share her struggles. Thankful God had brought her into his life.

His cell rang, and he reluctantly answered via Bluetooth, wishing for a few more moments of solitude with her. "McCray."

"Mr. McCray. This is Jim Trent. Arthur's brother."

"Yes." He looked at Finley with a smile. Maybe they'd get another lead. "Thank you for calling me back."

"Sorry it took me a bit. I was in Boca until late last night. I spoke with Art, and he said to help you in any way I can."

Thank you, Art. "I really appreciate it."

"So what would you like to know?"

"We're interested in Marley's relationship with her aunt. It sounds like your wife had a great impact on Marley and the direction of her career."

"Yes. Marley was like an eager sponge whenever Andrea spoke about her work in Bosnia, whenever she told stories of what she'd seen and experienced. Andrea loathed the injustice and suffering inflicted by the men in power, and Marley took on that crusade, following in Andrea's footsteps."

"We were told Andrea gifted her camera to Marley?"

"Yes. She took that thing with her everywhere."

Even to her death.

"As you know, Marley's body was found in Gettysburg. Would you have any idea why she'd be up there?"

"No. I couldn't say. Marley and I didn't really discuss her work."

"When was the last time you saw Marley?"

"Last year. Right around this time, actually. She came for Andrea's files."

Right after she'd seen the "ghost," as Ben had described it. Griffin looked at Finley, intrigue raking through him. "What files?" he asked.

"Everything Andrea collected, wrote, and photographed during her time in Sarajevo."

Griffin frowned. What'd that have to do with Perera? Had the timing just been a coincidence? "Did she say *why* she wanted the files?"

"Said she was curious about something and asked if I minded if she borrowed them for a while. I had no problem with it. I knew Marley would keep them safe, so I let her have them."

He hadn't seen any Bosnia files among Marley's belongings. "Where are the files now? Did she bring them back to you?"

"No. While she was alive, I figured she was taking her time to go through them. She worked hard and there was a lot to sift through—a half-dozen boxes. With her job, I figured it was a weekend hobby. Maybe her way of staying close to Andrea after her passing."

"And after Marley went missing?"

"I asked Art about them. He said they weren't among the things her co-worker sent up. I called her office and talked to the co-worker, and he said he couldn't find them among Marley's things. I figured they got lost in the shuffle."

"Shuffle?"

"The police taking stuff, her co-worker. Art with his health issues wasn't able to make it up to Marley's place, and I don't think it got handled like it would have had he been able. I offered to help, but by then it was already done."

"So you have no idea where those boxes are?"

"No, and I have to admit it makes me sad. That was my wife's lifework and something of great importance to my niece. I hate to think they're sitting in a landfill somewhere."

Oh, he doubted that was the case. They were either hidden somewhere they hadn't found or they'd been destroyed.

"Thank you so much for your time, Mr. Trent. If you think of anything else, would you give me a call?"

"You got it. I so appreciate you not giving up on Marley."

"She deserves justice."

"Yes. She does."

Griffin disconnected the call and looked to Finley. "Well, there's an interesting side note."

"You going to ask Paul about the boxes?"

"Most definitely."

They were still searching for a possible storage facility, but none were turning up. At least not under his name. Maybe it was time he asked Paul outright.

He dialed Paul, who answered on the third ring.

"Mr. Geller?"

"Yes?"

"This is Chief McCray."

"Yes?" he asked, his voice hopeful. "I hope you have good news."

"Actually I have a question for you."

"Oh?"

"We just hung up with Marley's uncle. He mentioned that Marley took a half-dozen file boxes of her aunt's from her uncle's house last fall. It seems those boxes are nowhere to be found. You wouldn't by any chance know where they'd be?"

"You searched my place. Clearly I don't have them."

"Not at your place."

"What is that supposed to mean?"

"Mr. Geller, do you have a storage facility?"

"That's none of your business."

"I'll take that as a yes."

"You can take that however you want. I'm tired of these boorish questions. The only person you should be questioning is Mark Perera." He hung up.

Griffin looked over at Finley.

"I'd say that was about as clear a yes as we're going to get."

"I'll talk to Declan about getting a warrant, but without any idea of where the storage facility is, I don't see how we can obtain one."

"And Paul's not going to offer anything up."

"But why hide her aunt's files?"

"Maybe he wasn't specifically hiding those. Maybe they were simply among the additional items he took that he's hidden away."

"I'm seriously starting to wonder if he was more than just obsessed with Marley."

"Yeah, and I keep coming back to the question of whether that obsession turned deadly." He'd seen it on the job way too much.

— 42 —

Griffin greeted Declan, thrilled to see his coloring returned and him sitting up alert and on the phone. He gestured them in, holding up a finger. "Okay, thanks." He hung up and turned his full attention to them.

"That was the sketch artist I sent up to Gettysburg after Parker called and told me the hotel owner saw our man or at least the man who apparently checked Marley out. He just finished working with Linda Jo Banks. A local officer is scanning and e-mailing me the image as we speak."

"Great. Parker and Avery called. They are on their way in from the lab. We got a hair follicle DNA match."

"So Marley definitely was there." Another concrete detail. Now if the pieces would just start fitting together.

"Kate and Tanner are on their way over. Kate said she found some interesting stuff in Marley's personal laptop browser history."

Parker and Avery entered carrying donuts from the Fractured Prune and coffee from Café Euro.

"I've got a call in to the man responsible for Gettysburg reenactment—Bob Ward," Parker said, biting into a chocolate-dipped donut. "Marley was asking Linda Jo a bunch of questions about him."

"Okay," Griffin said, "but I'm still not seeing how this all ties together—Perera, Gettysburg, reenactments, Marley's aunt?"

"I think I may know," Kate said, entering with the laptop under her arm and Tanner following behind, her face flushed with anger.

"What's wrong?"

Kate looked back at Tanner. "She's not thrilled with what I found."

"It's not that. I just think you're searching for another answer when Perera is right in front of you. He's a monster who wouldn't hesitate to kill Marley."

"And he admitted as much," Finley said. "Admitted he planned to take her out, but someone beat him to it."

"Likely excuse."

"Why admit he intended to kill her at all?"

"Because you wouldn't believe he was totally innocent. It admits guilt without holding him responsible for her death. You can't charge him for wanting to kill her, and he knows it."

"No, but with your evidence we can push to have her case against him reopened."

"And then the cycle starts all over. Authorities bribed, pressure to drop the case, files disappearing. We have to get him *now,* pin him for this, or he will just slip away again."

"I understand your frustration, Tanner, but our job is to find Marley's killer, and that's what we have to focus on," Griffin said. He wanted to get Perera too. The man had been in Finley's car. He'd made her feel vulnerable, invaded. But their focus, for the time being, had to remain on Marley's killer. And he wasn't convinced that was Perera.

"I may be able to help," Kate said.

All eyes were on her as Parker's cell rang. "Hold that thought. It's Bob Wade."

"Who's Bob Wade?" Kate asked as Parker stepped from the room.

"Mr. Wade, thanks for returning my call," Parker said, finding a secluded place to talk.

"Linda Jo over at the Gettysburg Inn said you had some questions about a young lady I spoke to quite a ways back. Linda Jo said she was murdered."

"Yes."

"How awful."

"It is, and we're trying to find her killer."

"That's great, but I'm not sure what any of this has to do with me."

"Not you precisely. We just need to know what you two discussed."

"All right. Well, I remember I found her interest odd."

"Odd how?"

"First off, I don't usually get a lot of women interested in participating other than in auxiliary roles, of course, but Miss Douglas was particularly interested in sharpshooters."

"Sharpshooters?"

"Yes. She asked me a lot about the men we have involved. I couldn't tell if she was interested in watching or doing some sort of article. I can't recall what she said when I asked the source of her interest, but I gave her Kevin's name and told her he'd be the one to ask about the history of sharpshooters."

"Kevin?"

"Yes. Kevin Murphy. He's one of our sharpshooter reenactors. Knows his military history."

"Any chance he was military or former military?"

"I got that impression."

"Did you ever ask?"

"Kevin wasn't the sort for small talk. You try to get personal and he just changed the subject. A lot of our reenactors are pretty private, especially those who chose to fight on the South's side. We've got a good contingent of former military, though. Wouldn't be surprised if he was."

"You have contact information for Kevin?"

"I got a phone number, but it is for an answering service. I leave a message about when we are meeting and he shows up."

"Does he live in Gettysburg?"

"Not that I'm aware. It's a small enough town; we have a good feel for most folks around. Many live in the surrounding area—cabins afford lots of anonymity."

"Ever see Kevin with anyone? Did anyone attend the reenactments to watch him? A wife, girlfriend, buddy?"

"Not that I noticed."

"Okay. Could we get that phone number from you?"

It was a start.

Parker jotted down the number, asked a few more questions, thanked Bob for his time, and returned to Declan's room. "That was Bob, and you're not going to believe what he just told me."

"So do you think our sniper is a sharpshooter reenactor?" Finley asked.

"Could very possibly be," Griffin said, the pieces starting to make a little more sense. "Former military tend to gravitate to a similar structure, and military reenactments provide a similar level of camaraderie and discipline."

"Okay, so what do we know about Kevin Murphy?"

"I've got a number." Parker handed it to Griffin. "Your area of expertise. Bob did mention it's an answering service."

"I'll get a warrant to access their client list," Declan said.

"I'll give them a call and see if we can't garner a little information in the meantime," Griffin said, stepping from the room.

He placed the call, spoke with the woman working the service, and returned to Declan's room, irritation sparking.

"That's not the face of happiness," Declan said.

"The woman at the agency said Murphy set up the service over the phone and pays by money order—always from a different location."

"Great. That's helpful. Sounds like a warrant won't do us much good, but I'll still follow through." With a sigh, Declan looked at Kate. "You said you had something?"

"Marley's browser history had been erased—or so the person who did it thought—but I was able to . . ." She shook her head. "Never mind. You don't need the details."

They'd never understand them anyway. Kate was a hacker extraordinaire.

"I was able to retrieve what had been wiped off, and it was not what I expected."

"What did you find?" Griffin asked.

"A lot of references to the Bosnian War. Marley was too young to have been involved working human rights stuff. She would have been a kid. Perhaps she covered it as part of her dissertation in college or something, but it feels more personal than that."

Griffin glanced at Finley. "I think we might know why."

They went on to explain to Kate what they'd learned about Marley's aunt Andrea and her work photographing the Bosnian war crimes.

"So how does Marley's research into Bosnia tie in with Perera?"

"I have no idea. I also can't figure out how a sharpshooter reenactor who is possibly our sniper would be tied to Perera."

"Maybe he's the sniper Perera hired to take Marley out?" Tanner said, a twinge of hope flickering in her voice. She wanted Perera bad.

"But," Griffin said, "how would she know that, and what does any of that have to do with Marley's sudden and intense fascination with her aunt's tie to the Bosnian War?"

"I found a lot of articles on a . . ." Kate opened the browser and retrieved the information. "General Rativik."

"Rativik," Griffin said. "His name has been coming up a lot lately. He was responsible for the genocide Andrea witnessed in Sarajevo. One of Mladic's right-hand men."

"Ratko Mladic?" Finley asked.

"Yes."

"They found him in hiding and tried him a few years ago," Avery said.

"Hid for nearly a decade," Finley said. Her beautiful eyes narrowed.

"What if this is a similar case?" Griffin asked. "What if Rativik has been in hiding?"

"Nope," Kate said.

"Are you sure?"

"Yeah. Marley pulled up a string of articles on his death. He died in an explosion."

"Was his body found?"

Kate shook her head. "Remains were too charred."

"Anything in Marley's research about a sniper?" Griffin asked.

"In a roundabout way."

"Meaning?"

"There was this U.S. Marine Marley did a lot of digging on. Peter Kovac. I wasn't able to find a whole lot on him after 1990, but he entered the Marines at age eighteen in '86. Attended sniper school in '88 and Marine Division Recon the next, and then he dropped off the records until he was killed in '95 while serving in Bosnia."

Griffin and Declan exchanged a look, and then Griffin asked, "Does it say how he died?"

"IED attack."

Declan shrugged his good shoulder. "Makes a great cover story."

"Cover story for what?" Avery asked.

"Covering up someone's death," Declan explained.

"Okay, so *if* this Kovac died in Bosnia, why was Marley so interested in him?"

"When U.S. soldiers are part of black ops, and Kovac's history would support that," Griffin said, "and they are killed doing something the U.S. government doesn't want to explain or acknowledge, the soldiers typically die from IED attacks, helicopter accidents, or friendly fire."

"Wait a minute." Kate shifted between windows, her eyes narrowing. "Rativik and Kovac died within a day of each other."

Finally Griffin felt the pieces coming together. "What if the ghost—to use Ben's words—Marley thought she saw in Gettysburg was Rativik?"

Finley smiled. "It would explain why she suddenly wanted her aunt's files on Rativik and his war crimes."

"And Kovac?" Avery asked.

"Could have been Rativik's way out of Bosnia," Parker said.

"Meaning the U.S. smuggled him out via one of their soldiers and have been hiding him here?" Avery said, frowning.

"Or what if Rativik paid Kovac to stage the explosion he supposedly died in and get him out of the country?" Declan said.

Avery shook her head. "Why would a U.S.

soldier do that? And how would they come in contact?"

"Again, it'll take some digging, but Kovac could have been sent in to kill Rativik. He'd possess the necessary skills. Maybe Rativik persuaded him to flip for a huge payoff," Griffin offered. "Kovac and Rativik staged the explosion and fled to the U.S."

"Meaning Kovac could be Kevin Murphy," Kate guessed.

Griffin nodded. "That's what I'm thinking."

"So Marley was researching Rativik and his death, trying to figure out how he could have survived, and she finds a soldier who died within a day of Rativik. Begins to track him. Maybe they find out she's on to them and they lure her to Gettysburg. She's busy taking pictures of Rativik while Kovac takes her out. And you know what sniper rifle Bosnian Serbs preferred?" Griffin said.

"The Dragunov?" Parker asked.

Griffin nodded.

"If Kovac is Murphy and participates in the reenactments, he probably knows the battlefield well," Finley said.

"Which means he may live nearby." Griffin shifted in his seat, staring back at the curtained window, thankful for the cover.

"So Perera was telling the truth?" Finley said.

Griffin looked at Tanner, whose eyes were filled with tears. "I'm afraid so."

This wasn't about Perera at all.

This was about bringing the man responsible for the atrocities Marley's aunt, family, and friends had suffered to justice. *Finally*.

Speaking of *finally*. "Park, can I speak with you outside for a moment?"

Parker looked at him, thoroughly confused. As did Declan.

"Sure." Parker stood and stepped from the room.

Griffin glanced back at Finley, whose amazing courage fueled his. To think of all she'd been through and the fight she continued to fight. It was awe-inspiring, and he loved her all the more for it.

The officer still guarding Declan's room glanced up at them.

"Let's see if we can't find an empty room," Griff said.

"O . . . kay."

It took a minute, but they tracked one down.

Parker hopped on the bed, one leg dangling off the side.

Griffin raked a hand through his hair. "I owe you a huge apology."

Shock rippled across Parker's face, his poor attempt at a guard fully slipping from place.

Clearing his throat, Griffin proceeded with what he should have said years ago. "Jenna's death wasn't your fault."

Parker sat shell-shocked.

"I'm not happy you two were sneaking around. I wish you had been honest with me. We were . . . we *are* brothers, but you could have never known she'd be abducted that night."

He'd never seen such emotion on Parker's face, not since the consuming sadness the day they found Jenna's body. "I should have told you about us. Shouldn't have asked her to sneak out."

"Yeah. You should have told me."

Parker shook his head. "It's no excuse, but Jenna begged me not to. . . ."

"And you were in love. I get it." With the amount of pain Parker still suffered, it was excruciatingly clear he still loved Jenna, still carried the burden of his guilt and her loss like a boulder on his back.

Parker swallowed. "*Very* much in love, and a big part of me will always be. She was . . ."

"*Special,*" Griffin said, clearing his throat as Jenna's vibrant, joyful face flashed before his eyes. That's how he wanted to remember her, not as they'd found her. Pain seared inside. When would the heartache settle? Maybe making amends with Parker was the first step. Not to forgetting, but for remembering the beauty of who his sister was. Who they all were, and that the Pirates were part of him—a huge part. They made him a better man.

He extended his hand. "I forgive you for not telling me."

The expression of undeserved mercy washed over Parker's face as he hopped down and strode to Griffin. "Thank you," he said, his voice shaking. He clutched his hand a brief moment, his eyes conveying the depth of his gratitude.

"You aren't responsible," Griffin continued, knowing it needed to be said and truly believing it. He'd just been so broken by her death, so pained, that it was easier to blame Parker than accept the fact Jenna's killer had gotten away. At least until now. "The man who killed her is responsible. And I think it's time we work her cold case. Bring her killer to justice."

Parker arched a brow. "We?"

"Yeah." He lifted his chin and then tilted it in the direction of Declan's room. "We all make a great team."

"Yeah." Parker slid his hands in his pockets, trying so hard to play it cool, but Griffin didn't miss the moisture welling in his eyes as he sniffed and swiped at his nose in a poor attempt to cover it up.

Griffin had no idea his forgiveness held so much weight for Parker, and at the same time, amazingly, freed himself of an equally heavy one.

— 43 —

"What do we know about Kevin Murphy?" Griffin asked, as Parker helped him set up the whiteboard in Declan's hospital room. Their talk, while difficult, had gone extremely well. Everyone in the room was studying them, but from the smiles on their faces, he could see, except for Tanner, they understood what had occurred. He and Parker were free men.

"We know he uses an answering service for his calls." Declan began with the task at hand—summing up everything they knew about the elusive Kevin Murphy in what would, until Declan's release, be their new center of operations.

Griffin nodded and wrote on the whiteboard. "Which probably means he has no direct phone line."

"He has a PO Box at the post office in Chambersburg," Finley said. "But of course he paid cash for that, as well, and never comes in to pay or pick up in any discernable pattern."

"He has nothing in his name," Kate said. "No driver's license, paycheck, property tax bill, cell phone contract." She shifted back from her laptop in frustration. "This guy really is a ghost."

Just like Luke—seemingly vanished from the

face of the earth. That was one area he and Parker still disagreed on, but one battle at a time.

"Okay," Declan said. "That tells us he's got a fake ID, not officially registered with the MVA, probably rents a place, paying cash or by money order, uses a burner cell . . . When do the reenactors meet next?"

"Not until spring, according to Bob," Parker said. "What if we got Bob to call him in for a meeting? We could have Bob call everyone in to avoid suspicion."

"I think a random meeting out of the blue would raise his suspicions enough on its own."

"Are there any other ties to him?" Parker asked.

"Vern Michaels," Finley said.

"Right." Griffin explained who Vern Michaels was and that he had died within a day of speaking with them.

"So Vern knew Kevin Murphy," Declan postulated.

"Or asked a question that generated Kevin's name," Griffin said. "Which means he probably shoots at one of the ranges in the region."

"All right." Declan climbed from his bed, slowly and with a muffled groan.

Parker whistled. "Nice legs."

Declan clutched the hospital gown. "Griffin, go in my duffel you brought and toss me my pants."

"Are you sure you should be out of bed?"

"I'm fine."

His fixed jaw said otherwise, but he returned from the bathroom a few minutes later clad in his gown and navy blue Joe Boxer sweats. "Let's throw up the map."

Parker flipped the board over and clipped the map of the region on it.

"We know Marley was buried here." Declan put a red X on the battlefield.

"He has a PO Box here." Finley pointed and Declan put an X on it.

"Vern Michaels shot and lived here." Griffin noted, and two more Xs went up.

"The answering service is based in Baltimore, so that doesn't really help," Griffin said. "But we know Marley spent her last night here." He put an X on the general location of the Gettysburg Inn.

"All right." Declan drew a large red circle encompassing all of the Xs. "This is our circle of interest. Griff, you and Finley follow up with the other shooting ranges in the area, and I'll get a warrant to access Vern Michaels' phone records."

"I'll also call Bob Wade," Griffin said. "Ask a few more sharpshooter-related questions and ask what kind of vehicle Kevin Murphy drives."

"None are registered in his name," Kate said.

"But he's got to have a mode of transportation."

A woman in her late thirties, wearing navy blue scrubs, entered and raised her brows at Declan by the whiteboard. "Mr. Grey."

"Amber."

"I see you're up and ready for PT."

"PT." He gave a forced smile. "Super."

Amber looked around the room. "If you all will excuse us, Mr. Grey has some exercises to do."

"It's kind of a busy time."

"Nah, we're all finished here," Parker said, smirking. "You go on with the nice lady."

"You keep him on task, Amber," Griffin said with a grin.

Declan attempted his best death stare. "Thanks, guys."

Parker shrugged. "It's what we're here for."

"They are on to us," Kovac said over the burner cell.

"Are you certain?" Rativik, aka Carl Hansen, asked.

"Yes. How do you want to proceed?"

Rativik exhaled. "I like my life here. My new family. I don't want to lose it all because some people couldn't mind their own business."

"Taking out the lot of them will draw some serious attention and heat. I don't know that it'll be safe to stay."

"What do you suggest?" Rativik asked.

"An exit strategy."

"No. I don't want to give up my family or the life I've made here. If we act swiftly, we can contain this."

"How do you suggest we do that?"

"Let me run the scenarios and I'll get back to you. I've got a few ideas."

"Okay, but we've got to move quickly," Kovac warned.

"They'll all be dead by tomorrow. I promise you."

— 44 —

Vern Michaels' death—which the ME Declan finally heard back from officially declared a homicide—clearly indicated Griffin and Finley's questioning at the shooting range had hit close to home with Kevin Murphy, aka Peter Kovac. That's where they needed to continue to press— the ranges. Griffin began with a list of shooting clubs, some in the area he was familiar with and others not so familiar. Visiting in person rather than cold calling dramatically increased the chances of gathering information.

Finley accompanied him, which in one sense he loved because it gave them more time together and he knew she was safe at his side, but at the same time, the thought of running into Kovac at one of the ranges terrified him.

They'd printed out a photograph of Kovac to show around in addition to their questions, though the obituary image was more than twenty years old. They'd separated the image from the context of the article, blowing it up from a two-by-two to an eight-by-ten image, thanks to Avery's meticulous attention to detail.

Declan had finally reached the ICE agent, Gabriel Rosario, who Declan explained was nothing but evasive. They'd be investigating him further.

Griffin pulled into the lot of the third range on their list and carefully surveyed the surrounding area, praying they weren't sitting ducks. They both felt on edge, watched, and it was a horrific feeling.

Parking in the most strategic and sheltered spot, he once again escorted Finley in, shielding her body with his until they were securely inside. He'd spend the rest of his life protecting her if she'd let him.

He shifted his thoughts from the woman he loved to the space surrounding them. The range was more extensive than Gunny's Red Barn—no doubt providing the patrons with a little more anonymity—and offered an indoor section for more comfortable year-round shooting.

From what Kate had dug up, the owner's name was Chris Abbott. Griffin prayed Abbott was friendly.

They moved down the aisles of ammo to the counter at the rear of the room. Gunshots sounded in the distance, the scent of gunpowder wafting in the air.

"Nice place you got here," Griffin said.

"How can I help you folks?"

"Are you Chris Abbott by any chance?"

"Guilty."

"Hi." Griffin extended his hand. "Griffin McCray."

"Finley Scott," she said beside him.

Abbott nodded.

"We're looking for a man who may shoot here," Griffin began.

"Let me guess. Weapon of choice is the Dragunov?"

"Yeah. How'd you know?"

"You're the third party who's been in here asking about a man and that gun."

"Vern Michaels one of them?" Griffin asked.

"Yeah. Shame what happened."

"Mind telling us what you told Vern?"

"Only if you explain what this is all about."

They explained what they could.

"All right. I'll tell you what I told Vern."

"And the second interested party?"

"Nope. Didn't tell that fella anything. He wasn't from around here."

"Oh? Could you describe him?"

"Five foot ten, squat, sturdy, bald, spider tattoo on his neck."

Simon Reuben—Perera's right-hand man whose burner cell had turned up nothing but dead numbers. Frustration flared. They were running out of time. They had to find Kovac before he found them.

"What'd you tell Vern?"

"There's a guy. Supposedly his friends call him Vector—not that I've ever seen him with friends, or with anyone for that matter. Likes the Dragunov. Heck of a shot. Vern recognized the name."

"So he knew Vector?"

"Nah, but he'd heard of him from someone. Imagine he went to ask that someone more about Vector."

"Any idea who Vector is? I mean his real name? Where he lives? What he drives?"

"No on the first three. Black pickup on the last."

Helpful, considering he hadn't heard back from Bob Wade yet.

"Any chance you noted his plates?"

Abbott hiked his brows.

Right. Not that kind of place.

"What about this?" Finley pulled out Kovac's picture. "He's about twenty years older."

Unfortunately the sketch from Linda Jo's description was too vague to use for identification. It certainly didn't rule out Kovac, but there was not enough detail to confirm it was him.

The man studied it. "Could be, but I'm not certain."

As they returned to Griffin's truck, Finley said, "Abbott was friendlier than the rest."

"Probably doesn't like the idea of an assassin using his range for practice."

"What now?"

"We call Declan and see where he's at on Vern Michaels' phone records." Abbott had refused to share the name of the man Vern questioned about Vector, and Griffin respected him for it. After what happened to Vern, Abbott was no doubt trying to protect the man's life. If he was still alive.

They all crowded around Declan's bed, Five Guys' burgers and fries spread about them.

"Vern Michaels made two calls the day he died. One to a man named Charlie Ricker."

"He's a shooter," Griffin said, popping a fry in his mouth. "Used to shoot against him at tournaments. And the second call?"

"To Kevin Murphy's answering service."

"Kate." Declan turned to her. "Pull up whatever you can on Charlie Ricker. Home and work addresses first priority."

— 45 —

They pulled up to Ricker's trailer. "Wait here," Griffin told Finley as he parked the pickup.

"What? Why? I've come on everything else."

"It's not like Ricker is Murphy or Kovac or *whatever* his real name is."

Griffin took in the solitary nature of the surroundings. It was quiet—*too quiet.* "I don't like it. Wait here."

"My presence will make him more likely to open the door."

He hung his head, knowing she was right.

He held her close to his side, sheltered as much as possible by his body as they approached the trailer. Two metal steps led to the door.

"Let me." She stepped up to the door and knocked. "Mr. Ricker. I'm hoping you can help me."

The front curtain slid an inch to the side.

"I just need a minute of your time," she said.

"We can come back with the Feds, if you'd rather," Griffin offered.

Finley frowned back at him.

"What?" He shrugged. This was taking too long.

The door opened and a burly man as wide and tall as the doorway stood staring down at them.

He glared at Griffin and then smiled at Finley. "What can I do for you, darling?"

"We need to ask you about Kevin Murphy and Vern Michaels."

He went to shut the door, but Griffin wedged himself in. "I was serious about the Feds. We don't want to cause you any trouble. Just ask a question or two."

"That's all Vern did, and he's dead." He looked past them, gazing at the ridgeline arching around them.

Griffin quickly shifted position to shield Finley.

"We just need to know what you told Vern and we'll leave," she pleaded.

"I can't do that. I've been warned."

"By Kevin Murphy?"

Recognition sparked momentarily on his face, but he remained silent.

"We just need to know where we can find him."

"You find him. You die."

"Please," Finley said.

"I'm sorry. I can't. I'm probably already a dead man." He nervously scanned the perimeter surrounding his home, sweat beading on his brow.

"Then help us catch him before he can kill you or anybody else."

"Springer Road. There's a gate at the end. Keep going."

Before they could ask anything else, he slammed the door.

Griffin pulled his cell as he escorted Finley back to his truck.

Declan answered on the second ring.

"I need what you can pull up on Springer Road. I'll text you the coordinates. I get the feeling we're close."

Springer Road was less than ten miles away. Declan instructed them to wait at the feed store a couple miles from the turnoff until he could provide Google Earth images, so they could at least have some idea of what they were walking into.

Nearly an hour passed, and Griffin's patience was evaporating. "I know how to scout. I can go in and assess."

"Declan said to wait."

"Listen to the lady," Declan said, rapping on the pickup window.

Griffin turned, ready to throttle him. He'd heard a car approach. Seen a man exit and move toward the store, but Declan was supposed to be in the hospital. "What are you doing? You're supposed to be recuperating."

"You didn't really think I was going to let you enjoy this one without me, did you?"

"Or me?" Parker said from Finley's side of the vehicle.

"Both of you?"

"Actually . . ." He gestured to his Expedition, where Tanner waved from the backseat.

Griffin looked back at Declan. "You can't be serious?"

"She hid in the back. Didn't know she was with us until we were halfway here. It's a wonder we were able to get Kate and Avery to hang back. Now, let's get to the matter at hand. I thought you and I would approach the house," he said to Griffin.

Parker shook his head. "No way I'm sitting this one out, especially with you not at full capacity."

"Parker's a good shot," Griffin said to Declan. "We could use him. There's a strong chance Ricker panicked and warned Kovac. And an even greater chance he's got the perimeter around his place rigged to alert him to intruders."

"All right," Declan said. "Let me call in a team."

"Kovac would see them coming a mile away, and we'd lose him. Us, he'd believe he could take."

"So essentially we're serving ourselves up as sitting ducks." Parker gave two sarcastic thumbs-up. "Good plan."

Griffin smiled. "Exactly."

They drove the couple of miles to the Springer Road turnoff, putting together their strategy. Declan and Parker would take the lead, and Griffin would follow behind, to provide cover. Fortunately, Finley and Tanner had agreed to remain in

Declan's vehicle at the feed store, at least until they'd swept and cleared the place, but he'd left his snub nose .38 with Finley, just to be safe.

Griffin stopped his pickup at the gate, and Parker looked back at Griffin one last time before he and Declan headed in on foot for Kovac's cabin. Griffin moved swiftly, having scoped out and studied the terrain via the satellite footage the Bureau provided.

Soon, cresting a low ridge, Griffin spotted Kovac's cabin—and with it, Declan and Parker. Declan signaled to Parker for them to split up so they could cover both the front and back entrances.

All was quiet. Maybe they had actually gotten the drop on Kovac.

Targets ripe for the picking thanks to Ricker's tip. Ricker—he'd take care of him later. Stupid man, thinking his confession would save him. Fact was, he'd still given him up, and for that he'd die.

Kovac tracked the two men moving across his property, deciding which to drop first.

He traced from one to the other. *Eeny, meeny, miny . . .*

Finley shifted uneasily in Declan's vehicle, Tanner doing the same.

"How much longer?" she asked.

"I don't know." Finley shook her head, her hand gripping the gun. "I don't normally work this end of things. I'm always called in after the fact."

After.

She prayed *after* included the man she loved and their friends all safe and sound.

With Kovac behind bars and Rativik on the way to stand trial for his war crimes. His new identity hadn't been cracked. Marley might have discovered his alias in her months of searching, but if she had found the evidence locating him, it was most likely in Paul Geller's storage facility, which they still hadn't been able to locate.

The window smashed beside her head, glass shattering. She swallowed her scream, lifting the gun as an armed man lunged at her, knocking the weapon from her hand with brute force. Shoving her aside, he retrieved the weapon and slid it into his pants while keeping his gun firmly fixed on her. With a grunt, he climbed into the vehicle beside her.

He pressed the muzzle of the gun under her chin. "Stay put or she dies," he told Tanner.

— 46 —

He exhaled, waiting for the natural pause before inhaling, his finger squeezing the trigger. *Moe.*

The rifle kicked from his grasp before he could fire.

McCray.

He rolled, leaping up into a crouch, pulling his knife.

McCray stood before him, gun aimed at his chest.

He rushed. The coward had left the profession. He wouldn't pull the . . .

McCray's gun fired.

Impact like a sledgehammer collided with his chest.

A second report and—

Griffin's breath moved in and out in white puffs, birds screeching from the trees, their wings flapping upward in a frenzy.

He took two steps and crouched over Kovac's lifeless form.

One shot to center mass. One to the head.

"Griff?" Declan called over the radio, his tone urgent.

"Yeah."

Declan's relieved exhale said it all. "How many shots?"

"Two, as always with a rusher. You heard another shot too?" He'd heard it in between his shots, off in the distance.

"Yeah. Sounded like it came from the feed store's direction."

Finley.

Finley squeezed her eyes shut as the gun fired and then opened her eyes, anticipating heaven.

But she was still in the Expedition, Tanner's shrieks ringing in her ears.

She glanced over to find Mark Perera pulling a dead man out of the car, letting his body slump to the pavement.

Finley looked at the man on the ground. He looked familiar. "Is that . . . ?"

"Rativik," Perera said with disgust as he opened her door and bound her hands with a zip tie. "You can thank me later." He slammed the door and she twisted in her seat as he opened the back door and bound Tanner as well. As he pulled the zip tie tight, he turned his head slightly, his gaze malicious. "Hello again, Tanner. Told you I'd find you."

Finley swallowed. So that's why he was in the U.S. Did he know about the evidence Tanner possessed?

Striding to the driver's side, Perera climbed into the Expedition, and shut the door. "He and Kovac knew you were coming. Rativik was watching when you arrived at the feed store."

"How do you know that?"

"You're an awfully bold woman asking so many questions with a gun at your side." The barrel pressed into her ribs. "I was waiting too. Tracking Rativik."

As Perera pulled out onto the paved road, he glared in the rearview mirror. "We're going to take a little drive. You try anything, Tanner, and what Rativik said goes—your friend dies."

Finley bit the inside of her cheek. If Perera was right and Kovac knew they were coming . . .

Her stomach burned. *Griffin.*

Please, Father, let them be okay. Let Griffin's plan work.

She glanced at Springer Road as they flew past, spotting Griffin's truck barreling down it toward them.

Thank you, Lord.

She needed to stall. To do something. Perera was intent on killing Tanner if not them both.

"Where are you taking us?"

He didn't respond.

"What are you going to do to us?"

He looked over at her as if they all knew the answer to that one.

"Then why bother saving us from Rativik?"

"He and his cohort tried to set me up for Marley's murder. That's unacceptable. Saving you was just a fortunate by-product for you."

"Until you kill us."

"You're still alive, aren't you?"

"For how long?"

"That depends on my needs."

She cringed at the darkness welling in hiseyes.

"Let me guess. We're loose ends, just like Rachel Lester."

He smiled. "Ah, so you figured out Rachel was my mole. Impressive."

"And you killed her."

"My associate handled that. I prefer not to get my hands dirty unless absolutely necessary."

"Where's he taking them?" Griffin asked, flying down the road.

Declan called in and arranged for the Bureau to track his car. "Uh-huh," he said over the phone. "What's ahead? Any exit strategy? How far? Okay." He hung up. "There's a small airstrip twenty miles from here."

"*Great.* If Perera gets them on that plane, we'll lose him."

"Not if we beat him there."

"What if we're wrong? What if he isn't headed there? What if he beats us there?"

Declan looked at Griffin. "You make the call."

Griffin pulled up a map of the area on his phone. "Call in a rapid-response team to the airstrip."

"And us?"

"We're going to intercept them."

Declan's eyes widened. "And then do what?"

Griffin accelerated. "You're going to have to trust me on this one."

Parker gripped the back of his seat. "Why don't I like the sound of that?"

— 47 —

Finley struggled to slip her hands free, but the zip tie Perera had slid on was too tight. She glanced back at Tanner struggling to do the same.

Perera cut right onto a side road, wheels squealing with the maneuver.

Think, Finley. She searched the vehicle for a weapon.

They approached another intersection, flying by it.

Where was he taking them? And what was he going to do when he got there?

Her stomach flipped, panic pulsating along her nerve endings.

Please, Lord, let Griffin reach us in time.

Hot tears streamed down her cheeks.

They flew past another intersection and quickly approached another. She needed to start paying attention to the street names and direction they were headed.

She turned to look at the green road sign, praying she'd be able to read it at the blinding speed they were traveling at, and blinked as Griffin's truck came barreling at them.

"Hold on," she screamed at Tanner as his truck plowed into the side of them, just front of center, veering them toward the tree line.

Perera cursed as they collided, wedging the Expedition between Griffin's truck and a tree.

Finley's head rung.

The air bags deflated and she blinked. Her door opened and Griffin's sturdy arms wrapped around her, lifting her from the crumpled vehicle.

She collapsed into his hold as he carried her from the smoke. "Tanner?"

"Parker will get her," he said.

He settled her on the ground and knelt beside her, examining her injuries.

"Perera?"

"Looked unconscious, but you were my priority. I'm sure Declan's on it."

He clasped her hand, then stood. "I'm going to grab the first-aid kit from the truck."

Truck.

"Did you seriously ram into us?"

"It was the best scenario."

"To hit us broadside?"

"Not broadside. A few inches to the right of it."

She stared at him as if he had three heads. Was he insane?

"It was the spot for the least chance of harm to you, but allowed me to maneuver your vehicle."

Parker sat Tanner on the ground beside her.

She looked woozy, but she insisted on getting to her feet, cradling her arm as she did so.

"I think it's broken," he said.

"Perera?" she asked, trying to push past him.

He stopped her. "Declan said he's pinned in the vehicle. EMTs are on the way."

Finley sat in the back of the ambulance, a blanket draped across her shoulders.

She'd been cleared to go home. Just a few bumps and bruises.

Tanner had a broken right arm but refused to leave until Perera was officially in federal custody.

With Tanner's evidence, Rativik's murder, and their abduction at gunpoint, Perera wouldn't be leaving the country or the penal system anytime soon.

Griffin took a seat beside Finley as another ambulance pulled away with Perera inside, trailed by federal escort vehicles.

"You doing okay?" he asked, brushing the hair from her face.

"Still in shock, I think. I can't believe you hit us, but . . ." She clutched his hand. "So thankful you did. We all are. You saved our lives."

"It was the safest calculated risk to rescue you. If Perera had reached that airfield . . ." He squeezed her hand.

They both knew what that could have meant.

She rested her head on his shoulder. "You owe me a date."

He chuckled. "I do?"

"Most definitely."

"Not that I'm complaining at the prospect of

an official date with the most beautiful woman I've ever seen, but why do I *owe* you?"

"First, you interrupted my last date halfway through, and second, you just sideswiped the vehicle I was riding in."

A mischievous grin quirked on his lips. "I'd ram your vehicle anytime if it meant protecting you."

She smiled back, a laugh at the precious absurdity of it all tickling her throat with a giggle. "And I love you for that."

"I love you too," he breathed against her lips.

— Epilogue —

Finley watched as Griffin ambled to her door, a swagger in his step, a soft smile on his lips.

He paused on her doorstep and took a breath before knocking.

"Pace yourself," she whispered, forcing herself not to lunge at the door. Anticipation had spiraled through her all night, giving her little sleep, and it was not relenting in the least now. All from the thought of spending the weekend with Griffin and his family. This was another big step in the direction she prayed they were moving.

"Hi," she blurted as she flung open the door.

Griffin's smile widened. "You look beautiful." His gaze thoughtfully lingered over her.

"Thanks. You look handsome, as usual."

He glanced down at his turkey sweater, and color flushed his cheeks. "It was a gift from my mom."

"That's sweet." She couldn't believe she was going to spend the holiday with Griffin and his folks. She was excited and antsy to get going.

He inclined his head. "You ready?"

"Yes. Let me just grab the cookies."

"Cookies?"

"Oatmeal raisin. I couldn't show up empty-handed."

"I'm sure my folks will appreciate them."

"It was no trouble." That was a lie. She could cook, but when it came to baking, something always seemed to short-circuit. She prayed they came out edible.

She climbed in his new truck as he held the door open for her, wondering again why she hadn't just used Le Mont's Bakery.

Because she wanted it to be from the heart. She just prayed it didn't give theirs an attack.

Griffin settled in beside her and pulled away from the curb.

"So tell me more about them." Their introduction at the hospital had been so short, and everyone had been focused and deep in prayer for Declan's recovery, not on chitchat. Griffin had introduced her to his folks, but today—this weekend—would be the first time she was truly meeting them, getting to know her possible future family, and she couldn't wait.

"Again?" he smiled.

She'd been asking questions since she met them at the hospital. "I'm sorry."

"Don't apologize. I think it's awesome you're so excited to get to know my folks better. They are going to love you."

"How can you be so sure?"

"Because I do."

She bit her bottom lip. "I love you too."

"Hopefully you still will after a weekend with the gang in Chesapeake Harbor."

"I'm so glad Avery and Tanner are going to join in." With Griffin's, Parker's, Declan's, Kate's, and Luke's families, it should prove to be quite the gathering.

"I've been there once," she said.

He arched a brow. "To Chesapeake Harbor?"

"Yeah. It was a long time ago and we weren't there long. My college roommate dated a guy from there for a while, and one weekend we picked him up on the way down to Ocean City."

"Remember his name?" Chesapeake was small enough. If this guy really was a local, Griff would know him.

"Craig."

"Craig Lewis?" He was the only Craig that fell in their general age range.

"Nope. It's been a bit, but I think his last name started with a B—Baxter. . . . Bates?"

"Craig Bateman?" he nearly choked. The man was fifty.

She snapped. "Yes. That's it. Bateman."

He shifted in his seat. "A little old for your friend, wasn't he?" Unless her roommate had been a much older college student.

"Serena had a thing for older guys. Craig wasn't the first, and I doubt he was the last."

"Odd."

"Not so uncommon. It usually starts with a flirtation with a professor and grows from there."

"So you . . . you experienced that?"

"Me?" She laughed. "No. Eww. I'm just saying it happens."

He'd never look at Craig Bateman the same again.

"We ate at this really cool Irish pub. Mc . . ."

"McCallahan's?"

"Yeah."

"It's my uncle's place. Brother on my mom's side."

"You're kidding."

"Nope. My mom's youngest brother. Started it about a decade back."

"They had this great—"

"Irish seafood chowder?"

"Yes."

"It's their trademark dish. Sort of like what Pat's cheesesteaks are to Philly."

"I can see why. On both accounts. So . . . you have Irish ancestry?" she said, pulling her legs up cross-legged on the seat.

"Most of the town does."

"Hence Parker's accent."

"Yeah. His family immigrated later than most in the crabbing community."

"Is that what your family does?"

"My dad did. My mom was a second-grade teacher. Both are retired now, though Dad still goes crabbing nearly every morning. Once it's in the blood . . ."

She would have asked how *he* got into law enforcement, how all the Pirates did, but she thought she knew the answer to that. Jenna's death had ignited their fire for justice. Declan had mentioned as much. And now Marley Trent's death had oddly enough reunited them, all but the mysterious Luke Gallagher.

The pieces of Marley's case had finally fallen into place, even locating Paul Geller's storage facility after a nonstop week of searching. Andrea Trent's files would be returned to her husband. Marley's casework on Rativik and Kovac, including the photograph she'd snapped of Rativik among the crowd at the reenactment in Gettysburg last year, would go to GJM. Along with her notes on the tracking she'd done to

Rativik and Kovac's meeting spot at the battlefield.

Marley's personal items, which Geller feared losing if he gave up the storage facility's location, would be returned to her father. Geller had been sitting on the evidence of Marley's killer all along but didn't even know it. He'd been convinced Perera had killed her, so he hadn't even bothered looking at anything that didn't pertain directly to him.

Finley wished Paul would be charged for stealing Marley's possessions and hoarding them away in some sick attempt to *"stay connected to the love of my life,"* as he put it. But at least upon learning the truth, GJM quickly fired him, which brought some small measure of justice.

The ride to Chesapeake Harbor was relatively traffic-free for Thanksgiving, and they arrived within a half hour. Griffin's family home was a breathtaking two-story shore house, complete with old-fashioned wooden shingles and edged by Chesapeake Bay.

Parker, Avery, and Tanner were on the lawn with a parcel of people playing touch football, but Finley didn't see Kate among them. "Kate coming later?" she asked.

Griffin shrugged. "I guess so. I don't see her car in the drive. She may still be over at her folks'. People file in throughout the day."

Her heart went out for Kate. It couldn't be easy loving a man whose fate she may never know.

"Took you guys long enough," Declan said, rising from his perch on the porch as they climbed from Griffin's truck.

"Perhaps they made a pit stop." Parker smirked.

"Actually, we did," Finley said, just for the joy of messing with him.

Parker nearly choked. "Is that right?"

"To get gas," Griffin said, deflating his bubble.

"Should have known better." Parker winked. "Now, you two lovebirds go get changed and join the game."

"Parker needs all the help he can get." Avery chucked the ball at him.

"Tate's a tad on the competitive side," he said.

"It is a *game*, after all." Avery pushed up her sleeves.

"Parker Mitchell, stop sassing the girls." Griffin's mom, Kay, walked down the front steps. Brown hair and bright blue eyes, just like Griffin. "They just got here."

"Hi, Mom." Griffin pressed a kiss to her cheek.

"Hi, Finley," his mother said. "So good to see you under better circumstances."

"Thank you for your hospitality. I brought some cookies." She handed her the tin, praying they were more edible than her baking history would suggest.

"Isn't that just the sweetest." Kay wrapped her

in a warm embrace, the aroma of stuffing and turkey swirling about her. She rubbed Finley's arm. "We're so glad you could join us."

"Kay, leave the poor girl be." Griffin's dad stood on the deck. Give Griffin twenty years and it'd be him.

"Thanks, Dad." Griffin waved.

"Oh, you both hush," Kay said. "Finley and I are just fine."

Griffin's dad rocked back on his heels. "I see you all wasted no time in tossing the old pigskin around."

Parker held the football aloft. "You want to join us, sir?"

"I'm afraid my football days are past. Besides, somebody's got to keep an eye on Kay and that turkey of hers." He winked at his wife.

"Yes," Parker said. "We don't want a repeat of last year."

"Or the year before." Griffin chuckled.

Declan smirked. "Or—"

"Declan Joseph Grey. Don't make me swat you."

Declan's grin turned sheepish. "Yes, ma'am."

"Ha. You got all three names." Parker jabbed Declan.

"Parker Mitchell, what did I just say about sassing? I *do* know your middle name."

Some of Parker's bravado momentarily eased. "Yes, ma'am."

"Now, you all go back to your game, while Finley and I get to know each other better." She wrapped an arm around Finley's shoulder and steered her toward the door. "Griff, get her bag, for goodness' sake."

Now she felt bad. Griffin had tried taking her bag, but she'd insisted on carrying it, wanting something to clutch in her nervousness.

"Yes, ma'am." He took it from Finley with a smile and followed her into the house, along with the rest of the gang.

Parker set the football on the table and pulled out a chair.

"Parker Mitchell, you did not just put that thing on my table."

He quickly removed it and rested it on his lap. "Sorry, ma'am."

Declan sniffed. "Are those yams I smell?"

Kay chuckled. "Declan, I swear you have a bottomless stomach."

"When it comes to your cooking, you know it."

"Come on. I'll get you a sample plate made up."

"Me too," Parker said.

Avery and Tanner waited politely at the edge of the room.

Kay shook her head with a touch of mirth, and then waved her arm, beckoning them. "Come on, the lot of you, but only a taster plate. Declan

351

and Parker, your folks won't be here for an hour and I don't want your supper ruined."

Kate entered through the back door, her blond hair pulled up in a ponytail, her makeup light and natural.

"Katie, there you are." Kay greeted her with a warm hug. "I was starting to worry."

"I'm sorry. I was busy with something. My folks will be over soon."

Parker stood behind her and swiped her ponytail. "Apparently Katie doesn't understand the beauty of taking a day off."

"Ha." Avery laughed.

Parker's brows arched.

"That's rich coming from *workaholic Sam*."

His lips twitched in amusement, but he simply took a seat at the table, lounging back with his hands linked behind his head. "Do you see me working now, love?"

"Not on the football field—that's for sure." She smirked.

"Really?" He cocked his head with an even wider smirk. "Repeat, then." He snagged the ball and headed straight for her.

"Bring it on." She turned and moved for the back door.

"What's up with those two?" Declan asked between bites of queso dip and tortilla chips.

Finley shook her head. When it came to reading women, Declan really was clueless.

An hour and a half later, Declan sat back, patting his belly. "That was delicious, Mrs. M."

"Thank you. And thank you, Finley, for the lovely cookies."

Parker tried biting into one. Tried valiantly, but after a moment set it back on his plate.

"Sorry." She bit her lip. "They're a bit hard."

"A bit?" Parker rubbed his jaw. "Nearly broke a tooth."

Declan elbowed him with his good arm.

"What?" Parker grunted, rubbing his side.

"No." Griffin chomped down with a hard crunch. "They're delicious." There was no way he was saying otherwise.

Finley erupted in laughter, and everyone else followed.

"Let's take coffee in the front room," Kay said, and everyone moved en mass, but Kate hung back, signaling the gang to do so too.

"What's up?" Declan asked.

She looked to make sure all the parents and siblings were occupied with coffee and the Ravens game before turning back to the group.

"What's up?" Griffin frowned.

"What I was working on before I got here."

"Yeah?" Parker asked.

"I think I just found evidence Luke is still alive."

Griffin saw Finley to his family's guest room, thankful she was spending the night and glad she'd be able to sleep in a real bed rather than on his couch, but he'd miss watching her sleep. Miss falling asleep to the sight of her across the room. He just prayed she had no nightmares. Prayed she never had them again, or if she did, she came to him for comfort. He wanted to be there for her in every sense of the word. His love for her was so strong he didn't know how long he could be a gentleman and court her without proposing. *A month, perhaps.*

She smiled as they paused in the open doorway to what would be her room for the night, and looked up at him with those gorgeous blue eyes he'd happily drown in.

A week?

"I can't believe what Kate found," she said.

"*Thinks* she found," he corrected. "It'll take more time and a lot more digging before we know if it's a solid lead."

"Well, it's got to feel like a sudden beam of hope after all these years."

"I agree." Hope was fighting to settle inside of him too. "I just don't want to see her disappointed." They'd all lost Luke once. He couldn't go through that again.

"But she can't give up hope. She needs to keep fighting. I can see the determination in her eyes."

"I see that same determination in yours. You're going to beat this fear Brent Howard filled you with. You are far stronger than he is."

"God is stronger. I've finally come to see that. I've been beating myself up for being weak when I should have simply been depending more and more on my Savior. I can do all things through Christ who gives me strength."

He had relied on the promise of Philippians 4:13 many a time. Through Christ's strength he'd found a place of healing, and he had no doubt Finley would too.

"I should let you get some sleep." It'd been a crazy few weeks.

She grabbed hold of his shirt. "Not without a good-night kiss."

His mouth went dry as she brought his lips to hers.

He kissed her with all the love and passion brimming inside, but after a moment restrained himself and pulled back ever so slightly.

"Good night," she whispered, her breath tickling his cheek.

"Night."

Stepping back, she waggled two fingers and shut the door.

He rested his forehead against it, every nerve ending in his body aflame. A week seemed a perfectly decent amount of time to pass before proposing. He could make it a week, right?

He turned to find his mom smirking at him from the end of the hall.

"Whoa. Mom. Didn't see you there. You're like a ninja."

"I haven't seen you smile like that in years," she said as he pressed a kiss to her cheek.

It was wiser not to comment. *Just let it slide.*

"Night, Mom."

"Night, Griff," she said, merriment dancing in her voice.

His heart swelled at hearing the happiness in his mom's voice. Finley had ushered in God's healing in a way he never could have anticipated, and he had no doubt God would work through her to bring a measure of healing to his family too. Finley brought light wherever she went.

Despite the darkness she'd witnessed and suffered, she shined. Just as Marley Trent had in her short life.

Thank you, Father, for bringing me the one person who could reach my heart. Thank you for creating her for me.

Acknowledgments

To God—for loving me, carrying me, and blessing me with the joy of getting to share stories. Thank you, Father. May every word glorify You.

To Mike, Ty, and Kay—for your constant support through every crazy stage of the writing process. You guys are the best. I couldn't do this without you. Love you guys!

To Calvin—for brimming my life over with joy.

To Becky—for your friendship, support, and most especially, your prayers. So blessed God brought us together. It's an honor to walk this journey with you, and a whole lot of fun.

To Dave and Karen—for your great guidance and input. I couldn't have been blessed with two finer editors. It's a joy working with you. Thank you both for your patience. I know I require a lot ;).

To everyone at BHP and Baker—for all you do and all your support!

To Janet Grant—for being such an awesome source of support, wisdom, and friendship.

To Dee—for your constant friendship, feedback, encouragement, and prayers. I'm so thankful for you.

To Dr. Megan K. Moore, Assistant Professor of Anthropology at Eastern Michigan University—for sharing your vast expertise in skeletal biology and forensic anthropology. I deeply appreciate all the time you spent with me and the wealth of knowledge you shared. Any errors are fully mine.

To Phil Muskett—for the amazing Gettysburg tour. I learned so much, and we had such a wonderful time.

To Kelli—for your amazing creativity, brilliance, phenomenal work ethic, friendship, and most of all, for helping keep my schedule sane. I appreciate you!

To everyone at the International Justice Mission —for all your help and insight. You were all so very gracious with your time. Thank you for all you do in God's name to help the suffering around the world. You are an inspiration.

About the Author

Dani Pettrey is the acclaimed author of the ALASKAN COURAGE romantic suspense series, which includes her bestselling novels *Submerged*, *Shattered*, *Stranded*, *Silenced*, and *Sabotaged*. Her books have been honored with the Daphne du Mauricr award, two HOLT Medallions, two National Readers' Choice Awards, the Gail Wilson Award of Excellence, and Christian Retailing's Best Award, among others.

She feels blessed to write inspirational romantic suspense because it incorporates so many things she loves—the thrill of adventure, nail-biting suspense, the deepening of her characters' faith, and plenty of romance. She and her husband reside in Maryland, where they enjoy time with their two daughters, a son-in-law, and a super adorable grandson. You can find her online at www.danipettrey.com.

Center Point Large Print
600 Brooks Road / PO Box 1
Thorndike, ME 04986-0001 USA

(207) 568-3717

US & Canada:
1 800 929-9108
www.centerpointlargeprint.com

3/16